Crimson Wing

Also by Robert Wallace

The Valentine Series

Valentines Cup
Crimson Wing
Monkeypuzzle
Operation Gunfleet

Standalone novels

One Single Ticket
A gripping Victorian thriller about Brunel.

Clara's Secret
A collection of urban ghost and mystery stories with factual origins.

Screenplays

JAX
Andrew is clearly not the man she thought she knew. The man she married.

About the Author

Robert Wallace was born and raised in Bristol and spent many years working in the medical field which took him to Europe, the United States, Japan, Australia and Scandinavia. It sparked a lifelong interest in travel. His work involves turning historical events into works of semi-fiction, retaining the factual background, creating fictional characters to share their lives with real people.

Praise for the Author

About *'One Single Ticket'* by Robert Wallace:

"A detective story told at a breathless pace, with a Richard Hannay type hero straight out of a John Buchan thriller, and it goes with a swing"
Professor Angus Buchanan, author of 'Brunel: The Life and Times of Isambard Kingdom Brunel

"The plot is so interesting, and the setting so well done; a delight to get a scenic picture of this special event in history."
Dr. Gabrielle Obrist, Museum of Modern Art, Zürich

ROBERT WALLACE

CRIMSON WING

THE SECOND STORY IN THE VALENTINE SERIES

TradShack

Crimson Wing is a work of fiction. Any resemblance to actual events or persons, living or dead, is entirely coincidental. The roles played in this novel by members of German military intelligence service, the chief executives of German industries and members of British intelligence however, abide by the generally known facts of their real lives, and I have sometimes quoted from their works and letters, et passim. The storyline . . . and all the passages relating to events . . . have no factual basis.

Cover design by www.tradshack.com
Published by www.tradshack.com

'Knowledge itself is power.' (Ipsa Scientia potestas est.)

Francis Bacon

Meditationes Sacrae, 1597.

Joselyn Foster, Martha's Vineyard, USA

October 1945, five months after Hermann Goering surrendered to the US 7th Army.

I FELT EXHILARATED, GRATEFUL TO BE ALIVE. And safe. The memory of killing Devlin – a Republican terrorist - was with me every waking morning. Joselyn Foster, government assassin and spy was finally free. But I wasn't free of the demons which haunted me; always there, lurking just below the surface. I took another deep breath and relished my good fortune. I prayed it would last.

Today was another day, sailing out on Nantucket Sound. It was just like all the others: sun, blue sea, a vast sky. I was standing at the helm of Uncle Mark's sixty-foot sailing boat – Orca – a mile off the coast of Martha's Vineyard. The scene was idyllic, but I was pre-occupied with dark thoughts despite the beauty of what surrounded me.

"You okay, Joselyn?" somebody shouted, breaking my

introspection.

"Sure," I replied, "why wouldn't I be?"

I had been back from Switzerland for eighteen months. And although I thought I had loved Alistair and life at Chalet Monte Rosa, I had started to feel stifled there. Nicholas Brimblecombe – Brim - head of British Intelligence, had sent me there Christmas 1943, for my own protection. It had started well. Alistair, Freddie and I had skied all over the Alps above Zermatt and into Italy. We had driven throughout Switzerland; it was stunning to discover such beautiful scenery. Then Freddie's wife Astrid had had the baby and the chalet had changed from being Herr Seiler's alpine retreat into something resembling a nursery.

The tide of the ocean was high, and we were very slowly drifting, not under sail, the Orca bobbing on the swell. Mark's instructions had been clear earlier that morning: Hold the wheel and watch young David is ready when we need the sails unfurled.

Then two events suddenly happened. I noticed Brad, a spoilt fourteen-year-old kid from New York, had inadvertently stepped into a coil of mooring rope resting on deck. He was fishing and oblivious to everything but himself. Mark and his cronies were at the stern; robust men, fishing, drinking bottled beers, talking about women and high stakes banking in Boston.

As Brad's foot became entangled in the coil, there was a sudden gust of wind; the wooden boom of the mainsail swung around and knocked him off the boat and into the freezing Atlantic. Where was David? Not watching the sails; he'd gone astern to see his dad. My reaction was quick, and I was back into training at SOE Commando school in Scotland.

"Somebody watch the wheel," I screamed. "Man overboard!"

I stripped off my baggy sailing clothes, grabbed a lifebuoy and dived in after him. I swam awkwardly, towing the buoy, catching my breath, and searching. There he was, just ahead now, his ginger hair floating on the ocean, like a lost wig. I couldn't see his face. Was he gradually sinking? I powered over to him with every ounce of energy I possessed, imagining that freezing Loch and my instructors shouting survival and First Aid.

"I got ya!" I panted, putting the buoy over his head and shoulders, forcing it down so his arms were free and resting on top of the buoy. I brushed the hair out of his eyes. They were wide with horror. He was trying to be brave, stifling tears, his teeth chattering uncontrollably with fear and cold. I knew his game: trying not to show fear in front of a girl, even though I was old enough to be his mother. Just.

"Come on, pal. Let's get you back."

I struggled back with him to the stern of the Orca; two men were already in the water and a rope ladder had been dropped over the side. Mark hauled the boy up onto the deck, followed by me. I quickly rolled him onto his side and slapped his back between the shoulder blades, until he spewed over the wood planks. It stank; I reeled away, disgusted: vomit and seawater is not a great combination at this time of day.

"Get off me," the boy shouted rudely. His father came over

with a large beach towel, wrapped it around his shoulders and tended him with words of placation. He ignored me completely.

I stood up in my soaking underwear: "I'll get my own towel then, right?"

I went below, found a rug and draped it around my shivering body. Uncle Mark came down with some hot coffee, asking me if I was decent.

"Never that decent!" I called back and he laughed out loud.

"That was impressive, Joss."

"Yeah. And not even a thank you," I replied, unable to conceal my anger at both the boy and his unappreciative father.

"Well, what do you expect; they're not Bostonians."

*

It was now the day after the Orca incident, and I was sitting in Uncle Mark's lounge. The clapboard house with picket fences was in the heart of Main Street; it was humble, cluttered and cosy. And I loved the casual feel of the place. More than anywhere else. The large coffee table was adorned with New England newspapers, most of them flash with copy about the aftermath of the war:

The final surrender of Japan, from a delegation aboard the battleship 'Missouri', is accepted by Supreme Allied Commander General Douglas MacArthur and Fleet Admiral Chester Nimitz.

My mug of coffee was stone cold. I wandered into the tiny kitchen, refreshed my mug from a large copper pot on the stove. The kitchen always smelt of maple syrup and boat varnish; aromas I had relished since childhood. Mark had been like a second father to me after my mom died and I adored him. He was wealthy but you would never know it. He owned a large mansion on Copley Square in Boston, this house and a chandlery in Edgartown. And of course, his beloved Orca.

I picked up the telegram for what must have been the tenth time, sipped coffee and re-read it: My daddy in London wants to see me. He wants to take me to some fancy bistro in Pimlico for a treat. But I wonder what he really wants. Why am I such a cynic?

The front door opened; Mark was there. Like my father he had a lumberjack build and a big grin. He clasped a canvas bag and immediately the familiar smell of the sea pervaded my senses: salt and fish.

"Since your rescue operation hampered our fishing yesterday, we took the Orca out again this morning. I didn't wake you because you were sound, Joss. Knocked out."

"Oh yeah?" I laughed. "Did he live? That ungrateful little perisher from New York City?" I made it sound like Noo Yawk, because that's how Brad and his father made it sound.

"Yeah, Brad made it. But I didn't get a cheque from his father."

"Neither did I."

"So, New England Clam Chowder, right?"

"Always great."

"How many times have you read that telegram, pussy cat? You'll wear it out."

I grinned at him: "Plenty and I still can't decide. What's the time?"

"Time you opened a bottle of wine and I got cooking ... just on seven."

I followed him into the kitchen as he removed his fishing jacket and placed fresh clams and some prawns on the sink drainer. He winked as I watched him.

"Maybe you should go see your dad. He'd love it." Mark was busying himself washing and sorting his healthy catch.

"I've left that life, Uncle Mark. I told you. Working for British Intelligence nearly killed me. I'm happy right here."

"Yeah, I know, Joss. Mr. Ambassador just misses you, I'm sure. I know he likes London. And now the war is over I guess he'll stay, right?"

I popped the cork of an expensive-looking bottle of California Burgundy and watched him skilfully top and tail the prawns.

"You never know with daddy. I guess I'll find out when I go. Shall I pour?"

"Nah, let it breathe. I need a shower. Back in ten."

"You'd better or I'll drink it."

"There's bacon, onion and celery in the pantry. Maybe peel some potatoes ...?"

“Sure.”

He clumped up the narrow stairs and yelled: “I’m goanna miss you, pussy cat; it’s been fun.”

He always called me that; because he wondered just how many lives I had left. I poured the daintiest drop of wine into a crystal glass – and sipped - my uncle’s tastes never disappointed.

‘Yes’, I thought to myself, ‘I will go back to London, because I feel I have no choice.’

London

Hurn Airport, Bournemouth, England.

THE PAN AM FLIGHT from La Guardia Field New York landed at Hurn with time to spare. It had been flying for just short of eighteen hours including stops: Newfoundland and Shannon.

Joselyn walked down the steps of the Douglas DC4 Clipper aircraft and stepped onto English soil for the first time in two years. In fact, it was Dorset soil, so she had been told by the English stewardess, as Hurn airport was only a few miles away from the seaside town of Bournemouth.

Joselyn had a sensuous, wide mouth, full lips and dimpled cheeks when she smiled. Which she often did. Her face, though not classically beautiful, was alluring and noble like an exquisitely crafted work of art. Her deep-blue eyes, however, did betray her mood: fire and fury one moment, deep serenity the next. This evening they should have looked tired. But she was lucky, she had slept on the plane. A little 'preparation' Uncle Mark had discreetly given her in a restaurant he knew near

Central Park before her flight. 'This will help, pussy cat,' he had said. And it had. She didn't even question what it was. Mark knew a 'tame' pharmacist in Manhattan who'd furnished him with a sleeping draught.

It was early evening, and a member of ground crew came over to greet the disembarking trans-Atlantic passengers – one of the first flights in a six-and-a-half-year absence – part of a new twice-weekly service. They all looked affluent; and she was sure she had spotted a well-known Hollywood film star at the front of the aircraft. He was being paid a lot of attention by cabin crew.

"Miss Foster?" asked an anonymous man in a grey suit.

Joselyn nodded, surprised.

"American Embassy. I have a car for you. I am to drive you to London, Claridge's Hotel."

"My father sent you." It was more of a statement than a question.

The man nodded as one of the Pan Am stewardesses brought over her solitary suitcase, a battered, pre-war item which had clearly seen better days.

"That it?" The man asked.

"Yeah."

"Lucky there's some shopping in the car for you."

The stewardess thanked Joselyn for choosing Pan American World Airways and hoped they would see her again real soon.

"Thank you," Joselyn said as the man stowed her case in the trunk of the limo. "Don't I need to go through customs or something? Formalities?"

"All taken care of, diplomatic privilege. Follow me."

The rear of the left-hand drive limo smelt sweet with fragrances: eau de cologne, soaps, toothpaste and talcum powders. They came in bags from addresses like Burlington Arcade, Bond Street and Piccadilly. Her head sunk back into the sumptuous leather and thought of her father; she could not wait to see him and wondered exactly where he was taking her for lunch tomorrow – a bistro in Pimlico? She wondered what exactly a bistro was. There were none in Boston and certainly not on the Vineyard.

"Why Claridge's by the way?" She asked the driver. "Daddy normally puts people up at the Savoy."

"Closed, Miss. Bomb damage. Bloody Luftwaffe."

"Oh." She closed her eyes and was instantly asleep.

"Welcome to London, Miss," said the man. Three hours later.

Ambassador's Lunch

Grosvenor Square, London, England.

MACDONALD HOUSE, THE AMERICAN EMBASSY was bathed in spectacular sunlight. A glorious late autumnal day when the trees in the gardens were splashed with vivid colours. Thin, wispy cirrus clouds drifted lazily across a deep-blue sky. The absence of iron railings, removed to support the war effort, made the square appear bigger. The sandbags had gone as was the barrage balloon the WAAF's nicknamed 'Romeo'. Slowly, things were starting to return to normal.

It was lunchtime, a matter of months after the end of the war and Britain breathed a sigh of relief. The gardens were full of people savouring peace. There was a feeling of optimism, almost celebration, in spite of the hideous bomb damage on adjacent streets. The Blitz and the attack of the Doodlebugs had caused devastation and death all around. But there was a spirit of 'rebuild' in the air; and for the first time in what seemed like ages, people were actually laughing and enjoying the freedom that had been fought so hard for.

Macdonald House was seven stories of administrative offices, political, cultural, economic, military and financial departments. A hub of American bureaucracy. And a luxurious top-floor apartment which had stunning views of the square and Hyde Park.

Joselyn's father, Deputy Chief of Mission, Ambassador Charles Foster, sat at his desk on the sixth floor and glanced at his watch for what must have been the tenth time. He was a tall New Englander with silver-grey hair, which had been carefully styled by an Italian hairdresser in Oxford Street. Foster was elegant; the weather-beaten features, etched into his skin, had been acquired from the many hours he'd spent sailing his schooner off the coast of Provincetown in Cape Cod Bay. With his pale blue eyes and film-star appearance, he cut an impressive figure in a handmade Savile Row suit, pressed white shirt and Stamford tie.

His desk was adorned with framed photographs of family and friends, eminent politicians, senior military and naval staff. And his fellow sailors at home of course, proudly holding their catch in front of the picturesque clapboard houses along the bay. Central among these treasured artefacts was a 10x8" colour portrait of his late wife Maria. Of wealthy Italian descent, she gazed confidently into the photographer's lens with a serene, almost regal, nobility. Not sad, nor smiling, but natural. And utterly beguiling, as was her daughter, Joselyn.

There was a soft tap on the door and a young woman let herself in without waiting for a response. She had a shock of jet-black hair and piercing blue eyes. Her face broke into a smile that was at once magnificent, captivating and utterly joyous.

Charles Foster looked up from his feigned administrative preoccupation:

"Hello, honey! Why, but you look just divine! Come in."

He made a show of brushing important papers to one side as if they now had no significance. His baby was back.

He stood up and walked around his desk and opened his arms to greet her.

"Hi, daddy."

"How was your flight?"

"Long. Thanks for the car."

They embraced and he hugged her like a big old grizzly bear, squeezing his eyes shut as he absorbed and enjoyed the closeness and her obvious affection. He couldn't shed a tear and show her just how delighted he was to see her. It wasn't his way or hers either for that matter.

"Let me look at you, Joselyn." He brushed a loose strand of hair from her cheek and she made a face, the way she did.

"Still me," she said coquettishly, "just prettier than last time!"

They both laughed because she always said that. It was their joke and she called him 'Grizzly' because of his lumberjack build, wide shoulders and hands that felt like sandpaper.

Joselyn wore a salmon-pink pleated skirt, cut very close and a white silk blouse.

"How was the Vineyard?" His voice was deep, mellifluous and tinged with an East Coast accent which had been gently anglicised over time. He could not hide the pleasure he felt.

"Oh. Exquisite. Sailing in the Orca on Nantucket Sound, walking, fishing, I worked in the Chandlery quite a lot of the time. Uncle Mark was fun and generous as always, we ate fresh fish and drank some wine. I've put on some weight, don't you think?" She twirled around like a dancer, showing off her perfect curves.

"I'm insanely jealous. And don't be crazy, you always look great. It's all that energy you expend out there on the ocean. Here, come and sit down. Do you want some tea? Or a cold lemonade?" He grinned; he knew it would rile her, it was another of their in-jokes.

"Lemonade! Hell no, Mr. Ambassador! What am I? Thirteen? You promised to take me to lunch. At least, that's what you put in your cable. And I quote: London's finest. Fit for the daughter of the American Ambassador."

"Then what would you say to angels on horseback, served with crusty bread and a cold bottle of Alsace? No New England Clam Chowder in London, I'm afraid. Not even in peacetime."

"Mama's favourite, mine too," Joselyn said solemnly. They both looked at the photograph of Maria and there was an awkward little silence. They let it pass; she looked him in the eye.

"Daddy, you have something on your mind. Now do you mind telling me what it is?" She delivered the line in a perfect

Katherine Hepburn voice, which always made him smile. Except that she really could read his mind. "Come on, Grizzly, what gives?"

"Ah, well. The thing is, Joss, we're being joined by two people you know."

Her face became manifestly disappointed: "Suddenly it's a party. I thought it was just us. Your cable and all."

"It was, but something has come up. And I'm afraid it involves you."

She twigged and frowned: "Now, don't tell me. Professor Brimblecombe, my former boss in British Intelligence?"

"I'm afraid so, yes."

"Daddy. I told him I was out of the Service. And I am. Period. That world is not for me; I did enough for British Intelligence, and he knows it."

"I understand that – they understand. God knows, I don't want you placed in the line of any more danger...they're not trying to rally you. I'm sure of that. Not in that sense, at least."

"Really? I know Brim, remember?" She shook her head, "May I go up to the apartment and freshen up? I've been travelling for hours. New York is a mighty long flight; well, series of flights, I guess. I'm beat, but hungry. And I can taste that wine!"

"Sure."

Joselyn stood, stretched and smoothed down her skirt. It fitted like a glove and she knew she looked stunning, no matter how tired: "Same bedroom?"

"Yes, it's all made up ready for you. Fresh sheets, towels, soap. I've even had a shower fitted and a decent American refrigerator installed in the kitchen. These Brits are okay, but they need civilising! They drink warm beer and take cold baths; shouldn't it be the other way around?" Charles tried to sound jovial. He could feel her disappointment. He felt dissatisfied too.

"Twenty minutes," she turned.

"Honey?"

She stopped, froze, and didn't face him: "Don't even ask, Grizzly. I'm not going anywhere. Not when there's Alsace on the lunch menu. Trust me, I'm your favourite daughter, remember?"

"Sure." His only daughter.

The sound of Hepburn hung in the Ambassador's office as if the actress had actually been there. Charles smiled and looked at the image of his dead wife. And a single, involuntary tear ran down his right cheek. This time there was nothing he could do, but at least Joselyn wasn't there to see it.

Bistro

Belgrave Road, London, England.

"Giles Walcott didn't entirely own Needle's Eye House, is what I am trying to say, Joselyn," said Brim, dabbing his chin with a napkin. A trickle of Vermouth had missed its mark.

They were sitting in a quasi-French style in Pimlico, an establishment known as Bistro. She had gone there with her father, and later met Brim and Alistair. At first, she was shocked to see Alistair, but he was so charming and evidently pleased to see her that any frostiness soon melted.

She was on her second glass of a wonderful Gewurztraminer; smoky, sweet and scented. The bistro was empty save for a number of waiters, many of whom were clearly Secret Service; disguised very unconvincingly as waiters. A six-foot man with a crew cut didn't look right wearing an ill-fitting dinner jacket, at lunchtime. He was obviously assigned to Embassy protection.

"Then who does?" asked Joselyn; she took a generous sip of wine and smiled at Alistair in a conspiratorial way. Hell, she was supposed to be on vacation. Wasn't she?

"You do," said Brim. "That is to say his seventy-five percent of the asset has been passed to you as his legal beneficiary. The other twenty-five percent belongs to somebody else. As yet unknown. That's the legal position."

"He is dead then. Giles? No question?"

"Yes, he is," said Brim, "no question."

Did she detect that Alistair looked just a little sheepish – for a split second – or was it the wine playing tricks? She would find out, that was certain.

"And how do you know all this?" asked Joselyn.

Brim fixed her a stare: "An Official Notice appeared in 'The Times' newspaper; it's not uncommon. A firm of Solicitors, Carter and Jackson, from Weybridge, Surrey made an announcement saying they were looking for persons connected with Needle's Eye House ... your former home ..." He finished on cue and looked at Alistair.

"We knew of course, that's where you lived with Giles Walcott."

"Yes."

"One half of the London Sleeper Cell - Gertrud Wolf – told me that's where they had met Giles and Michael Devlin, the night before the attempt on Windsor."

"Did she indeed? I met Gertrud at the house. She was a treacherous bitch, but quite beautiful. And where is she now?" Joselyn's tone was perhaps a little aggressive.

Brim interjected: "It must be explained the Windsor incident is an Official Secret, Alistair. Neither Charles nor Joselyn know the full story."

"Gertrud isn't an Official Secret." said Joselyn suddenly. "As I told you, we had dinner with her before I was dismissed by Giles that night. The night I pursued Devlin to Southampton ..." Her words trailed off ...

"And it was reported in the newspaper, Brim," volunteered Charles.

"An incident was reported, that is true. But not the names of the people involved or the nature of the threat," said Brim, clearly annoyed. "But since you ask, Gertrud Wolf is being held at a secure facility under my orders. Trent Park."

Joselyn: "I see." She calmed down. "Go on. You were telling us about the announcement. I have 'inherited' Giles's seventy-five percent of Needle's Eye House. Do I presume you have contacted this law firm on my behalf?"

Charles touched his daughter's wrist in paternal admonishment: "Easy, Joss."

"Yes," said Brim, "I did contact Carter and Jackson. I explained I was a close family friend acting in your best interests after your husband's tragic death. Clive Rowlands, the lawyer there, was happy with this clarification and was pleased I had your welfare at heart ... "

"I'm sorry," Joselyn said meekly. "This is all a bit of a shock. I wasn't even expecting to see you today. Or Alistair." Her apology worked; Alistair gave her his winning smile and said:

"Maybe we should have said, but there we are."

She sipped some water: "And the rest? Who owns the remaining...twenty-five percent?"

"We have absolutely no idea; this is the point. But according to Rowlands, a Peter Braun, from Switzerland, is acting as that person's lawyer; his, or indeed her, notary."

"So, what's the deal?"

Brim pursed his lips: "Rowlands seems to think it would be, what, prudent for you to go to Switzerland with Walcott's Death Certificate and settle the matter. I haven't spoken to Braun yet, of course. I wanted to speak to you first. And with your father present and in agreement."

She wanted to say she wasn't a damn child and didn't need her father there as a witness. And they could all see her mulling these thoughts over in her mind. Her 'marriage' to the treacherous Walcott being one of them:

"But I don't want it. I don't want seventy-five percent of anything to do with Giles Walcott. The 'marriage' was a sham. We organised this duplicity together; you wanted intelligence about his activities."

If Charles Foster had been shocked at this revelation, he made no sign of showing it. Perhaps he had known all along.

"A point well made," agreed Brim. "Braun hinted to Rowlands they might want to trade some information in exchange for your share," said Brim.

"Trade? Trade what?"

Alistair spoke firmly: "The position is, we really want to know who owns that twenty-five percent of Walcott's estate."

"Why?"

"Because" said Brim, "there is an outside chance they may be the same people who financed the whole operation. Windsor. The aerial attack. All of it."

"But it was the Nazis, surely?" said Joselyn.

"Yes. But the Third Reich was backed by industrial cash in 1933. We know that. But we don't know who. This could be vital intelligence."

"How do you know that?"

"Restricted, I'm afraid. Even from you."

"You are making it impossible for me to say no," said Joselyn.

Ambassador Foster looked sheepish; Professor Brimblecombe looked imploringly at her; Alistair took her hand: "You've done so much, Joss. Really you have. This is the last hurdle. Freddie and I will be with you. What do you say?"

"Yes, is all I can say, isn't it?"

Brim pursed his lips, the way he did: "I suggest we skip lunch and get on to this right away."

British Intelligence

St. James's, London, England.

THEY RETURNED TO BRIM'S office. He immediately picked up the red phone, a scrambler and dialled a number in Switzerland he had written in his notebook. The answer was swift:

"Braun." Brim tilted the earpiece so the others could hear as much as possible.

"Good afternoon, Mr. Braun. I represent Mrs. Joselyn Walcott."

"Ah, yes."

"Your name and number were given to my firm by Mr. Clive Rowlands of Carter and Jackson. Weybridge, Surrey."

"You are her lawyer?" asked Braun.

"More than that, but yes. I work for HM Government."

"I see, yes. I understand."

"No names."

"Of course."

Brim looked up at the others. Caution was paramount:

"We understand you have some documents you wish to exchange for Mrs. Walcott's seventy-five percent share in Needle's Eye House, her matrimonial home." Alistair smiled at Brim's description – matrimonial – it amused him.

"Too delicate for the telephone, sir," Braun said emphatically.

"St. Moritz is a long way from London, Mr. Braun. This is a one-time offer. Take it or leave it. My client has the legal right to claim her percentage in Court. She is a bona-fide beneficiary."

Silence.

Brim covered the mouthpiece and whispered: "Let's see how serious they are."

"Very well, if that is your, how do you say, position."

"I regret it has to be."

This time the silence on the other end of the line was palpable. Brim wondered if there were other people in Braun's office, frantically instructing him.

"Very well. What position do you hold in HM Government?"

"That I cannot say, Mr. Braun. But senior enough to be able to negotiate on behalf of my government, if need be," said Brim with pompous authority.

There was another pause and then the bombshell:

"Very well. My client is in possession of a copy of the former German leader's will. You know who I mean, of course?"

Brim remained quiet for five seconds: "And who is your client?"

"The person who lent Giles Walcott the twenty-five percent in the first place. Cash. I cannot and will not divulge their name at this point. Mrs. Walcott has no need to know the name of the benefactor. That is my one-time offer, sir. Your government may take it or leave it."

Brim looked at Alistair, Joselyn and Charles Foster. They were all blank faced, astonished as Brim continued:

"May I ask how your client came by such a document."

"I do not know how they came by such a document. But it has been verified by an eminent historian from the University in Zürich. There is also a diary. It is not that of the leader, but someone else. No names."

"I see. I will have to consult with my client and call you back tomorrow morning."

"Very well," Peter Braun said again and hung up; he wasn't a man to mince words. Brim replaced the red receiver on to its cradle and looked once again at his visitors.

"You got the gist of that, I am sure."

"How can a Swiss law firm possess such a document?" said Alistair. "Hitler's will, for God's sake."

"What do we know about the circumstances of Hitler's last moments?" asked Ambassador Foster.

Brim explained that British Intelligence believed that it must have been rescued from the Führerbunker in Berlin, where Hitler and his wife Eva committed suicide along with Joseph and Magda Goebbels and the others.

"Rescued by whom? Didn't they all die?" asked Foster. "That

was my take on it."

Brim looked at the group: "Permit me to explain what we know. On April 29, 1945, Hitler ordered a copy of his Will to be couriered out of the Führerbunker – right through the Russian lines – to Field Marshal Ferdinand Schörner in Czechoslovakia. Rumour has it that Karl Doenitz and Paul Giesler were also sent political testaments of some sort...

"But the courier in this case was almost certainly Major Willi Johannmeier, Hitler's trusted adjutant. He took the will out of the bunker and delivered it to Schörner."

Joselyn and the others remained silent; this was news to them too.

Brim continued, his tone flat: "Besides Johannmeier, Heinrich Müller of the Gestapo was the only other occupant of the Führerbunker whose death – and corpse – had not until recently been accounted for. They alone had the motive, means and certainly the opportunity to liberate Hitler's will and possibly other documents. We just don't know which."

Joselyn was concentrating, her eyes flicking to the others: "What about Doenitz and Giesler? Those other political testaments you mentioned?"

Brim puffed out his cheeks: "Well, if they existed, either the Russians or the Americans have them and neither are admitting to it," he glanced at Foster, "and Traudi Junge, Hitler's secretary – who was also present – is unclear. Amid the confusion she cannot recall exactly who took what and where. You can't blame her. It must have been grim."

Joselyn looked at her father: "I see."

"I think we must assume Peter Braun's documents are genuine, and, if so, it is vital that we retrieve them. Braun mentioned a diary. It is just conceivable it may be Himmler's. And if so, at a stretch, it may provide evidence of the locations of the underground factories where the Tabun gas was manufactured. Probably situated somewhere remote, in the east of the country. Although we don't know who owns or controls it. Or, more importantly, how it was financed." Brim looked directly at Joselyn. She reacted immediately.

"I see. Then it seems I have no choice but to go to Switzerland and sign these papers."

"Correct," said Brim. "With the support of Alistair and Freddie."

Joselyn bit her lip and tried her best not to scowl at Brim: "Very well, I will go."

"Good. I'll telephone Braun in the morning. Let him sweat on it overnight."

Alistair, Joselyn and the Ambassador stood to leave. Just as they did, Brim opened a drawer of his desk and pulled out a sealed envelope.

"Miss Trueblood will organise your travel arrangements to St. Moritz; hotel and so on, but you'll need this." Brim handed the envelope to Joselyn.

"What is it?"

“Walcott’s Death Certificate, issued by HM Coroner, West London. September 1943.”

Joselyn sliced the envelope open: “Fishing accident, that’s cute.”

“The perils of angling, my dear. Perhaps Alistair will treat you and the Ambassador to a late lunch. Sorry we had to cut it short earlier. But, as you see, it was worth it.”

They turned to leave. But they could all clearly see Brim wasn’t sorry at all.

Mountain Train

Switzerland.

"IT'S SO WONDERFUL to see you again, Freddie," Joselyn said as she gazed out of the carriage window. "How's fatherhood?"

"Wonderful." He paused. "Astrid and baby Christina are in good health."

"Good."

"They missed you, you know, when you left Chalet Monte Rosa." Freddie didn't want to embarrass Joselyn, but he was keen to find out why she went back to Martha's Vineyard. He picked up on her mood; he knew she would explain when she felt like it. Joselyn experienced a sense of déjà vu, similar to how she had felt when she first came out to Switzerland, on Christmas Eve two years previously.

"Penny for them?" asked Alistair, his face cracking into a charming smile.

"No. They're not worth a penny," she said and gazed out of the window. "They ain't even worth a dime," she said in her

Katherine Hepburn voice.

"That was perfect," said Freddie, laughing. "I'd forgotten your skills for mimicking. That's how you picked up German so quickly, taking off Astrid and her mother. God! We had some fun in the mountains, didn't we?"

Alistair, Freddie and Joselyn were sitting in a first-class compartment on a SBB/CF train from Zürich via Chur south to St. Moritz. 'Four hours' they had been told on arrival at the airport, 'via Liechtenstein'. But it was longer; winter had arrived early in the Swiss Alps that year.

Her meeting with Herr Braun – the notary - was scheduled for 9.00 the following morning: Braun and Weber, Via Maistra. Third floor. The cable to Brim had confirmed the solicitor's address and added the word precisely rather unnecessarily. Braun was, of course only expecting Joselyn Walcott, together with her Marriage Certificate, her British passport and the cable as proof of her identity. And, of course, Giles Walcott's Death Certificate.

Alistair stole a glance at Joselyn: she looked wonderful. He thought about their time together and wondered why he hadn't treated her better; he couldn't explain it, even to himself. And he dared not broach the subject with Freddie, who could be quite prim about such matters.

Joselyn consulted the railway map she had picked up at the Swiss Air arrivals desk and ran her index finger across the unfolded page:

"Good. I can see where we are. This country confuses me with all the different cantons and regional dialects."

"Well, you have seen a lot of it, Joselyn. Many people haven't."

She sat back and said, almost to herself, "Mom would have loved Switzerland, you know. I wonder if she ever came here?"

Change

Switzerland.

THE TRAIN PULLED IN TO Chur station with a screech of brakes. Outside it was dark and a flutter of snowflakes was illuminated by the station lights. It was here they had to change for the last part of their journey, but there would be a ten-minute wait.

There was a loud clatter of carriage doors opening and being slammed shut, of people calling out in various European tongues, children crying for their parents and the sound of distant car horns. Joselyn looked out of the window with a dreamlike expression on her freckled face; she seemed oblivious to the loud commotion outside on the station platform.

Almost to herself she said again: 'Yeah. Mom would have loved this place.'

She traced a pattern in the condensation on the carriage window and watched the rivulets of water as they trickled down like tiny tears. Freddie wondered what it would have looked like from the other side of the glass. The expression on her face: sad, angry, resentful - but enigmatic and maybe hopeful. It was a curiously childlike gesture which Freddie found most endearing.

"What happened to her?" asked Alistair, genuinely interested. And she could see it.

"She was killed in an air raid. Bethnal Green. East London. She was delivering soup to a shelter."

Alistair: "So is that what motivated you to join British Intelligence? Did Brim approach you?"

"Yeah, via my father, I think. There is a lot going on there I don't know about, I'm sure. And it looks like I'm still doing it, aren't I? No escape."

Alistair and Freddie weren't quite sure what she meant but decided to say nothing. A station official called out it was time to disembark and board the narrow-gauge train destined eventually for Engadin via St. Moritz.

Grill

Badrutt's Palace Hotel, St. Moritz, Switzerland.

THE REDOUBTABLE MISS TRUEBLOOD, Brim's secretary had booked their hotel as instructed. The three of them were now ensconced comfortably in a spacious and sumptuous suite at Badrutt's Palace, in St. Moritz. The palatial rooms – including their own private lounge - overlooked the frozen lake, just a few metres below them. A joint concession, it seemed, by both Charles Foster and Brim, believing that they 'deserved a little luxury for their combined efforts'.

"That should cover it," Brim had said to Freddie with a twinkle in his eye, "and more besides." Their dinner was served in the Grill Room, a traditional wood-panelled dining area which also commanded extensive views of the lake and the Engadine mountain range beyond it. The tables were candlelit; the service discreet, but formal, in that conventional way that defines Swiss etiquette.

The main dish was a speciality: Alpine Macaroni – Aelplermagronen – a recipe made with caramelised onions and buttery cinnamon apples, slightly nutty Gruyère cheese from the canton of Fribourg and diced potatoes. The exquisite meal was accompanied by several bottles of Pinot Noir from Valais and served chilled, in tall-stemmed glasses.

"That was an experience not to be forgotten," said Joselyn, gently caressing her stomach, "and this wine is perfect with it."

Freddie made apologies and decided to turn in early; his prosthetic leg was aching from sitting in the train for so long and he knew they had an active day ahead of them: "I'm sure you understand," he had said and disappeared through the maze of busy dining tables. His motivation was clearly designed to give them time to reacquaint.

Joselyn looked into Alistair's blue-grey eyes once more as the candlelight flickered and danced in his face. She was thinking about all the times the had spent together in Zermatt after Brim had exiled her from London.

"I miss Chalet Monte Rosa, Alistair," she said without even realising she had said it.

"Would you like to go back?"

"Would you want me to?" Typical of her to be so direct.

"That's not fair, Joss, answering a question with another question."

She touched the top of his hand: "You've never called me Joss before."

"No, I haven't." He flashed her his winning smile; but something was on his mind.

"Well?"

"I don't know. It felt more intimate."

"And do you feel like being intimate, Alistair?"

"You have an effect on me."

She smiled: "A good one, I hope?"

"That night at Monte Rosa ..."

"Christmas Eve."

"We drank 1918 Hermitage Cognac and listened to the carol singers: 'Alle Jahre Wieder', with the Alpine horns." He said with a very fond memory.

"Every Year Again.". It was magical.

"It was magical for me, Joss." He took a deep breath. "You were the first woman I – loved - since my mother died."

This time her face creased into tears: "You – you never told me."

Alistair said nothing. He could not. He was choked. She finally knew the truth he had been concealing and it broke her heart.

"I'm telling you now."

"Thank you for confiding, because I wouldn't have known. If you know what I mean."

Alistair smiled: "I know what you mean. And thank you."

"I want to ask you something; something else completely."

"Go on."

"Is everything alright between you and Freddie? Tell me if I'm being impudent. Tell me if it's none of my business. It's just that I'm very fond of you both. More than fond; I love you both in different ways."

"And we love you – in different ways ..." Alistair paused to collect his thoughts ...

"But since you ask, everything is fine. You know we had that stupid disagreement about a letter from our mother to Herr Seiler. We refer to it as the 'Waterloo Station incident.'

"Yes, I remember." She smiled at his explanation; it was so like him.

"History now."

"Good. Life's too short. Herr Seiler must have been a character!"

"He certainly was."

She paused.

"What was he like, Alistair? Tell me about him. If you feel like it. of course."

Alistair sat back, considering the question. And the answer.

"What was he like? ... you have to put it into context really ...

"After our father died during the 'Great War', our mother decided she wanted to return here - to Switzerland – her birthplace. The three of us were, how can I put it, adopted by Herr Seiler ... but, what was he like? ... that's a good question ...

A garrulous old ruffian," he smiled at some memory, "a self-educated man who spoke five languages; he could cook, farm, ski, climb and debate history and politics with candour and impartiality. I have never known a man who embraced life with such forthrightness, simplicity, honesty and vigour. That was Herr Seiler...you would have liked him...everybody did, he was larger than life..."

Joselyn nodded and tried to imagine the avuncular figure who had obviously played an important part in all their lives.

"Oh. And he had a deep mistrust of religion," Alistair paused. "Faith, Hope and Charity was his favourite toast. Speaking of which ..."

He ordered two schnapps from a passing waiter and continued: "He died in a hotel room in France, a few years ago. Freddie was the last person to see him alive."

"That's sad. But he had a good life, judging by all the artefacts at Monte Rosa."

"He certainly did. Fearless."

The waiter presently returned with two Bon-Père William; strong pear schnapps that was a favourite apéritif and digestif in Switzerland. Alistair downed his in one go and chased it with the remains of an earlier beer.

"Prost! Now, down in one, Joss. Take that leap of faith."

She did so and raised her eyebrows in shock; her voice quivered: "Actually, not bad. Is gasoline good for you?" She almost gagged.

Alistair chuckled: “It worked for Herr Seiler for 75 years.”

Joselyn re-composed herself after the brutal drink: “I have a proposal for tomorrow.”

“I’m in the mood for a proposal.”

“After the appointment with Braun tomorrow, why don’t the three of us go skiing? You can check on my turning skills ... not bad for a girl from Massachusetts.” A trace of Hepburn.

He laughed: “Perfect. But what about tonight?”

She leant forward, emboldened by the pear schnapps:

“Wasn’t intimate the word you used earlier?”

Notary

Via Maistra, St. Moritz, Switzerland.

THE LAW OFFICES of Braun and Weber on Via Maistra in the centre of St. Moritz were as anonymous as they were functional and well positioned. Outside, a freshly polished brass plate announced: Advokaturbüro und Notariat. It looked impressive and described their principal services; one of which Joselyn would be using that day.

An open steel cage lift took their clients from a draughty downstairs entrance hall to equally anonymous offices on the third floor. They were blandly decorated, but a few odd, framed certificates hung on the plain walls. The office's small windows overlooked the snow- covered street below. There was no furniture save for the occasional metal filing cabinet and a spare desk. Not the most inviting premises, but adequate and convenient.

Alistair had escorted Joselyn as far as the corner of Via Maistra. And it was here that he left her to her own devices.

Alistair and Freddie decided it was far preferable for Peter Braun to believe that she was travelling alone; at least for as long as was credibly possible.

Braun was an impressive-looking character; tall, broad-shouldered, and impeccably dressed. In his late fifties, he had a full head of sandy-coloured hair, greying only at the temples. His tie bore the emblem of Friedrich-Schiller University in Jena and his suit was well tailored.

They had exchanged introductions as she alighted from the noisy and ancient Schindler lift and he greeted her warmly:

"Would you prefer to speak English, Frau Walcott?" he inquired diplomatically.

"If you don't mind." Alistair and Freddie decided unfamiliarity with the language was the best policy; she was here to play the role of the grieving American widow, after all.

"As you wish." He beckoned her into his office.

There were no other partners present – no Herr Weber – or indeed any secretarial staff, which one might have imagined at such an establishment. At such an hour. They sat down at his desk without preamble or offer of refreshment, which she found strange since it was she who had made the effort to travel.

She felt suddenly wary. It was her instinct and her training: Could this all be a set up? No. The documents must be genuine. Her father knew about it. Brim had been in contact with the law firm in England. It must be alright. She closed her mind to negativity.

Braun cleared his throat to gain her attention:

"We are all, of course, sorry to hear about the passing of your husband. But that is why we are here." He gave a brief bow of his head to show that he was sincere and straightened his already perfectly knotted tie.

Joselyn gave him a grim nod of agreement. What else was she to do?

"I am obliged to ask you, by law, for proof of your identity, if you please."

She produced the various documents from her handbag, including the cable, all of which he studied meticulously: "I am sorry I have to ask at this difficult time."

"Sure. I could be just anyone, walking in off the street," she said casually, "at nine precisely."

A flash of a smile to show that he understood her quip: "But you are not just anyone."

"No, I am not, Herr Braun. I am Joselyn Walcott; you can be quite sure of that."

"Good. Then I think we may proceed."

He handed her back the Marriage Certificate and British passport, but retained the cable, folded it and put it in his jacket pocket.

"This you do not need, as you are safely here in St. Moritz. Yes?" He continued without making any eye contact; he was business-like and to the point:

"Ah. One more thing, please. Do you possess a Death

Certificate for Herr Walcott?"

Joselyn rummaged in her handbag and found the certificate Brim had given her at his office in London. She handed it across; he studied it carefully.

"Cause of death: drowning." Braun frowned and looked at her as if waiting for an explanation.

"The perils of angling, Herr Braun." She echoed Brim's words without humour. He handed back the certificate without further comment.

"Good. So, then really all I need you to do is to sign these previously drafted transfer papers and the, ahem, items you require are yours."

Joselyn glanced at the first page with confusion: "Drafted? But they are written in German!"

"Ja! Of course!" He raised his eyebrows as if she had made another joke. "But the Deeds to Needle's Eye House, which I also have here are written in English. As are all the other documents from a law firm in Weybridge, England: Carter and Jackson, as confirmed in a letter from me to England. To Clive Rowlands. I have the correspondence and Property Deeds and Titles, in English."

"Who is the beneficiary of this transaction, Herr Braun?" asked Joselyn, removing her immaculate fur stole. "The remaining twenty-five percent?"

He looked contrite: "Schwarz GmBh, a German corporation headed by Dr. Karl Schwarz, an eminent chemist. Part of a group of German companies involved in research. I understand he loaned your late husband the money in May 1936, when he was studying Chemistry at the University in Dublin. I imagine they were friends, or maybe business acquaintances."

"Why did this – Karl Schwarz – loan him the money? My husband never mentioned it; at least, not as far as I can recall."

"I cannot say why Dr. Schwarz loaned him the money." The emphasis was on the word doctor. Braun was embarrassed at such a vulgar question of money.

"Cannot or will not?" She sounded firmer than she had perhaps intended; but it seemed to get his attention.

"Mrs. Walcott. I am merely a notary carrying out legal instructions on behalf of a client. Nothing more or less. You are, what is the word now, 'gifting' your 75% share of the asset in exchange for some 'items'."

Joselyn smiled. Her dimpled cheeks and blue eyes clearly registered with Braun. He was not used to dealing with beautiful young widows, especially Americans.

"And where are these items of which you speak?"

Braun opened a desk drawer and produced two 10x8" black and white photographs.

"Not here." He handed the photographs across the desk to Joselyn and gave her a knowing smile, because he knew the images depicted were exactly what she wanted. What she had been instructed to collect by the firm in England.

The first photograph was of a leather-bound diary with the

words 'Heinrich Himmler' embossed on the lower right-hand side. It might have been in gold; she could not tell.

The second picture was more impactful: "The Last Will and Political Testament of Adolf Hitler. April 29, 1945. Dictated at 8.00am. Führerbunker, Berlin. Notes taken by Gertraud Junge and witnessed by Martin Bormann and Joseph Goebbels."

Joselyn put the two photographs back on the desk, her face flushed. Braun nodded; his brown eyes shone with moisture; he had relished watching her discomfort.

"Where are the actual items?" she asked again.

Braun composed himself: "If you would please first sign these documents in ink where indicated – with the initials 'JW' in pencil – this is, of course you, Frau Walcott. And I will witness them. This is the legal procedure I am bound to comply with under English and Swiss law. The canton of Graubünden. You understand this?"

"Yes, Herr Braun, I do understand this."

Joselyn did as she was bid. Braun carefully watched her, running a crescent-shaped ink blotter over each signature she completed. She noticed a woman's name on several of the documents concerning the loan. She would commit it to memory. And mention it to Alistair and Freddie.

"Good," he said and placed the collection of documents into a wire 'in-tray' on the desk. He continued:

"The items you require are waiting for you at a property

owned by Dr. Schwarz called Villa Languard. It is near to a small town called Pontresina, the Via da Bernina at the foot of the Alps. There is a Piz Languard. The Villa is the Doctor's holiday home, so I am given to believe. When he is not working in Germany ..." He paused ...

"A horse and carriage will take you there; it is very remote and in the middle of a meadow now covered with snow. I have taken the liberty of booking one for you. It leaves St. Moritz Bad, the lower part of town, in an hour." He fussed with his tie again and gave her a hint of a smile. "Braun and Weber will be happy to cover this unforeseen expense; but of course, only one way. That is fair, I think."

"Why can't Dr. Schwarz come here himself to meet me? I have come a long way," Joselyn asked, a little irked at this discourtesy.

"Alas he is unable to, Frau Walcott. I am given to understand Dr. Schwarz is infirm and is - wheelchair bound – is this the correct expression? – and widowed last year. But his housekeeper is expecting you with the items, as arranged. In a sealed envelope, you understand."

"Yes, I suppose so."

Braun smiled meekly, his task now done: "And don't forget your fur stole. Although the Alpine carriage is open, it has blankets. But the journey by the lake is quite delightful in the snow and today you have sunshine. So, all is good, yes?"

Joselyn said suddenly: "I'm glad I have my brother with me. He is waiting outside. He's been a brick since Giles, well, I am sure you can imagine how difficult such a bereavement can be; he was much older than I."

"A brother you say?" Was there a flicker of surprise on Braun's furrowed brow?

"Yes, he travelled with me. It's a long way from London for a woman on her own to contend with; all those train changes and that complicated timetable."

"Of course."

Braun stood up from his desk and gave her his little bow: "It is fortunate the firm of Carter and Jackson were able to find you. And your lawyer was most discreet on the telephone."

Joselyn thought of Brim's conversation with Braun: "Yes, he always is."

"Good."

"By the way, who is Rosa S? I noticed the first name and initial on several of the documents I signed."

Braun raised his eyebrows: "I cannot say. Perhaps an administrator or witness. It is not a name I recognise."

"But they are your documents, Herr Braun," Joselyn said in German and smiled warmly. The dimpled cheeks, blue eyes, jet-black hair.

Braun was shocked: "Es is ein Mysterium, Frau Walcott."

"It sure is," Joselyn said, this time real Massachusetts, for effect.

She picked up her stole and headed for the staircase, pounding down the wooden stairs for the solace of fresh air. She could not wait to get out of the building to see Alistair and Freddie.

"St. Moritz Bad," Braun called after her. "Don't forget."

But she was already gone. Slowly he picked up the black handset and dialled a number. He was a serious man with little humour. And he did not like surprises: the name and initial was a serious oversight by someone. Why hadn't he noticed it and why the hell did she sign it?

Villa

Pontresina, Switzerland.

"DO YOU KNOW, they've been playing competitive ice hockey on that lake since the nineteen- twenties," Freddie called out breathlessly.

"And polo," added Alistair.

The three of them were on their way to the villa. Alistair and Joselyn on foot and Freddie poling down behind them on a pair of Langlauf skis rented from the Skiraum at Badrutt's Palace. The instructor who had helped him into the bindings was impressed that he was even prepared to ski at all, given his prosthetic limb. He had also equipped Alistair and Joselyn with sturdy spiked mountain shoes for walking.

All around them, the mountains and glaciers were bathed in a soft golden sunlight that made them appear majestic and permanent. The dry cold had preserved the freshly fallen snow so that the contours of the landscape had retained their white, fairy-tale appearance. And yet the sky was as blue as a Caribbean morning. Joselyn was spellbound and felt curiously content; her spirits lifted.

The road from St. Moritz Dorf, the upper part of the village, descends along the lake to St. Moritz Bad, the lower part and into a vast plain towards the little town of Silvaplana. Here, on the edge of town by a farm, they found the awaiting horse and carriage, together with a friendly middle-aged driver by the name of Wolfgang Koch. He was surprised to be greeted by three of them, since he was only expecting two after the phone call from Peter Braun, who had claimed to be the head concierge of the Badrutt's Palace Hotel. It was a conversation he would remember because he hadn't been paid for the fare and wondered who would reimburse him.

Slowly they made their way towards Villa Languard, Swiss holiday home of the elusive Dr. Schwarz. Maybe he'd be there? The three of them had conjured up images of how he might look. How old was he? If he'd been a contemporary of Giles Walcott in 1936, when the loan was made, they'd be more or less the same age. Why was he in a wheelchair? Polio? War injury? They'd find out soon enough. If he was there.

Alistair and Freddie were able to communicate competently with Wolfgang Koch, in a combination of Schweizerdeutsch, Romansch and German. Their wishes were made clear though: Alistair and Joselyn would ride in the open carriage, while Freddie would be towed on a length of rope.

They approached the villa from the lakeside aspect and stepped down from the carriage, grateful for the offer of blankets. Wolfgang said he would wait, after Freddie paid him in full, once the confusion had been sorted out.

Joselyn walked towards the wood-and-brick structure. It was a typical Alpine chalet: two storeys, with a slanted roof and wooden shutters. There were attractive carved window boxes, bereft of any floral content given the time of year.

"Wait a moment," called Alistair, looking up. "That chimney stack. There's no smoke. It is December, after all."

"Maybe the good doctor doesn't feel the cold. Maybe he too enjoys smelly old horse blankets for warmth," replied Joselyn.

Behind them, Freddie painfully unclipped his skis and leather bindings and scanned the horizon with a pair of binoculars also borrowed from Badrutt's. Even though his training had been less intense than Alistair's, and shorter, the practice of caution was always encouraged by Brim. No matter the situation, no matter the place. Joselyn watched him carefully.

Alistair advanced cautiously towards the front door of the villa. His training took over as he unclipped his gun holster, his eyes flitting left and right, up and down. He noticed the stacks of logs piled either side of the wooden terrace, covered with a tarpaulin; they added to his confusion about the lack of smoke. But then, it wasn't that cold. There was a dog bowl, but no sign of a dog.

"Hello!" he called out firmly. He looked around: there was no sign of life. The snow-covered meadow on which the remote villa stood was barren and a cold mist was slowly starting to drift from across the frozen lake nearby. He called out again and moved in closer to the door and gently pushed it.

"The door is not locked, look," he called over his shoulder to Freddie and Joselyn, who were a few paces behind, "that's odd, isn't it?"

Even Wolfgang looked up, startled at the sudden use of English words. Joselyn suddenly thought of her parting words with Peter Braun. The signatory on some of the loan documents. What was it? Damn. She should have ...oh ...

"By the way, does the name Rosa and the initial 'S' mean anything to you two? Braun was really cagey earlier ... Rosa S?"

Alistair edged forwards about to push the door open wider. He stopped dead in his tracks.

"What did you just say, Joss?"

"The name Rosa and initial 'S' was on the loan documents."

Alistair stepped back; they could not see his face, but it was white. His mind was a whirl of sudden realisation:

"Get back, both of you," he screamed out, "back! – back! – back!"

"What is it?" yelled Freddie.

"Throw me your ski pole, quickly!"

Alistair caught the pole and cautiously advanced, like a soldier clutching a rifle, head down. He pushed it against the half-opened door. It was stiff. What was that smell? Almonds?

Musty. Damp. But something else. He was conscious of a resistance behind the door, as if some counterbalance mechanism was forcing it shut. He jabbed the pole forward with all his might, turned and charged backwards, shouting at the others to get back out of the way.

A fraction of a second passed and he heard a click: the scratch of ignition. Then something ignited, it had to be dynamite. The explosion was not massive, but it would have killed him, had he been nearer, or inside the villa. The sound was horrendous. He felt the heat sear his back as he was thrown down on to the ground by the overwhelming power. He crawled through the snow toward Freddie and Joselyn who were crying out with utter disbelief. His clothes were on fire:

"Roll over on your back, Alistair," she shouted. "You're on fire - over, over, over."

Wolfgang came running over, hysterical: "Mein Gott!"

Alistair rolled over on his back like a child playing in the snow. Freddie and Joselyn came to him – the two of them utterly shocked. The snow had doused the flames.

"What the hell ...?" Freddie sobbed and hugged his brother.

"A trap ... a trap ..." Alistair could not control his breath; he was shaking.

There was a second explosion; less powerful than the first, but still violent. The heat from the combustion was intense and relentless. Wolfgang's horse reared up in fright and bolted. It snorted, wild with panic and galloped off; the carriage, out of control, twisting and turning. The bitter smell of cordite was rank and sickening, redolent of a battlefield. The three of them huddled together, a bodily heap of quivering emotion. And unity.

Wolfgang said something incomprehensible and charged after his horse and carriage. Alistair, Freddie and Joselyn caught their breath, struggling for air. It had all happened in seconds. The flames were wilder now, engulfing and devouring the pretty little villa like some hungry orange monster from hell. Nothing could be done, but to watch it. Suddenly Joselyn screamed out:

"It was meant for me!" The tears poured down her face. The words came out disjointed, interspersed with sobs.

Alistair suddenly stood as if some defensive instinct had kicked in. He had to protect his younger brother Freddie as he had always done – and the woman he now knew he loved beyond question. He held out his hands – palms down – telling them to stay put. The two of them looked up at him, puzzled. The training at Sgian Dubh: demolitions and explosives. Primers, detonators, switches and fuses, mines, incendiaries, booby traps. But it was more than that. It was ...Survival. This was a professional hit. Military precision and planning. Somebody wanted Joselyn dead and he knew who.

Rosa.

What had Brim told them in the car that day? A conversation overheard at Trent Park. Giles Walcott had had a love affair with Rosa Spengler. The daughter of a German industrialist named

Erich Spengler. The man Admiral Canaris had warned him about that day in Berlin.

Spengler: Der Jagdhund.

One of the ten men who attended the Nazi fund-raising meeting, 20th February 1933, Bavaria. The financiers of the Third Reich. It was unquestionably Spengler who had financed DAS SCHLOSS and the planned aerial assault on England. The one Joselyn had helped prevent by killing Devlin in Southampton. It all fitted.

But how could Spengler possibly know?

Could there now be an ambush? Soldiers? Snipers? Could there be men in hiding, with their telescopic sights trained on them? Alistair's eyes scanned the horizon, taking in every detail. But all he could see was a blanket of snow, the buildings and bare trees all too far away. And certainly, out of range, even for a high-powered rifle. Was there the reflection of binoculars somewhere, a distant observer.

He was sure there was no one.

Behind them, across the snowfield, the local villagers approached in their dozens: horses and carriages, people running, skidding and slipping on the snow, children, cross-country skiers. Everyone came to try and help them. And there was even a fire tender, useless, its fire bell ringing in an urgent alarm that now meant nothing.

Alistair turned to Freddie and Joselyn, with one overriding thought in his mind: Rosa Spengler must now presume Joselyn was dead.

They must keep it that way. And Peter Braun had questions to answer.

Swiss Detective

Badrutt's Palace Hotel, St. Moritz, Switzerland.

IT WAS LATE ON FRIDAY EVENING, and he should have been snuggled up on the sofa with his third wife, Elisa, after a good dinner. Instead, Detective Leo Hoffmann, forty-eight, was sitting in a leather club armchair in a luxury suite at Badrutt's Palace Hotel. The setting was indeed palatial: luxuriously appointed without being too opulent.

Hoffmann spoke perfect English and nursed a malt whisky and water, gazing into a log fire, intrigued. Not bad, except he was on duty and had been busily occupied since the sudden explosion at Pontresina had been reported to the local police. And he had sped to the scene – 'get there early' – was his watchword – 'before things change. Evidence is absolutely vital.'.

Hoffmann, with his dome-shaped head and broad shoulders looked tough; because he was tough, ex-Swiss army and a character to be reckoned with. And with a reputation that had spread throughout the canton of Graubünden since before the war. But he liked to savour the occasional treat, particularly when it was at someone else's expense. The suite was warm and comfortable. Hoffmann's questions had been straightforward, their answers necessarily evasive. At least, they were for the moment. Hoffmann had spent more than four hours with his suspects; still he knew little about them.

Joselyn sat curled up on a sofa, while Freddie stared out of the window at the frozen lake and flickering Christmas lights below their terrace. Hoffmann felt he needed to address his questions to her as much as possible, since she had been the person summoned to Peter Braun in the first place.

The two brothers were merely accomplices and he needed to discover why they were there at all. What their role was. Alistair sat at a writing desk committing his thoughts to paper, an exercise he liked to carry out while things were fresh in his mind. These words would form the basis of his report to Brim. He would want to know everything. Exact times, a detailed account of what could have easily spelt death for all of them, had it not been for his quick thinking.

And Joselyn's timely mention of the name Rosa S.

"This is an extraordinary situation," said Hoffmann, for what might have been the third time. "An explosion in Pontresina, unheard of. It is a peaceful town. My officers are trying to discover who owns Villa Languard. But it is now Friday evening and the Rathaus – town hall – is closed for the weekend. They are trying to find the senior administrator for archives and records.

But she is not there. Frau Monika Gessler is either shopping or at her husband's art gallery. But rest assured, we will find her."

"It certainly isn't owned by Dr. Karl Schwarz, a disabled gentleman in a wheelchair," said Joselyn with a trace of anger, "as I was led to believe."

Hoffmann sipped his malt: "Before we establish why you were there ... on what errand ... I must tell you this ..."

Alistair looked up from his notes: "As we explained, why we were there is a matter of National Security and I have made a call to London. But as you say, it is a Friday there too. And Whitehall closes down by 3.00pm," he glanced at his watch, "let alone 7.00pm."

"I am aware of the delicacy of your mission. You have explained, and I respect that. But a crime has been, yes, perpetrated, on Swiss territory and it is my duty to investigate it."

"That's fair," said Freddie. "Please tell us what you have discovered so far."

"Thank you, Mr. Valentine, Frederick. Frau Walcott, there is no law firm on Via Maistra by the name of Braun and Weber. A number of others, I agree, but none by that name." He sipped his malt again with undisguised pleasure, absorbed by the sight of the flames. And by her; she was an extraordinarily attractive woman, he thought. What was the word? ... elegant. She could be the face of Vogue.

"But that's impossible, I tell you. I went there." Joselyn huffed and looked across at Freddie. He felt awkward because there was so much they couldn't say.

"And as I have already explained, those offices are empty. I also went there, to check. The third-floor offices used to be occupied by a firm of accountants, but they moved to Bern two months ago. The offices are vacant. And the letting agent confirmed there have been no further lettings. And therefore, no occupants. This is the dilemma, or at least, it is one of them."

"We're going around in circles, aren't we?" said Freddie irritably. "Clearly our friend Joselyn has been duped." The emphasis was on the word friend as he turned to face Hoffmann; it implied a disassociation, which was unconvincing. Freddie felt exhausted by what had happened, probably still in shock. Alistair appeared composed, despite having borne the brunt of the explosion at Villa Languard.

"Have you any idea who would want to kill you in such a violent manner? This was clearly no accident."

"No," said Joselyn, "I haven't."

Hoffmann told them his officers had found evidence at the scene: two empty cans of aviation fuel and charred debris suggesting use of dynamite. The sort used for avalanche control. Not to mention a 7.65mm Luger, or at least, what remained of it. There were a lot of questions that still required answers.

Alistair looked up again: "I think until we have spoken to our superiors in London, it is best for us to say nothing. Mrs. Walcott has obviously been misled" ... He paused ...

"The person behind this attempt could be anyone. We just

don't know."

Hoffmann nodded: "Alright. Let's just get back to this Peter Braun character you allegedly met ..."

She cut in: "I did meet him, Detective Hoffmann. Not allegedly." Her American accent was always pronounced when she was angry.

"Mrs. Walcott, I appreciate your dilemma. And, gentlemen, I appreciate yours too. But my superiors will want some answers and they'll want them tonight."

"Appreciated," said Freddie. "You'll have to tell them something."

"Yes," Hoffmann said, still fascinated by the flames. "You claim this Braun character retained all the documents he asked you to sign. Deeds to this rather grand house in England. Is that right? Owned by your late husband, Mr. Giles Walcott?"

Joselyn nodded. "Yes. I already told you on the way back here from the police station. And I made a statement to your colleague."

"So, you have no physical evidence or any paperwork to support your claim? Or any correspondence from Braun?"

"No," Joselyn said and folded her arms. Braun had deftly kept the cable, the only tangible evidence she had. She was desperate for a strong drink but decided to hold off until Hoffmann had left. She stole a glance at the decanter of vintage Rémy Martin.

Alistair: "Not at the moment. We can get you the evidence to support your investigation. But probably not until Monday. We are not being difficult."

Hoffmann sighed. He didn't believe any of it. But what was the alternative? He knew there was a lot more than was being said.

Alistair, Freddie and Joselyn decided they had no choice but to fabricate a story to the Police; they'd had no time to pre-plan to make such a narrative sound plausible. Except, not to mention her real name; not to mention that her father was the American Ambassador in London; not to mention they were British spies trying to acquire Nazi items they now knew not only didn't exist and were certainly never available for barter. It had all been an elaborate trap. There was no Dr. Schwarz in a cosy Alpine villa. No Himmler diary and no Hitler Will. Somebody wanted Joselyn dead and Alistair knew there was only one contender:

Spengler.

But he had no concrete proof either. The only evidence was an overheard conversation between Gertrud and her husband recorded at Trent Park. Alistair needed to speak to Brim; they needed to escape from the clutches of the Swiss Police as soon as possible, no matter how reasonable Hoffmann appeared to be.

Hoffmann said: "Wolfgang Koch, the driver of the carriage, has made a full statement which confirms many of the points you have made ..."

Alistair rose from the writing desk: "Good. All the points are true."

"Koch also stated his carriage had been booked by the

concierge of this hotel, to guarantee his payment for the journey to Villa Languard. That statement is not true. We checked. He also said he was surprised that three people turned up, not two. That is what he had been told by the so-called concierge: a woman and her brother. This is important because he clearly didn't know there would be a third person."

"Braun told me his law firm had booked and paid for the fare one way," Joselyn added weakly.

"His firm doesn't exist, Frau Walcott," said Hoffmann impatiently, "and neither does he. But somebody must have made that call to Wolfgang Koch. The question is who?"

"Braun?" Joselyn said.

Hoffmann chuckled; she wasn't going to change her mind: "No. Not Braun."

Freddie wandered over to the drinks trolley, poured himself a stiff whisky from a crystal decanter and took a sip. He joined Joselyn on the sofa. Hoffmann thought this was a curious relationship: two brothers sharing a suite with a beautiful widow. What were they up to? He could not make his mind up. And just who could afford a suite like this?

"We've done nothing wrong," said Freddie again.

There was a sudden, unexpected knock on the door. Hoffmann sighed and rose from his chair:

"This may be for me, if you don't mind."

They shook their heads as the detective ambled over to the door. He opened it to reveal a tall, uniformed policeman. They spoke in whispered tones for five minutes.

*

Alistair, Freddie and Joselyn remained silent, before Hoffmann returned to his chair and sat down. He returned his gaze to the fire before resuming:

“It seems there has been a further revelation at the scene of the crime.” He paused to allow the word ‘crime’ to linger in the air. They waited. He was used to this game of ping-pong. Shots were exchanged, placed and parried with more or less power and then a killer shot was delivered:

“A wheelchair was recovered at the rear of the villa; this may mean something or nothing at all. There is no evidence of an occupant, or indeed, any mortal remains. The heat was extreme and the remains of the property dangerous. But a snowfall has, most fortunately, made things easier for my team to have a look around at the rear of the villa, where the second explosion occurred.”

“Wheelchair?” asked Joselyn warily.

“This means something, yes?”

Joselyn: “Yes. We told you Dr. Schwarz was supposedly disabled. But he doesn’t exist. So what? The wheelchair is either an elaborate prop or a total coincidence. Nothing more.”

Hoffmann sighed audibly.

“My officer finally found Frau Monika Gessler in a local

restaurant. Today is her wedding anniversary. She grudgingly went back to the Rathaus and consulted her records. Villa Languard is owned by Schwarz GmBh. A German company. That is the name registered. But she said the property has apparently been unoccupied for many years. The company pay a Communal Canton Tax once a year in full. It is up to date. A good evening's work by my officer."

"The company must be phoney, "said Alistair. "The villa is actually owned by someone else. We'd need to discover how the Canton Tax is paid. By whom. There must be a trail. No, it's all a clever façade to hide the truth."

"Possibly."

"Probably," Alistair insisted.

Freddie was about to say something, but Hoffmann cut in:

"Please let me continue. So, we may have a possible victim. Maybe, maybe not."

"Not without a charred body you don't," said Alistair. "So definitely not. The wheelchair was a total coincidence, as Joselyn said. Or somebody put it there; a red herring."

"A red herring?" Hoffmann repeated the phrase as if he had not heard it before. He made a mental note to remember it.

"Yes," said Joselyn.

Hoffmann: "And, Wolfgang Koch is an eyewitness, don't forget. But before we say any more, I have a question ...

If it was your appointment, Frau Walcott, for a simple meeting to discuss property ownership, why did all three of you go? I am mystified."

"Only I met Braun, don't forget," said Joselyn. "Alistair and Freddie waited outside."

"Ah yes, of course." He paused. "But the three of you went to the villa?"

The three of them nodded. It was Joselyn who actually said 'yes.'

"And why was that?" Hoffmann was getting close, but he didn't realise it.

"Just to help her," Freddie volunteered.

"But why did you go at all? Was your so-called business not concluded at Braun's office? The documents you supposedly signed?"

Joselyn improvised wildly, looking at Alistair: "There were a few other papers I had to collect ... I was told Dr. Schwarz had left them with a housekeeper ..."

"That sounds most unusual, but let's leave that for a moment. Three of you went to the villa?"

Alistair: "Yes."

"Were you expecting trouble of some sort?" The question was directed at Alistair.

"No."

"Then why were you carrying a weapon?" Hoffmann liked verbal fencing. The question was very deliberately directed at Alistair.

"I wasn't," said Alistair. "It must have been there before,

outside the villa, under the snow."

"But Herr Koch said he saw you had a holstered weapon and then approach the door of the villa first, with the weapon drawn; ahead of you, Frau Walcott and Mr. Freddie Valentine."

"Herr Koch is mistaken." Alistair's denial simply did not sound genuine and they all knew it. Hoffmann nodded:

"Because you have no permission to carry a weapon in Switzerland. No licence."

Alistair resisted the temptation to make a second denial.

Hoffmann sighed and looked at his watch: "I am going to ask you all to surrender your passports to me tonight, until we are able to contact the British Embassy first thing on Monday morning. There will certainly need to be a lot more questions about why you were there at the villa ... and why you were armed. "Was there a hint of something hidden in his words? Freddie was too tired to tell.

"Monday is two days away," said Freddie.

"Indeed, it is," said the genial detective. "You will be able to enjoy a restorative weekend in St. Moritz. I notice you paid cash in advance on arrival. So, in this instance, you are covered until Monday."

Detective Hoffmann stood: "Thank you for the drink. I will collect your passports from the concierge at reception..."

Hoffmann put on a substantial fur greatcoat and leather gloves. He finished off by confirming he'd be back at the hotel first thing on Monday and instructed them not to leave St.

Moritz. That it might well be out of his hands. More a matter for the police in Zürich or the British Embassy there. Hoffmann left the suite with a courteous nod at the three of them.

Joselyn went to the trolley and poured herself a substantial cognac: "What do you think?" she asked, enjoying the burn of vintage Rémy.

Alistair shook his head with a vague smile, a memory: "Hoffmann's clearly no fool. And his superiors will want answers. I should not have lied about the gun. Freddie?"

"Agreed. Interesting about Schwarz GmBh and Villa Languard."

"Yes, good to know," said Alistair.

"But before we call London again, I'll speak to somebody tomorrow. Somebody we know we can trust."

Joselyn swirled her cognac and savoured the fragrance: "Are you saying we can't trust London? You left a message, didn't you?"

"Yes," said Freddie. "What I am saying is London led us into a trap; knowingly or unknowingly. That's the evidence."

Freddie's tone had an air of Detective Hoffmann; it implied suspicion and downright disbelief.

Joselyn finished her drink: "Shall I telephone my father at the Embassy?"

"No," said Alistair and Freddie in unison, implying – that's the last number she should call.

Joselyn was too tired to be offended. And she wanted another drink. To calm herself down.

Nexus

Hotel Reception, Badrutt's Palace.

THE FOLLOWING MORNING, Freddie went down to reception and asked for the concierge. A few moments later a largish man of Italian descent greeted him.

"Buongiorno, signor. I am Marco Palledri, the senior concierge. How can I help?"

"I need to make a person-to-person call from one of your private booths. But I don't have the person's telephone number. It is within Switzerland." He spoke in English.

"Give me the details and I will call the operator," said Palledri helpfully.

Freddie gave him a piece of paper and read out the name: "Helmut Siebenthal – Streitgasse – Basel."

"Momento."

Siebenthal was the chief of Nexus, the Swiss Secret Service, who had been responsible for safely transporting him and Herr Seiler to Mulhouse by barge on the Canal du Rhône au Rhin in

August 1943. A central figure in the Operation Windsor case. Siebenthal's credentials were exemplary, a key ally of Brim's and British Intelligence.

Ten minutes later, Freddie was in the telephone booth and the number was ringing.

"Hello," a familiar voice answered cautiously.

"This is Taurus, remember?" Freddie used the codename assigned to him by British Intelligence. The one he had used before. He recognised it.

"Yes." To the point, as always. Not even surprised.

"Problem. Mission. Someone tried to kill us."

"When?

"Yesterday."

"What do you need?"

"Evacuation. The Police have interviewed us."

"Have you told London?"

"Left a message."

"Where are you?"

"St. Moritz, Badrutt's Palace Hotel."

"Good. That is good." Siebenthal sounded positive, "We have someone in St. Moritz. A very good man. Do you have a pen?"

"No need."

"His name is Leo Hoffmann, and his number is..."

Freddie laughed: "You mean Hoffmann the detective? He's the Policeman who interviewed us."

"Hmm. I see. Give me half an hour. Stay within reach of the

telephone and either I will call you back or Leo will come himself. Either way, you will have support."

Freddie sighed: "Your network is everywhere."

But the line was dead. Freddie wandered back into the reception area and waited. There was a crowd of wealthy-looking faces and any one of them could have witnessed the carnage at Villa Languard, and any one of them could have caused it.

Enemies

The port in Cuxhaven, Germany.

DR. ROSA SPENGLER sat in her upstairs office in a building adjacent to the port in Cuxhaven. She was concluding a difficult, animated telephone conversation. Sitting with her was her unwelcome, uncouth visitor, Patrick Devlin. And with him, an associate whom she assumed to be his bodyguard, given his build and distinct lack of conversation. Devlin listened to her part of the conversation with interest.

Rosa was forty-five years old; about Giles Walcott's age, had he lived. She had been Walcott's friend – and then lover – during her days studying chemistry at Dublin University. She knew the truth and all the lies about Walcott. Every last detail. But it was more than that; she had been a crucial part of his life at that time. She and Walcott had a shared past; a bond of love and ambition that held no boundaries. Despite, or maybe because of these intimacies, her patriarchal father Erich had insisted Walcott sign a document confirming the loan Rosa's personal trust fund had made in order for him to buy Needle's Eye House. Such a valuable country pile would have been well out of Walcott's financial reach without it. Recently it had, of course, been used as a lever against Joselyn Walcott, to get her out of hiding and lure her into an intended fatal trap.

Spengler GmbH had been formed in 1890 – and started in this very building – a work shed and offices – beside a key port near to the Netherlands. And even though Cuxhaven had been a major target for the keen pilots of the RAF, the buildings had miraculously survived intact. Spengler was involved in shipping, mining, railways, industrial construction, chemicals; and most important of all, armaments. They had supplied the Luftwaffe, the German Navy and the Wehrmacht. By 1939, it was one of the wealthiest and most important companies operating inside Germany. It employed more than 1,800 people in four plants across the whole country and Austria.

Because of his status in German society, Erich Spengler was very well connected. He knew the Nazi elite well; indeed, he had been a party supporter and backer.

When the agreement between Germany and Ireland was being brokered, it was Patrick Devlin, his son Michael, Giles Walcott, Himmler and Erich Spengler who were its key architects. Spengler facilitated money transfers from German to Irish banks and set up secret but legitimate bank accounts.

Patrick Devlin had a permanently bemused expression on his face; with owl-like eyes which never seemed to blink. He was over seventy, but unlike his late son Michael, was tall and broad shouldered. He was a tough old Republican, and very self-opinionated. A latent aggression lay in every movement he made and every word he uttered.

He watched Rosa Spengler carefully as she concluded her telephone conversation with Peter Braun in Switzerland. The wily old man understood enough German to get the gist of the bad news.

"It seems our attempt failed," she said precisely, casting her level eyes over Devlin and the other man. Despite German heritage, Rosa Spengler had that Russian appearance evident in old photographs of the Romanovs. She closely resembled Tsarina Alexandra and had a serene composure. Even though the situation in her office was serious, she remained placid and calm. She waited patiently for the inevitable response.

"Your attempt failed," snapped the old man spitefully.

"No. Not mine," she replied haughtily, as if to put the record straight there and then. "It was Braun's job to have Joselyn Walcott terminated, after she'd signed the Deeds. It was to happen at our company villa in Pontresina, its ownership buried in trusts. And he failed. Not me."

"So, that American bitch got away? Is that what you're saying?" said Devlin. "That slut who killed my son?"

"Yes," she replied warily, "she did."

"Tell me what you know." The intense eyes pierced her brain like drills.

"Apparently, the rumour being circulated in Pontresina is that a woman and two men escaped an explosion ... an accident at a villa, caused by unstable dynamite ...

... Braun just told me he phoned the local newspaper yesterday ... the Police aren't saying anything, except no fatalities. Explosions are bad for tourism, harmful to the town's image. But dynamite is used for avalanche control. So, the rumour has credibility with the public."

"Where are they now? Hospital?"

"No one knows."

"Police custody?" Two words loaded with malice.

"I told you, Mr. Devlin, I don't know."

"Braun must be an idiot. And don't look at me like that, Rosa. You told me he tried it on with you many times," he laughed, "when you were younger."

Despite the insult, Rosa remained composed. She hated this spiteful old man; scared of what he might do. But reassured by the presence of her secretary Gisela, who was sitting downstairs in the reception office.

Rosa Spengler let a few moments pass. She took a deep breath and continued:

"My contact at the American Embassy in London is convinced Joselyn must have been a British agent when she married Giles. It's the only explanation for – "

Devlin cut her off: "The bitch is a Yank."

He shot out of his chair. The bodyguard touched his arm, which Devlin snatched sharply away like an irritable child.

"How can she be an agent for the Brits?"

"I don't know. Please sit down." Rosa tried to conceal the fact that she still felt deeply hurt by Giles Walcott's marriage to this American beauty he had barely known.

Devlin sat; his face flushed. He wanted blood and right now he didn't care whose.

She continued: "She must have been spying on him; that's all we can think. We don't know. I'm trying to find out who she is. The Embassy man says it seems no one there has heard of her. It's a mystery. She's very well protected."

"Your father told me in October 1943 he was sure Joselyn killed Michael. The question is: how did she get from Needle's Eye House to Southampton?"

"I don't know."

Devlin was enraged; he didn't hear her: "In the middle of a black-out. No road markings. How the hell did she manage that?"

"I told you, I don't know," Rosa said again. But was there just a trace of admiration for this mystery spy? A woman who, no matter her cause, had taken enormous personal risk against an armed terrorist? A brutal thug like his father. And she had succeeded, no matter the odds.

"She must have had help," Devlin speculated, as if reading her mind. A deep, knotted frown formed on his face, which brought his bushy eyebrows closer together.

Rosa was desperate to be on her own; to finish this discussion:

"Look, Mr. Devlin. For whatever reason, Michael failed. The air-strike was prevented. By Joselyn Walcott, with or without help. She tricked Giles. But then, she evidently tricked everyone."

Patrick Devlin could not face the truth. He took a tin of tobacco out of his pocket and lit a pre-rolled cigarette. His gnarled hands and fingers were stained yellow with years of tobacco tar. They trembled as he inhaled.

"I'd rather you didn't smoke. It makes me sick."

But it was too late; his jaw muscles were clenching with tension, as he smoked and spat loose strands of tobacco on to her carpet:

"I want her head in a bucket ...she deprived us of a free Ireland...and murdered my son."

"And how do you think we feel, Mr. Devlin?"

"What?"

"Spengler GmBh put in millions of Reichsmarks to support Germany."

"Screw Germany! You got what you deserved. Hitler was a madman."

"Alright. But millions of innocent Germans died. Women, girls, raped by the Russians when they invaded Berlin. We did it for ..."

"I did it for Ireland," spat Devlin with a vile laugh. "Spengler did it for money. Nothing else."

"That's enough, Mr. Devlin."

She was at the end of her tether. It took every ounce of self-control she possessed to stop herself from being physically sick. She wanted these men out of her office and out of her life forever. She struggled to continue:

"My father will deal with it all from now on. I'll telephone him. He has contacts. Now please leave."

Devlin stood in a haze of smoke: "You just make sure you do. Or the Donoghues in Boston will be brought in to sort the matter. The Irish-American clan don't piss about when it comes to revenge."

He turned and walked out, slamming the door behind him. The bodyguard followed without a word. Rosa stood and went around to the other side of her desk. She noticed his cigarette butt smouldering in a mound of yellow spit. She stood on it and breathed a sigh of relief; she knew perfectly well who the Donoghues were.

She stretched out for the telephone; the instrument was still warm from her last call. Hesitantly, she dialled, she knew her father's private number by heart. And she knew he'd want Joselyn Walcott dead as badly as Devlin did. Probably more. He had lost most of his money. And Germany, his beloved Fatherland had lost the war. And he frightened her more than ten Patrick Devlins. She had witnessed his brutality first-hand and could picture him in his office in Berlin as he tore the receiver from its cradle:

Spengler was always at war with someone. He'd told her often enough.

"Ja," the old man barked on the other end. No hellos. No pleasantries and he knew very well who the caller was.

Braun

Thusis, Graubünden, Switzerland.

PETER BRAUN SAT IN THE workshop below his apartment at Thusis, a small town between Chur and St. Moritz. He had worked as Erich Spengler's second-in-command for more than fifteen years, apart from a brief spell during the war. He had originally trained as a lawyer and worked briefly for a law firm in London. Consequently, he was familiar with English law regarding property, deeds, titles, and land registry.

On the bench in front of him were all the documents he had fooled Joselyn into signing. The envelope in which they were sealed was stamped and ready to be posted – recorded delivery – to Mr. Clive Rowlands, Carter and Jackson, in Weybridge, Surrey, England.

He admired the brass advocate plate, a nice little extra touch, he had thought, which was propped up against his Adler typewriter: Advokaturbüro und Notariat. It glistened with authenticity. He'd been clever, he thought. It had been so easy to trick Joselyn, that gullible American widow.

But Braun was not happy. He had just put the telephone receiver down from a call with Erich Spengler. He told Braun he would send two ex-Wehrmacht mercenaries from Berlin to St. Moritz immediately; they would arrive at the resort the next day – Saturday.

Erich Spengler's tone had been persuasive, but held an edge:

"Peter, don't concern yourself about Villa Languard. Go to the post office in Chur, post those documents to England. Probably best to return to your apartment and stay there. You can't take the risk of being seen by our adversaries."

Braun agreed. It made sense. The line went dead.

Despite their long association, Braun didn't trust Spengler. Or Rosa for that matter. How easy it would be for Spengler to instruct the two Berlin killers to stop off at Thusis on their way back. And kill him. Who would know? Or was he being paranoid? This time tomorrow he might be dead unless he thought of something clever – a counter plan. He always thought of something. Mounted on the wall behind him was a Mannlicher-Schönauer 6.5x54mm military rifle with sights. He'd used one similar in the Army. This one was for hunting: and he was a damn fine shot. A marksman.

Peter Braun went to a beer crate, plucked himself a bottle and forced the cap off with his thumb and forefinger. He thought about Joselyn. How beautiful she was. Her deep blue eyes; and that figure. He fantasied about her for a moment and then realised he had dribbled beer down the front of his shirt. He laughed out loud at himself: a fifty-year-old bachelor dreaming about a twenty-five-year-old girl.

What the hell, it could be worse.

Allies

Badrutt's Palace Hotel, Switzerland.

DETECTIVE LEO HOFFMANN and Freddie Valentine were sitting on the ground floor of Badrutt's Palace hotel in an opulently appointed grand salon. It was famous for serving gastronomic afternoon teas. This morning, however, strong Swiss coffee was the order of the day. And it was served in tiny cups and saucers on two solid-silver salvers.

"How unpredictable can a Saturday morning turn out to be, Herr Valentine?" Hoffmann was proud of his language abilities and communication skills. He completed an English, a German and an Italian crossword everyday – it was his lunchtime recreation – along with the plat du jour at the Café Union in the main square. He always lunched alone, and this was his daily sanctuary.

Freddie was tired. He'd had a restless, shallow sleep, his mind chasing the images of the previous day's explosion at the villa. How lucky they had been. He couldn't wait to return to his beloved Astrid and daughter Christina at Chalet Monte Rosa. He wondered if Alistair and Joselyn would come back to Zermatt with him. Or would she lure him to Martha's Vineyard? And where was Alistair now? He glanced at his watch.

"Unpredictable?" said Freddie. "How so?"

"Is your brother not joining us?"

Freddie thought of the revealing négligée Joselyn had been wearing when he caught a brief glimpse of her pouring orange juice in their suite earlier. Alistair was probably still tucked up in bed. With her.

"A late breakfast, I should imagine. He'll be with us shortly."

Hoffmann smiled at Freddie. He had imagination too.

"Yes, unpredictable. Two phone calls. But firstly, a conversation with my senior investigator, Heinz Johner. An intelligent and thorough young man. My protégé if you like. He buys me a packet of cigars, the last Friday of every month," he chuckled, "as a thank you for my guidance and wealth of experience."

"And?" asked Freddie.

"You know Alistair asked me to find out about a Rosa Spengler."

"Yes, it was a name that had been overheard in the UK."

"A German national, born in Berlin 1901. She is forty-five years old. A skater and a known champion of the Cresta Run. You are familiar with the- "

"Yes, yes, of course. Go on." Freddie was anxious to know.

Hoffmann consulted his notebook, "She studied Chemistry at the University of Dublin, but most importantly – "

At that moment Alistair joined them without a word. He pulled up a chair, poured himself a coffee and said:

"Sorry, most importantly what?" He flashed them both his winning smile usually reserved for women. When he wanted something.

"This will interest you, gentlemen. Rosa Spengler is the daughter of Erich Spengler. His company is alleged to have been very pro-Nazi, during the war. Does this ring any bells?"

Alistair: "Yes, it does. Spengler GmBh were a supplier of armaments to the Third Reich. Supposedly they attended the infamous fund-raising meeting in Bavaria in 1933. When Hitler needed Reichsmarks to fund his rallies."

"Yes," said Hoffmann, "but they also supplied the Wehrmacht, Luftwaffe and Kriegsmarine from the mid-Thirties until the end of the war. As did many German companies: Bayer, Agfa, Opel, IG Farben, Siemens – a long list of reputable companies."

"Is this public knowledge?" asked Freddie.

"It is intelligence within Nexus," said Hoffmann, "from reliable sources."

"Reassuring to hear Rosa is who I thought she was," said Alistair, thinking of Gertrud Wolf. And Joselyn's timely words at the villa."

"You mentioned two phone calls?" asked Freddie.

The wily detective nodded, pleased the information about Rosa was useful. He waited a moment:

"Yes. One from my old friend Helmut Siebenthal in Basel. But then you know about that since it was you who called him. You need to get out of St. Moritz. Fast."

"And the other call?" asked Freddie.

"Anonymous. But the telephone operator managed to trace the call to Thusis, a small town not far from here. In fact, you would have passed through it on your mountain train from Chur." Hoffmann flashed him a dark expression because he knew what was coming.

"And?" Freddie was fascinated.

"The caller warned me that two ex-Wehrmacht mercenaries were on their way to St. Moritz to kill you. They know Frau Walcott has two accomplices. I fear you are all in grave danger."

Freddie: "Who was it?"

Hoffmann chuckled to himself: "Who can say? That is the beauty of anonymity. The very purpose. But my best-educated guess would be that it was Frau Walcott's elusive Peter Braun. The notary."

"Braun? But why?" Alistair asked, but he knew why.

"Because he knows she – Joselyn – has you two."

Hoffmann paused and sipped some black coffee from the tiny cup:

"And, because if Braun was acting under orders with this whole charade, which I strongly suspect he was, he expected only

Frau Walcott at his 'office' yesterday to sign these papers. Now he has you both to contend with. So, in a sense he is back to square one. Joselyn is alive with you two to protect her."

"Yes," agreed Freddie. It was all logical.

"Therefore, Braun's superiors want the job finished. By warning us, that is me, he saves his own back too. Because he knows we will intervene. Quite clever really, when you consider his lack of options."

Freddie acknowledged, with a brief nod: "You believe Joselyn now?"

Hoffmann caressed his bald head and smiled: "Of course. And naturally, with Helmut's involvement..."

Alistair said: "All that is true. But who are Braun's superiors?"

Hoffmann: "You tell me."

"I believe, Detective Hoffmann, they are Erich and Rosa Spengler. They have the greatest motive. And, if you can discover Villa Languard is owned by them, that's all the proof you need."

Hoffmann tried not to look surprised, but clearly was:

"You obviously have a good reason to say that, and I won't press you. If you have worked with Nexus, it must be an Official Secret. Correct?"

Alistair and Freddie both nodded, said nothing.

Freddie said: "How can you help us with our dilemma? What can we do?"

Hoffmann finished his coffee and placed the cup and saucer back on the silver salver and continued:

"Let's consider the options, shall we? If you run, they will pursue you and they won't stop until they find you. Whatever Frau Walcott did – during the war, I imagine – to anger these people, has driven them to try and kill her. They lured her into a clever trap – with some kind of mysterious bait – and their job is not done. They want revenge. Quite simple, to me."

Hoffmann sat back, pleased with his summation.

"And if we stay?" asked Freddie, already sensing the answer.

"The Swiss police can protect you, up to a point."

"I feel there is something more, Herr Hoffmann. An alternative?"

Hoffmann lent back and closed his eyes as if imagining a scenario: "What if you gave the illusion of running ... um?"

Alistair grinned: "I like that."

Hoffmann opened his eyes and latticed his fingers together like a physician delivering a tricky diagnosis to a patient:

"We need to be vigilant. I can have the local airport and railway station discreetly watched. And most of the centre of town staked out."

"And our passports?"

Hoffmann's walnut-like face creased into a smile: "I never even looked at them, let alone confiscate them.".

Hoffmann stood, put on his greatcoat, and held out his hand which both Freddie and Alistair shook in turn. Hoffmann's grip was strong and dry, like his sense of humour.

His tone became serious:

“These mercenaries don’t know what Frau Walcott looks like. Or either of you. And they have no idea where you are staying. Not yet. They will be searching, watching, maybe asking questions, in hotels, bars, restaurants. But we will recognise them first, you can be quite sure of that. They’ll stick out like a sore thumb, I am sure.”

Hoffmann gave them one last look, pleased with his use of the vernacular, turned and left the grand salon.

Freddie grinned. Their passports. He had spoken to the concierge twice this morning and it hadn’t occurred to him once to ask about them. Hoffmann was like a Swiss version of Brim.

Cunning. And that’s what they all needed now – allies.

Descent

Via Traunter, St. Moritz, Switzerland.

SPENGLER'S TWO HIRED mercenaries from Berlin, Dieter Schmidt and Werner Kocher, stood in the main square in St. Moritz, watching the front entrance to the town's police station. The two men had been keeping a silent vigil – four hours on – four hours off - with a discreet change of jacket on each shift. Schmidt had the build of a boxer, a barrel-chested thug. Kocher was a wiry figure, perhaps a climber. But the face was that of a hunter, wary and alert.

Everything looked normal. There had been a fresh dusting of snow and the square was festive. It was just after two in the afternoon and there was a discernible change of light and temperature. A street vendor was selling piping hot Glühwein and roasted walnuts from a small wagon. The square was crowded with skiers, skaters, and tourists; the air rich with exotic aromas and wood smoke.

One of the two men carried a pair of old ice-skates and a sack of authentic-looking Christmas parcels. The other had a pair of battered old skis and poles slung over his left shoulder. To all intents and purposes, they resembled holiday makers in the Alps for the season. Their ruse was deceptive and convincing. The twin room they had rented in a cheap hotel added to their credibility as Alpine enthusiasts on a tight budget. Their papers confirmed them as Austrian citizens from Vienna.

Schmidt came to relieve Kocher for his next shift. Kocher looked cold and shook his head:

"This Joselyn Walcott woman is supposed to be very attractive, great figure," he said, "with dark hair and blue eyes. I've seen hundreds that match that description. It's like a fashion parade here."

"I know. But all we can do is watch and wait. Something will happen. She may be with someone. I haven't got any more information than you." He touched his temple, "Rely on your instincts. It's what we were trained for. And we know that the local police must be involved by now," said Kocher and turned to leave.

Schmidt shivered; he didn't want to be there. He felt out of place. But their instructions had been brutal and blunt and had come from Erich Spengler in Berlin: 'One last mission for the Fatherland,' he had told them, 'And don't bother returning if you do not fulfil it completely."

Neither of them dared argue. Nobody crossed Spengler.

*

It was two hours later that Leo Hoffmann emerged from the police station. A dark-haired woman was being escorted by another officer. She looked angry, as if she had been wrongfully arrested and was protesting her innocence. Hoffmann scanned the square quickly and signalled for a car.

Whoever she was and whatever she was doing, she was the right age, dark haired and very attractive. Schmidt tensed: It had to be Joselyn Walcott, didn't it? What the hell should he do now? He looked for Kocher but knew he would be back at the hotel, most probably supping a Swiss beer.

At that moment, a horse and carriage slowly ambled past the police station, its driver talking to the horse affectionately in a regional dialect he couldn't understand. Another driver sat beside him, similarly dressed. The carriage was decorated with garlands of holly and ivy, like a scene from a Christmas nativity play. The back was covered in old blankets.

A black police Mercedes-Benz appeared from the Chanterella road, the gold Graubünden motif on the driver's door and the word: POLIZEI. As it approached the station, one of the rear doors swung open and a uniformed officer climbed out. He approached Hoffmann and saluted. The dark-haired woman was arguing with another officer as she was handed across to her new guard and driven away. It had to be Joselyn Walcott, surely? Schmidt didn't know what to do, but he decided to run...

"Thank you, Wolfgang," Freddie said to the familiar carriage driver sitting beside him, in German, then English, then Romansch. He hadn't felt so relieved for months.

"All is good, I think," Wolfgang responded in Romansch, "so far."

"Are you two alright in the back there?" Freddie asked.

Alistair and Joselyn were huddled together, hidden out of sight, under a pile of horse blankets in the rear footwell of the carriage. They were jolted and jarred around as the carriage skis sliced a trough through the compacted snow on their descent to Pontresina.

"It's certainly cosy, Freddie, "Joselyn called out breathlessly.

Alistair said nothing. A sure sign he was irritated.

"CELERINA-STAZ!" shouted Wolfgang Koch, a short time later, straining to be heard above the sound of the horse and carriage; the creaking of wood-and-leather harnesses. The horse snorted and whinnied in the cold late afternoon air, almost as if he were replying to his master's voice.

Joselyn stroked Alistair's face: "Do you think we'll make it?"

"Yes." A few moments later, he felt Joselyn stir against him: "I think we're slowing down, Joss. Listen. Be ready."

"PONTRESINA-BAHNHOF!" shouted Wolfgang to his three passengers.

"Do you think our decoy worked?" Joselyn sounded uncommonly anxious.

"Yes. But not for long."

Alistair swept the blankets back decisively, letting a waft of cold air into their cosy nest. The horse and carriage ground to a halt, but the whole contraption still felt in motion, bouncing on primitive springs; the animal's breath hot in the cold air and its excretions smelling foul.

"Come on, let's get off," Alistair said, lowering himself down on to the wooden step, "before we're poisoned by that bloody smell. You alright up there, Freddie? Do you want a hand?"

"I'm alright." He climbed off the driver's passenger seat and manoeuvred himself down to the wooden frame and on to the snow.

"Here we are, Wolfgang. Please stay with us and don't forget our suitcases are here."

Freddie handed Wolfgang a banknote from Brim's money clip and thanked him profusely. It was getting dark now. He looked into the distance and spotted a pair of bouncing headlights. A vehicle was descending the 'Celerina-Staz' route they had just taken. It was either Leo Hoffmann with flasks of hot coffee and crusty ham sandwiches from Café Union, or a couple of killers hot on their trail.

"All we can do is wait," said Freddie.

"Yes. And hope," said Alistair. He felt for the police-issue weapon Hoffmann had lent him and helped Joselyn out of the carriage. She dusted strands of straw from her coat and kissed him on the cheek affectionately.

"Danke schön," she said with a delightful twinkle in her eye.

It was going to be a long night.

*

Leo Hoffmann saw the man across the square start to run. As soon as his raven-haired assistant Monika was thrown into the police Mercedes-Benz, he knew it was one of the two Berlin killers. She had done a good job posing as Joselyn Walcott for those vital few moments, deliberating drawing attention to herself. The two men would now be confused; but they'd have to act. There was no other choice.

But now, Dieter Schmidt couldn't get away. The whole square in St. Moritz had been staked out. Armed police officers were stationed on the rooftops of adjacent buildings. But just how far would these two men go? Hoffmann needed to find out.

He stood in his long greatcoat, lit a small cigar. His protégé investigator, Heinz Johner sidled up to him and he too lit a cigar. There had obviously been some action in the square among the crowds.

"Both the men are now covered, sir. It looks like your man here met his colleague near that Glühwein stand. What shall we do?" They stood a few moments in companionable silence, enjoying the tobacco and watching the scene in the square. Hoffmann looked at his colleague, lowered his voice:

"I've sent another car down to Pontresina-Bahnhof to observe Joselyn and the Valentine brothers. They're catching the Poschiavo train. Soon." Hoffmann glanced at his watch.

He continued: "There they will meet the liaison team I have arranged. This is all confidential. Do you understand? Not official." Hoffmann looked at his colleague.

"Yes, sir, I do," said Johner, thrilled that Hoffmann had confided in him.

Hoffmann turned up the collar of his coat: "Good. So, to answer your question. See what the opposition do next. Leave them alone for the time being, but keep an eye on them. Be wary, they are extremely dangerous."

Hoffmann went on to say that if they apprehended the suspects now, they would have nothing. They had to get evidence of their intention to murder the escapees in cold blood. Proof was paramount. And the Divisional Commander had been absolutely clear about it.

"I understand completely, sir," said Johner. They waited a few more moments.

Hoffmann stubbed out his cigar: "My hunch is that the two men will soon realise Wolfgang's horse-and-carriage ruse was a decoy and head down to Pontresina themselves. They have no other option."

"True," agreed Johner, "but how will they get there? Aren't we assuming they have no car?And, we have alerted the only two taxi companies. Everyone is on the look-out."

Hoffmann frowned and mulled it over: "Ski? Walk? Bus?" He paused; all three options were unlikely:

"You're right. Damn good point ... how would they get there? Let's go. Get another car. Quick."

"Sir." Johner ran like hell.

Sprint

Pontresina-Bahnhof, Switzerland.

DIETER SCHMIDT AND WERNER KOCHER drove cautiously down the icy slope in a hijacked police car. Overpowering the two shocked police officers had been straightforward and extremely quick.

The car approached Pontresina-Bahnhof with a crunch of tyres on snow-chains, powerful headlamps casting beams out into the fading daylight. Faint specks of snow were illuminated, hovering, and bouncing in the cold air. The engine ticked over. And they waited. They were both wearing the police tunics they had stolen from the hijack: caps and holstered side arms completed the picture. They looked convincing and dangerous.

Just below them, Alistair, Freddie and Joselyn were studying a Swiss-Bahn railway timetable under the light of a solitary carriage lantern, while Wolfgang dutifully fussed over his horse. Freddie looked up at the police car. He smiled and said:

"Ah! The coffee and sandwiches have arrived for our journey

to Italy. Detective Hoffmann is as good as his word. I wonder if he remembered the Dijon mustard."

Alistair: "Why aren't they getting out? The Poschiavo train leaves soon." He sounded anxious. "What are they waiting for? Surely they can see us."

"Strange," said Joselyn and looked up at the police vehicle and the two beams of light pointing at nothing. The daylight had almost vanished now, and a few passengers had gathered near the platform for the narrow-gauge train to the local villages.

Inside the police Mercedes, the two men watched. Schmidt, ever brazen, reloaded a separate Walther pistol and blew into the firing mechanism to clear any dust. He said firmly:

"We've got five minutes before they're on to us."

The radio crackled: "Mobile 3. Come in. Officers down. Urgent. Respond."

Kocher was anxious, afraid: "Not here, Schmidt. On the train would be better, then we can escape into Italy. No one likes cop killers. The train is due in less than ten minutes."

"No. Here. It's too late to wait any longer and we have the opportunity. I can handle any back- up they send." Schmidt slipped a pair of leather gloves on to his meaty hands and flexed them. "Go, Kocher. You go now."

Kocher got out of the car and slowly walked down towards the railway station where his quarry were standing waiting for the train. Wolfgang watched Kocher carefully. Kocher concealed the

Walther behind his back with his right hand:

“Good evening,” Kocher said in a heavy Berlin accent.

Wolfgang put the bundle of hay down and called out at the ‘police officer’ in Schweizerdeutsch, the local dialect. But Kocher didn’t understand him. Wolfgang’s tone was bright, so he tried again in Romansch:

“Your sister is as fat as a pig! I pity the poor bastard who has to fuck her! It must be a horrible chore!”

Freddie and Alistair were shocked; they both understood the meaning of the words clearly:

“What are you doing, Wolfgang?” Freddie said, and then it dawned.

Joselyn was bemused.

Dieter Schmidt swaggered down the bank and joined his colleague. Behind, the car radio squawked again. There was a hiss of radio static as the same message was repeated again with much more urgency.

Why didn’t one of them answer it?

Wolfgang said: “Because they are not real Police, Herr Freddie. I know all the local Graubünden force. Better still, they all know me. I transport them around after parties; and I take them to their girlfriends at all hours. Ours is a mutual bond of trust.” Wolfgang smiled with a hint of mischief.

“I see. They look real enough,” said Freddie, but he could follow Wolfgang’s logic.

Alistair nodded, took Joselyn’s hand.

"Believe me. They are not." Wolfgang was emphatic.

"What's going on?" asked Joselyn. She folded the map. "I can't understand a word of this."

"I think we are about to be ambushed," replied Freddie mildly. "Stay calm." He felt for the weapon in his coat pocket and he knew it was loaded...the safety off...

At the other end of the platform, a figure dressed entirely in black, with a balaclava and full-face mask had Werner Kocher focused in the telescopic sights of his very powerful hunting gun. The Zeiss lens switched on 'night-vision'. The two red lines in the sights, criss-crossed Kocher's stolen green uniform tunic. He steadied the gun on the station fence and gently started to squeeze the trigger. He knew where the 'catch point' was exactly; and how much pressure needed to be applied.

Kocher ignored the quip about his sister because he didn't understand it. He continued:

"I am Captain Horst Kopleck of the Graubünden Police." He angled his head at the motif on the car, as if to make his claim appear to be genuine. The others watched him as he struggled in broken English:

"The good news is we have found them, yes? The two Nazi killers from Berlin and Peter Braun. The two men were staying at some second-rate hotel near to Signal-Bahn and the Detective Inspector is pleased."

Joselyn clutched hold of Alistair's arm and whispered

"Braun?"

Freddie quietly: "It's a trick."

"Lucky really," continued Kocher, with rising confidence as he believed his performance was becoming more convincing: "a house-to-house search, hotels, pubs, yes, ski bars." He picked up speed and was now less than ten metres away from them.

Schmidt was now at his side. Kocher put his left hand into his right tunic pocket:

"I have something for you, Frau Walcott, from Braun. A document." Kocher produced an envelope. "It would be better if I gave it to you personally, before you leave."

He pointed at the railway track in a persuasive manner and looked at his watch. There was urgency in his voice. Joselyn moved away from Alistair and Freddie for a second and she was now blocking the crucial line of sight between the sniper and Kocher's uniformed body.

*

Just up the hill behind them at CELERINA-STAZ, Leo Hoffmann and Heinz Johner were in hot pursuit in the original black Mercedes in which Monika had been 'abducted' by his deputy.

Hoffmann was on the police radio, voice raised in shock: "Both officers shot in the legs? Critically injured? This is madness. Why?"

"Because the German killers needed the Police tunics to fool us all," said Johner and accelerated as much as he dared on the icy descent, the snow chains biting into the snow.

"Of course. Damn it," Hoffmann said angrily and hung the radio microphone back on its hook.

*

"Stay absolutely still, Joss." Alistair's tone was harsh, and it shocked her. She stepped back beside him, and he pulled her in sharply. A split second elapsed. The sound of an unexpected shot jolted them: CRACK.

Kocher was still pointing at the railway track with the envelope when the front of his tunic imploded simultaneously with the impact of the round. He clutched the deep open wound in disbelief, stumbled and fell back, dropping the concealed Walther. It emitted a single blunt shot into the late afternoon air. Schmidt went for the police holster, but the gun was clipped in with leather straps and studs. He struggled, moving backwards into the shadows.

Alistair, Freddie, Joselyn and Wolfgang simultaneously spun around to see where the sniper's shot had come from as the assembled passengers shouted and screamed and ran for cover in the platform's waiting room...

Hoffmann's car pulled up and the two of them were out of the doors, guns at the ready. At that moment, the Poschiavo train chugged into the station. Its passengers disembarked, locals, farmers and the odd tourist. Then it fell quiet.

Joselyn could hear the sound of the weapon being reloaded. It was all she needed. Immediately her training took over. Every nerve in her body was taut. Ready for this moment. She turned and pounded down the platform towards the direction of the mechanical sound, her elbows pumping.

Alistair screamed at her as she ran: "You haven't got time!"

Hoffmann and Heinz approached Alistair, taking in the scene. Wolfgang looking shocked acknowledged the two officers, but in the sudden moment of violence, Schmidt disappeared.

"Where the hell did he go?" Alistair shouted, furiously looking around.

Joselyn covered the distance in seconds, sprinting like an athlete. She saw the crouching sniper... and dived blindly into the dark shape, simultaneously slamming the weapon out of the way with her fist. She wrestled the figure to ground, pinning it down into the snow with brutal force. But there was no fight, the figure was defeated. She lifted the head, tore at the mask screaming:

"Who are you?"

"Joselyn!" Freddie was just a few metres behind her now, shuffling down the platform as fast as he could: "You could have been shot."

Joselyn was on fire with anger, ripping the mask and balaclava away, tearing tufts of hair, to reveal the twisted face of... Peter Braun.

"Frau Walcott," he whispered almost apologetically.

She was shocked: "You?"

Alistair heard the sound of a footfall from out of nowhere. Suddenly Schmidt kicked him in the back of the knees from out of the shadows behind. Quick, fast, effective. Alistair fell forward to his hands and knees, dizzy, disorientated and shocked. Damn! The oldest trick in the book. He staggered up on to his feet, desperately trying to focus ...

He heard the burly German laugh, saw a vague outline of his raised fists, dancing around like a triumphant boxer about to win a round.

Hoffmann and Johner had run down the platform to where Joselyn was crouched over Braun, Freddie beside her.

Hoffmann: "One dead. One missing. Who's this?"

"Are you going to tell him," hissed Joselyn, "or shall I?" She dumped his head down onto the icy ground with so much force the ice nearly cracked.

"Peter Braun," she screamed and cuffed Braun's face with the back of her hand.

"Ah," was all Hoffmann could say. They were suddenly aware

of the combat taking place at the other end of the platform. Freddie, unable to speak, shuffled toward his brother and Schmidt. Alistair was wavering ...

Alistair countered two blows to his face from the powerful German. Suddenly Schmidt executed an uppercut towards Alistair's stomach. He stepped back just in time to avoid it. But the man was back, jabbing with his left, sparring with his right. Moving in close. Alistair appeared to be flailing, slowing ...

Joselyn was shocked. Alistair appeared to be losing the fight. She ran along the platform, catching Freddie up, overtaking. She was shouting at Alistair, telling him to stop and run. She believed he was beaten.

Alistair was now close to Schmidt, in hand-to-hand combat mode. Exactly what he wanted. He suddenly spun around, twisting his body and inflicted a right elbow strike to Schmidt's solar plexus. It was so powerful that Joselyn could hear the breath being knocked out of him. A second. Alistair's left fist struck his opponent's Adam's apple with colossal force. A twist punch. His lethal calling card. The cartilage broke. Schmidt went down, blood and gristle blocking his airway ...

"Jesus!" Joselyn watched Schmidt choke to death.

Alistair was breathing hard as Freddie, Hoffman and Johner approached, their eyes wide with shock. None of them had ever witnessed such brutal violence before.

GUARD

Pontresina-Bahnhof, Switzerland.

MOMENTS LATER, there was an urgent, prolonged whistle from the station guard and then he shouted:

"POSCHIAVO! PRONTO!"The train was waiting to depart. The guard was looking across at Hoffmann, as if waiting for an instruction. What should he do: hold the train? What about the two passengers waiting to depart – the man and the woman? What had they seen?

Johner bent down, handcuffed Braun and dragged him to his feet. He picked up his rifle in one fluid movement.

Hoffmann: "Who were those men, Braun, dressed in Police uniform?"

For a moment, Braun said nothing, as Hoffmann continued:

"They shot two of my officers in the legs; one lost a kneecap, shattered by a bullet. Now you tell me who they are, or so help me God ..."

"Mercenaries sent here to eliminate Frau Walcott and these

men," said Braun pointing at Alistair and Freddie, "then me, I am sure."

Hoffmann went close to Braun: "Sent by whom?"

"I cannot say."

Freddie suddenly grabbed a hold of Braun's black jacket and with immense physical strength, dragged him out of Johner's grip. They were all shocked at his aggression, even Alistair:

"You were asked a question, Braun."

Braun bent forwards, his cuffed hands on his thighs, as if he was going to vomit, but Freddie was not going to be deterred:

"Alright then. You planted the bomb at Villa Languard, yes?" Freddie said again in German, his tone was brutal.

A deep sigh: "Yes."

"Why did you try to kill Frau Walcott?"

"Orders." Braun was pale with shock. "I had no choice."

The guard looked at Hoffmann and Johner, checked his watch, blew his whistle. The driver looked out of his cab...

Hoffmann pleaded to them: "You must get on that train." he said, "This is now a crime scene. I cannot protect you. Go now please. Leave him."

Freddie: "I want to hear him say the word."

"You cannot question Braun further, Freddie. He is now in Police custody for murder and we are all witnesses. You must go, all of you." Hoffmann was deadly serious.

Braun said nothing. A man who would rather die than betray Spengler.

*

The guard blew his whistle one last time. Leo Hoffmann acknowledged the urgency with a brief wave of his hand. He, Alistair, Freddie and Joselyn hurried as fast as they could towards the departing train.

Hoffmann said: "Helmut Siebenthal and his team will meet you at Poschiavo and take you to Zermatt. I have a hell of a mess to clear up." He spoke in English – raising his eyebrows momentarily at Joselyn – an impolite word was not his style. Not in front of a lady.

Joselyn went over to Hoffmann, stood on tiptoes and kissed him on the cheek:

"Thank you for everything."

"My pleasure, Joselyn – it's certainly been an experience."

The three of them boarded the slowly moving train. Wolfgang hurled the suitcases into the carriage, as it chugged out of the station.

"I don't know what Hoffmann did to deserve a kiss, do you Freddie?" Alistair asked.

"Quite a lot. Have a look outside."

They looked out of the window. Werner Kocher's fatal wound had bled into the snow and the full moon illuminated the ghostly scene. Frightened faces stared out of the waiting room windows.

The two Police cars, their headlamp beams pointing into the darkness; the horse and carriage and the group of policemen. Schmidt's body had been covered with a horse blanket. Braun was being walked, handcuffed over to a police car.

Alistair watched him: he had tried to kill Joselyn – or at least, someone had – and so far, they had got away with it. Alistair could not see his face and in that instant felt bitterly angry. He tried not to show it.

Freddie sensed his feelings and tried to lighten the atmosphere: "I've never seen anyone run as fast as that, Joselyn. I'm astonished."

"So am I, Freddie." She looked at Alistair's dark expression. "Believe me."

But Alistair's mood had now changed from its former joviality completely. He was rubbing the knuckles of his right hand, lost in thought. Joselyn put her arm around Alistair and drew him close:

"Penny for them?"

Chalet

Zermatt, Switzerland.

“FREDDIE, could you fly an aircraft?”

“What do you mean?” replied Freddie. “Would I like to? Ha! I don’t think Squadron Leader Squires would take me back into the RAF, do you?

Alistair laughed: “No, I mean physically fly an aircraft; you know, if you had to. With your prosthetic limb. Control the pedals or whatever it is you pilots do with your feet.”

“Douglas Bader did.”

They were sitting in the Stübli at the old Matterhorn Hotel in Zermatt, drinking their second pear schnapps, with two steins of Swiss beer on the bar in front of them. The atmosphere was familiar and convivial in the ‘Whymper,’ as it was locally known. It was named in tribute to the English climber who had originally scaled the Matterhorn in 1865 with his team.

Alistair saw three girls came into the bar and one of them looked directly at him. They were ebullient; the name: ‘Valle

D'Aosta Curling Team' was embroidered on their jackets. Alistair's admirer ordered carafes of Glühwein from a very attentive waiter.

Alistair smiled: "So you could, in theory, fly an aircraft. Twin prop?"

"What are you thinking?"

"I'm not sure yet. I just want to put it in my information resource file" – he touched his temple – "you know, for future reference."

The Curling Team became more animated as their drinks arrived and were poured by the expectant waiter.

Alistair and Freddie chinked their glasses of schnapps and downed them in one.

"I'd have a go in an Airspeed Oxford trainer, to answer your question. I haven't thought about flying for a long time. The RAF seems like another world," said Freddie.

"It was a while ago," Alistair admitted, watching the Curling Team.

"How do you feel about being back in Zermatt?" asked Freddie, sensing his brother had moved on from the flying question.

"Good to see Astrid and your little princess Christina," said Alistair. "She is my niece, after all, and yes, good to be back. It's all Joselyn could talk about on the train."

"Manfred and Ingrid adore her," Freddie said as they finished their beers. In the back of his mind was Alistair's question about flying. What on earth was he thinking?

*

"Leo Hoffmann is an honourable man," said Manfred Lochar pinching his nose and raising his eyebrows the way he did. "Fortunate for all of you he was a key member of Nexus, otherwise your trip to St. Moritz would have ended differently."

Alistair glanced at his watch: "What time are we expecting Brim?"

"This afternoon. Zermatt will be busy with visitors by then. The first Christmas after the war in Europe it will be something special," Manfred said, looking out of the window at the passing skiers, skaters and holidaymakers.

They were sitting in Herr Seiler's study in the rustic old chalet, drinking a glass of Riesling before lunch. Freddie and Astrid with their two-year-old daughter Christina; Alistair and Joselyn; Manfred and Ingrid Lochar.

Outside, the snow was gently falling, but inside the wood burner kept the spacious living area warm and cosy. A large, decorated Christmas tree stood in the corner. The chalet smelt of pine, wood polish and old leather, the air was redolent with ancient cigar smoke and Eau de Cologne. Herr Seiler's influence was everywhere: on the walls hung old skis and bindings, sepia photographs of long-forgotten ski teams. The shelves were stacked from floor to ceiling with vintage Burgundy, Grappa and

Old Cognac. As a mark of respect and also out of practicality, they had kept the chalet much the same as it had always been. With the addition of Christina's baby paraphernalia.

Joselyn had first come to Chalet Monte Rosa Christmas Eve, 1943 – two years previously – and much had happened in those ensuing years. And although she knew Martha's Vineyard was her spiritual home and birthplace, she had come to love Switzerland and Europe in general. Falling in love with Alistair was the reason. He had taught her so much. And so had Freddie. The Valentine brothers had opened up to her a world of culture, sophistication, and danger. Fine wine and good food didn't detract from the fact that she worked in a world of espionage and uncertainty.

Seeing Alistair in a combat situation had both frightened and reassured her. It was all part of the mission: the unexpected was always just around the corner.

But she realised their mission was far from over. All was now clear in retrospect. They had been summoned to Villa Languard in Pontresina on a fool's errand.

Since they had returned from Poschiavo a week earlier, she had heard Alistair and Freddie talking – in Schweizerdeutsch – and caught the odd word, often 'Braun' and 'Spengler.' She wondered what the future held for her. She saw Brim's telegram balanced on top of a French carriage clock and wondered what he wanted. A debrief of some sort presumably. And Brim didn't want the three of them travelling to London; that was clear. Manfred and Ingrid were understandably concerned about Freddie's well-being now he had a baby daughter to look after. Not to mention their precious daughter, Astrid ...

"You look very deep in thought, Joss." Alistair came and sat beside her.

"Yeah, I was thinking about 24th December forty-three."

"Your first visit, Joselyn, I remember," Manfred chipped in.

Joselyn: "We drank 1918 Hermitage Grand Champagne Cognac – remember, Alistair? It was extremely special because of the significance of the date."

He kissed her on the cheek: "Of course I remember. You know I do."

Freddie knew just how significant that evening had been for his then, troubled older brother. It was a secret he had shared. And Joselyn knew it too.

*

"I feel responsible for the events at Pontresina, Joselyn," Brim said. "I am truly sorry. That's why I came out here to see you all."

"You weren't to know it was a trap, Brim," said Joselyn very reasonably.

"That's most gracious."

Brim was wearing a Savile Row suit, handmade shirt and club tie. His only concession to the Alpine conditions had been a stout pair of Lobb's walking boots and a Naval Commander-style greatcoat. A Cambridge scarf had completed the sartorial appearance when he had arrived at the chalet an hour earlier. Now he was holding a glass of Riesling and studying his protégée's face. That she still looked wonderful in spite all she had been through, was all he could think.

"As I put in my report to you, Brim, it was Joselyn's mention of the name Rosa S which alerted me to the danger at the villa. Very timely," said Alistair, keen to make sure Brim understood the horrendous significance.

"Quite." Brim brushed imaginary flecks of dust from his immaculately pressed pinstripe trousers; a custom familiar to all of them when he was about to deliver a serious message. He glanced at the faces around the room:

"I went to see a certain Clive Rowlands at Carter and Jackson Solicitors in Weybridge. A bull of a man with a soft voice. Went there with a lawyer friend from the Cavalry and Guards Club in Piccadilly. Fellow by the name of Pickering. This is his sort of thing: land, deeds, wills, family estates, etcetera. Rowlands was quite forthcoming ... but strangely, he was keen to know where you were, Joselyn. In fact, he asked me twice."

"That's more than suspicious, Brim," said Alistair.

"It is," he agreed, "and I have taken steps to address that suspicion. I'll come to that later."

Alistair looked at Joselyn and then Brim with concern: "In what capacity did you contact this Rowlands character, Brim?"

"I merely said I was looking after 'the widow's interests' and hoped they'd received the paperwork from Switzerland. Rowlands was happy with that. But I wanted to discover as much I could."

Joselyn grinned at his choice of words but said nothing. Only Alistair seemed to pick up the irony. But it was clear Brim wanted to set the record straight. This was the principal reason for his visit to Zermatt.

"The documents you signed, Joselyn, were all genuine. Mailed from a Post Office in Chur to Carter and Jackson in England. Rowlands let us see them. Authentic. Pickering agreed. That's why I was keen for him to accompany me," ... he paused ...

"... In that respect Peter Braun was genuine ..."

"Genuine? How can he be genuine? He set me up to die," Joselyn said angrily.

Brim raised his left palm: "What I mean is Pickering felt the way he handled the documents was competent. In fact, all he had to do was get you to sign in the right places and send them back to England."

"So how did Erich Spengler get to Braun?" asked Freddie, sharing Joselyn's annoyance.

"That's the key issue here, how? We know why, but not how."

"Maybe this Rowlands knows? asked Alistair.

"If he does, we'll find out. And I'll explain how. Let's just turn to Braun for a moment."

"Alright," said Joselyn, still not placated.

“Helmut Siebenthal put me in touch with your friend Leo Hoffmann ...”

“Braun is in prison and has made a statement. What the Swiss decide to do with him is up to them. Britain has no jurisdiction in their legal process and the crime he committed was on Swiss soil.”

“Snow,” put in Joselyn with more than a trace of sarcasm. She was not happy.

Alistair waited a few seconds: “Did Braun’s statement mention Erich Spengler?”

“Apparently not; although I did ask the question.”

“Why would it?” retorted said Joselyn.

Alistair: “Is there anything that links Braun with Erich Spengler?”

“No. And Leo Hoffmann’s team have searched his apartment.”

“If Braun’s a blank,” said Alistair, “then what are we left with?”

Brim finished his drink and put the glass on the table: “We believe Spengler is behind the trap at the villa, and we are assuming it is for revenge. But we have no legal redress against him, because we have no evidence ...” Brim paused to make sure he was understood ...

“and, in a way, that is for the best. Hoffmann can do no more than he already has, which is a considerable amount. Let’s face it, he facilitated your escape from St. Moritz into Italy.”

"What are we left with, Brim?" asked Freddie. "Our options appear limited."

"On the contrary, Freddie. Our options are considerable." Brim's face lit up; he was a master at delivering the unexpected.

Freddie looked baffled: "How so?"

"The Tabun cylinders and warheads recovered from the scene at Windsor. The MOD and War Office technicians are confident they were manufactured by Spengler GmBh. They have dismantled and examined the components thoroughly. Spengler assumed, understandably so, that they would have been destroyed by the explosions they caused. Fortunately for us, they were not. "

"I see," said Alistair, with more than a trace of excitement.

Brim continued: "What we need is evidence. Get the evidence and we nail Erich Spengler for War Crimes."

Alistair: "And you need us to get it?"

"In a word, yes." Brim stood.

"That way we get our retribution for what Spengler tried to do to Joselyn," said Alistair.

Brim chuckled: "That would be an agreeable outcome, would it not? Spengler in front of a Court at Nuremberg – or wherever."

Alistair, Freddie and Joselyn were elated at the prospect. It was only Manfred who looked doubtful and for good reason: Freddie might be in danger. Brim addressed them all:

"I'm going to pop back to my hotel and get my head down for an hour, if you don't mind; long day ... I will catch up with you all later. Maybe we can dine together? My hotel restaurant has a mouth-watering menu ...” Brim looked around at his friends knowing that he had scored a coup ... of reassurance ... with the Spengler situation:

“Manfred, they have both cheese raclette and entrecôte this evening.”

“As it is Christmas, a very rare steak and Rösti would be perfect. Thank you, Brim.” Manfred could sometimes sound formal, but he smiled at Ingrid to show her he was not being serious.

“Good,” said Brim, “and I have spoken to Fräulein Greta – the Kindermädchen – she is happy to look after Christina for an hour, Astrid. Give you a little respite.” Brim thought of everything and they all recognised that skill of forethought and planning.

“I know Greta, of course, thank you Brim. Most kind,” said Astrid, glancing at her parents and Freddie.

Alistair and Freddie also rose to see their guest out.

“By the way, Brim. This Rowlands character. You are obviously suspicious about him?” asked Alistair.

“Ah yes, I’m having him tailed, you know, DS ...”

Everybody in the Service knew the acronym stood for discreet surveillance. This meant a series of agents in shifts watching a suspect, normally around the clock.

“As I said, he asked where Joselyn was, twice. Now why would he do that?”

Pub

Salmon and Ball, Bethnal Green Road, London, England.

"HER MAIDEN NAME IS JOSELYN FOSTER; her father is Charles Foster, the bloody Deputy Chief of Mission, right here in London. Macdonald House, Grosvenor Square. Where I work," said the man in the blue raincoat.

He was average height, with auburn hair cut short and straight, almost military. He had energetic eyes and an academic manner. His accent was Irish American, specifically Boston. He tried to disguise it, given the circumstances.

He regarded Rowlands with disdain.

"Ambassador Charles Foster. Are you sure?" asked Clive Rowlands. He had the build of a loosehead, or tighthead prop, yet was eloquent and softly spoken. Blue Raincoat noticed he had extraordinarily long eyelashes which fluttered as he spoke.

"Too damn right. I checked with Records. To me there is no doubt he is her father."

"She told Giles Walcott she was orphaned. Parents killed in a train crash in the mid-west of the United States, when she was ten." The soft voice of Rowlands sounded a little piqued that Joselyn had misinformed his client.

Raincoat: "She lied. It seemed Joselyn fabricated an entire life story. None of it was true, apart from Cambridge University, which Giles did check on. And her love of tennis of course, that much was true. The rest of it, bull."

"Giles was clearly a fool to have been misled by such a woman," said Rowlands with a trace of envy. He was betraying Carter and Jackson. Treachery was ugly. And discovery even worse.

"He was a guy in love," said Raincoat, "besotted. And you cannot blame him. She is a stunner as they say back home. And what a figure, boy!"

"Even so." Rowlands mulled the idea over in his mind; his little pink tongue brushed his lips nervously.

Blue Raincoat watched him, said nothing.

"And you are sure she works for British Intelligence? Set Giles up?" Rowlands tried to sound casual.

"As sure as I can be. That's what I am trying to find out. But she has covered her tracks. Or someone has covered them for her. I won't find out much from the Embassy."

Rowlands: "And yet she's American, like you. I wonder how she was recruited." There was a tone of speculation in his soft vowels. He thought about the two men who had visited his office in Weybridge.

"Who knows?"

Blue Raincoat and Rowlands were sitting in the Salmon and Ball public House at 502 Bethnal Green Road, in the East End of London. It was six o'clock in the evening, busy with exhausted commuters emerging from the Tube station next door. There was plentiful evidence of the London Blitz all around the old pub, of relentless night-time bombing raids by the Luftwaffe in 1940/41. Bombed-out buildings, piled up bricks and rubble where people's homes had once stood. It was a sorry sight. Grey streets and thin faces, the result of rationing and dismal nights spent down in an air raid shelter.

They sipped their watery beer in the public bar, watching two old men throwing darts at a twisted old board. The radio was playing BBC Light Programme, a dull music hall farce that was far from comedic. There were no women in the room, except for the barmaid Lucy, a buxom creature in her late twenties - and the surly landlady Mavis. She resented the lewd comments of her customers, but encouraged Lucy's ample cleavage all the same. It was good for business. The Off-Sales counter was busy selling bottles of brown ale, pickled eggs and the odd pack of black-market butter. No coupons were needed at that particular counter.

"Yes, Joselyn is almost certainly British Intelligence," said

Blue Raincoat, "and I'm taking a hell of a risk coming here. If anyone at the Embassy found out, they'd fucking hang me." Blue Raincoat was senior staff and the London contact of Rosa Spengler. He was also a lot more.

"Anything else," pressed Rowlands. He wanted value for money.

"She visited her uncle in America. I snooped around in Immigration Records one evening, had a good look. There is no record of her outward journey to New York – possibly a troop ship – but we know that she came back to Europe because of what happened in Switzerland. After that she vanished again."

Rowlands sighed, absorbing the information, but he needed more.

"Where is she now?"

"No idea."

"Does she have an address in London?"

"Yes, it's called the American Embassy."

"She stays there?" Rowlands could not hide his surprise.

"Foster has an apartment on the top floor. I'm told it's sumptuous. All-American luxury, care of the taxpayer. And no expense spared. I ought to be jealous, but I'm not."

"Do you like Foster?" Rowlands asked with a sideways glance, "considering you are betraying him."

"Yeah, he's alright," he said ignoring the jibe, "well-connected. Well-paid ... speaking of which ..." Blue Raincoat drained his pint and the look on his face showed he hadn't enjoyed it. But Rowlands was paying, so what the hell.

Rowlands lowered his voice:

"Our friends in Cuxhaven want to know where Joselyn is." Rowlands discreetly handed him an envelope which he took, opened, and looked inside greedily, not caring who saw the exchange of cash.

"Subtle as an earthquake."

"I'll do what I can ..."

"Get into Foster's office, search his desk, his files. His diary. He may be meeting Joselyn somewhere. Find out. We need to know where she is. At least, Rosa and her father do."

"That's damn risky. It's guarded."

"Then search his apartment. You have a pass to go anywhere in the Embassy."

"Not his private quarters."

"Do what you can," said Rowlands. "We'll meet here in one week's time."

Blue Raincoat didn't like being pressured: "No, Mark's Bookshop, Charing Cross Road, like before. Same time. Same aisle."

"Alright," Rowlands lightened his tone, tapped him on the arm. "Buy your wife some nylons with the money. You never know, she might even let you sleep with her!"

"I don't have a wife."

"Someone else's then. You must have quite a choice at the Embassy; office girls on tap."

"Sure." Blue Raincoat stuffed the envelope hurriedly into his jacket pocket and left without another word.

Rowlands laughed at his vulgar joke and ordered a double scotch from Lucy. He gave her far more than the drink was worth and told her to keep the change. As she dinged the cash register's keyboard with a 'No Sale', she turned and gave him a cheeky smile. The money was dropped into her apron, with a look of promise:

'Oh good,' he thought, 'I wonder what she likes on her fish and chips."

*

Across Bethnal Green Road, a man was having immense trouble lighting a pipe. It was rather windy and, truth be told, he did not smoke. He had followed Rowlands all the way from the Weybridge law firm: train, tube and on foot. He had noted everything. This evening was an interesting rendezvous. He did not know who Blue Raincoat was, but he would make it his business to find out. A separate tail. But he did know who Rowlands was and that he had handed the other man an envelope, a bribe. He would send a telegram to Professor Brimblecombe in Zermatt tomorrow. He had not even known where it was until he'd consulted his son's Worldwide Book of maps, published by HMSO in 1937.

'Switzerland,' he had thought. 'Lucky blighter.'

Fifteen minutes later the pipe-smoking man would be relieved – wordlessly – by another tail. The man would watch Rowlands leave the Salmon and Ball at closing time with a busty-looking woman in her late twenties. They would head toward Roman Road and he would follow. No doubt to a seedy guest house or b&b. He had seen his sort before: married, affluent, probably with children, seeking sexual gratification on the cheap. Better still, for nothing.

Another long night for another lone watcher.

Listeners

Beaufort Lodge, Middlesex, England.

THE STORY OF 'The Listeners' was one of the earliest brainwaves of British Intelligence in the Second Word War and began in the most unlikely of locations; the Tower of London. It soon became apparent that the iconic fortress would prove insufficient to cope with the growing number of captured POWs, of all military ranks, and some civilian spies unlucky enough to have been caught.

Beaufort Lodge in Middlesex was seconded by the War Office in 1940 as a Debriefing Centre to replace the Tower. Ten miles north of the capital, Beaufort was set in 400 acres of secluded woodland and park and relatively easy to protect, and defend, if need be. A convenient distance from London, yet within easy reach, the estate would be perfect for a clandestine unit. Safe from the public, interfering journalists and the prying eyes of politicians of all persuasions. The owner, Dutch businessman Maximillian Hendricks had died in 1939 from acute appendicitis and the WO recognised the building's potential for 'special purposes.' It was not dissimilar to Trent Park at Cockfosters, where Listeners also overheard and recorded conversations between senior German Military Personnel.

A bugged conversation at Trent had provided MI19 the location of the scientific production plant for the hydrogen peroxide needed for the V-2 rocket programme. It was a stunning and critical piece of information. And all this covert intelligence was translated by German émigrés who had fled Hitler's tyranny. The key was that the relaxed atmosphere caused the inmates inadvertently to relax and let down their guard.

At Beaufort, the team of Listeners had crucial words to listen out for: the names of escaped or unaccounted-for Nazi High-Command, SS, Gestapo. Plus, one or two Luftwaffe and Kriegsmarine officers unlucky enough to have been found and captured by either the British or Allies.

Two other names had also been requested by Brimblecombe: Dieter Scheiderbauer and Erich Spengler. Both crucial players, in their own way, in the DAS SCHLOSS scenario:

Dieter Scheiderbauer had been helmsman of the 'FV Clarissa,' the vessel which had transported the Tabun cylinders from France to England in 1943. He had been detained in Poole Harbour and then transferred to Beaufort. One evening, the unsuspecting Scheiderbauer was overheard to say to a fellow inmate:

"I wonder what happened to Captain Richard Lambert. If ever there was a war criminal, he was one. I bet Spengler shot him for failing Himmler."

And that is exactly what had happened to him.

Gertrud and Harald Wolf, the treacherous London sleeper spies were also being detained at Beaufort. One night after a few too many drinks Gertrud had let slip that 'Giles Walcott had a serious love affair with the daughter of a wealthy German industrialist, while she was studying in Dublin. Her name is Rosa Spengler, daughter of the Nazi funder Erich.'

To the Listeners, it was a golden nugget of intelligence and was reported immediately back to Brimblecombe.

When Joselyn had asked Alistair if he knew the name Rosa S, it had saved their lives at Villa Languard in Pontresina.

*

Alistair and Freddie were being driven by Captain Clitheroe in Brim's Humber, from London to Middlesex. They noticed newly replaced signposts to places such as Uxbridge and Harefield before arriving at Beaufort Lodge. The impressive estate had a gated entrance which was discreetly manned by armed agents. The long driveway was lined with trees; the immaculate lawns, last mown in the late autumn of 1945. The car pulled up with a scrape of gravel outside the front door.

“I’ll go and see Gertrud first,” said Alistair, “and then we’ll both interview this Scheiderbauer character. Don’t forget we’re being recorded.”

“No,” Freddie agreed, with a smile. He could only imagine why Alistair wanted to see Gertrud on his own. It was Alistair’s instinct about Gertrud which had led to the successful outcome at Windsor in 1943: a slip of the tongue – Verdammter Mist!

“It’s you again. What do you want?” said Gertrud in a brusque manner. Alistair found her in her comfortable quarters, sitting at the window, smoking a cigarette. The sky-blue eyes, high cheek bones, blond Victory Roll style hair, a look of regal haughtiness. She was enchanting. Alistair knew he needed to be professional and distant. There was no sign of her husband Harald or of any of his possessions which should surely have been in evidence. Alistair did notice a little stack of paperbacks and wondered if they were the ones she had bought from the Priory Bookshop in Windsor, the first time he had ever spoken to her.

“Last time – “

“Last time we met you found me attractive.” She inhaled her cigarette through shiny, red-painted lips and exhaled with a smile. She eyed him carefully.

“I have no time for games, Gertrud.”

“Ah, so this time it’s Gertrud and not Frau Wolf. You must want something. It is the nature of the English etiquette. That use of my first name breaks with convention. And yet you are not

English, Herr Valentine. Are you?"

She looked at him, stubbed out her half-smoked cigarette, stood, smoothed down her dress and wandered slowly towards him. She moved with a slow sexual insouciance, holding his gaze, electrifying. Instinctively, he stepped back.

"I won't bite."

He ignored her quip: "Yes, I am English."

"Alright, you might be. But there is a trace of something. Although I remember from last time your German is excellent – better than mine."

"But you are German," he said in an accusatory way, which bordered on offensive and yet he didn't mean it to be.

"Of course. What do you want? I can tell that you are short of time. Are you seeing another prisoner ...?"

Before he could answer, she continued: "Who was the man you arrived with? Your brother? He looks like you. Same build, same colouring, but with a limp. I have seen him before. At Windsor, I think. He was there, yes?"

He ignored her because he recognised the tactic of engagement; for her it was natural:

"You are not a prisoner, Mrs. Wolf."

"Ah, then what am I?" She said the words in German, and she was now less than a metre from him. Then closer. He caught her fragrance; she caressed the lapel of his jacket; it was a coquettish intimacy. Everything about her was provocative. And she milked it.

"A detainee." He touched her hand to move it; brushed her skin. She should have flinched, but she did not.

"The same." She looked up into his eyes; she was captivating, intense. Her glossy lips looked too inviting.

"No. Believe me. Prison is far worse."

She snapped her hand away, sensing he wouldn't play: "Is it? What do you want, Herr Valentine? You didn't drive up from your office in, where - Whitehall - with your brother to pay me a social call, did you?"

She turned and went back to where she had been sitting, in a chair by the window, overlooking the sweeping drive. 'Bad security', thought Alistair. He must remember to raise it with Brim. Or Colonel Thomas who had greeted them earlier.

"Rosa Spengler," said Alistair.

"What of her?"

Alistair had to tread carefully, he could not betray the nature of the eavesdropped and recorded conversation.

"You know the name."

"Yes."

Alistair said nothing, watched her.

She sighed: "What's it worth, if I tell you what little I know?"

"I don't know, Gertrud. Possibly quite a lot."

"Ah! Can you get me out of here?"

"Maybe."

"And Harald?"

"No."

She watched him, calculating her chances: what did she have to lose? the chance of freedom, could she trust this charming man? Why should she? But then, why not?

"Giles Walcott the man you killed at Windsor?"

"Yes." Alistair watched her eyes.

"He was our handler, our intermediary with Germany."

"Alright."

"I've already told your people this."

"Tell me, Gertrud. It's important."

She took a breath: "Walcott came over to our hotel one night in Kensington. Harald had gone to bed. Walcott got very drunk. Gin. Not used to it."

"And?"

"He started to reminisce about Dublin in the Thirties. The countless number of female students he had seduced at the University."

"Oh?"

"One of them was Rosa Spengler. Except she was quite different from the other conquests."

"Conquests?"

"The word he used, yes. He told me he'd had a serious love affair with Rosa. He was quite graphic actually ... about the physicality of their relationship ... it was quite an eye opener, you know. Also, she was wealthy. At least Erich is."

She waited for a reaction; he gave nothing.

"Old man Spengler was important to Hitler, the Reich. But

you know all this."

"Not really."

"Why do you care? It's history. The war is over."

Alistair found he had to take a breath: "Erich Spengler tried to murder a friend of mine."

Gertrud was incredulous: "Spengler? No, not him."

"Somebody else then?" He stopped in case she knew who it was and might tell him.

Gertrud stood and faced him as if she was uncomfortable, sitting while he stood. She almost purred the words:

"And you care, because that friend of yours is a woman." She was near to him again. "A woman you love, but you didn't realise it at the time."

"Yes."

"And you want to get to Spengler? What, for revenge?"

Alistair said nothing but watched her again. She met his gaze once more. Her face, her eyes, imploring, wanting him to kiss her, just for the hell of it. He resisted.

"You'll never get to him. He's too well-protected."

"I see."

Gertrud sighed; the moment was lost forever: "Rosa."

"Rosa? What do you mean?"

"She is the only way you'll get to him ... Spengler warned Walcott off, you know. He didn't want his precious only daughter involved with an Irish gangster, a man in league with a savage killer like Michael Devlin. For her he wanted German

Aristocracy; a man of breeding and cultural significance."

Alistair blinked his eyes tightly, the way he always did. He thought of beautiful Joselyn and what she had had to sacrifice:

"Oh really," he said as casually as he could. "I understood Walcott had met someone else."

Gertrud smiled; it was as if she had read his mind. She whispered: "Maybe he did."

Alistair swallowed; how close she had brushed with the truth. But did she know it? Of course, she had met Joselyn at Needle's Eye House. With Walcott.

Suddenly Alistair needed to get out of her room.

*

"You look as though you have just seen a ghost," said Freddie, holding an armful of transcription notes from the radio room.

They were standing in the grand entrance hall at Beaufort Lodge, at the foot of the sweeping main staircase and ornate balustrade.

"Not a ghost. I feel as though someone has walked across my grave. Isn't that what people say?" said Alistair quietly. He had sensed the spectre of danger, that menacing feeling of thin ice: Gertrud had got into his soul: she knew the woman he was protecting was Joselyn.

Before Freddie could answer Lt. Col. Kirkpatrick's colleague from Cyphers and Codes came over to greet them, his hand outstretched:

"Gentlemen, David Fox. Army Signals. You wanted to speak to Dieter Protz?"

"Yes," said Freddie. "Scheiderbauer said he knew all there was to know about the German underground tunnels at Mittelwerk and the V2s."

"He did."

"Did?"

"Protz was found dead in his room this morning."

"That's bloody inconvenient," said Freddie and then, "God! Did I say that out loud.?"

"Yes, I'm rather afraid you did," said Fox. "But a lot of what he knew we eavesdropped and recorded in the snooker room."

"When was this?" asked Freddie.

Fox looked at the transcript: "Yesterday, as it happens."

"And this morning he dies?"

"Yes."

"Will there be a Police investigation?"

"An investigation, yes. Probably an internal matter. A German national dies ... while in custody ..."

"A captured POW," Alistair reminded him. "What of this transcript? Is it of any interest?"

Fox's tone lightened: "Interest? Yes, I would say so. All we generally hear is the clack of snooker balls and the odd German expletive." He looked at the two brothers ...

"Protz played with Harald Wolf; you know, Gertrud's

husband. Goodness only knows why he doesn't spend more time with her. Shame really."

"Tragic," said Alistair.

"Captain Fox, I wonder if we could go somewhere quiet and you could read out this transcript," said Freddie. "I think your knowledge of the people involved might lend it an air of authenticity."

"I'd be glad to; and please call me David." He took the bundle. "Follow me."

Fox cleared his throat and started to read, not really taking in the content until he had actually uttered the words; he carried on, regardless:

"Your Gertrud has a great figure, if you don't mind my saying, Harald."

"Harald (laughing). She has a great everything. The trouble is, I rarely see any of it."

"Dieter Protz: Pity."

The sound of snooker balls being dropped into the frame, a cue being chalked. No other POWs in the snooker room.

"You should have seen her when she was twenty. Heads turned all ..."

Fox: "I won't read any more of this. It's just idle chit-chat. Wait." He read from further down the transcript:

Protz: "Did you know that in October '43, the German company Mittelwerk GmBh was issued a War Contract by

General Emil Leeb, Head of Army Weapons. 12,000 missiles at 40,000 Reichsmarks each. Work it out."

Wolf: "Who authorised it?"

"Who do you think? The rocket weapons project was important."

Fox: "Shall I carry on?"

Alistair: "Yes."

Protz: "Peenemünde was bombed by the RAF, the tunnels of Mittelwerk. They had to move their operations elsewhere. Spengler was clever. He carried out his development away from the new locations. His factory produced at least ten high-speed ballistic missiles, each with an explosive warhead. The missiles were primed with pressurised Tabun. A gyroscopically stabilised fin was designed to guide these weapons to the target."

Wolf: "Why Spengler?"

Protz: "Orders from Himmler. The problem was that Von Braun's V2s were erratic and unreliable. The possibility of launching Spengler's missiles from an aircraft made them more accurate, especially when there was a specific target."

Wolf: "Where?"

Protz: "The south of England. They could reach an astonishing speed, powered by a mixture of alcohol and liquid oxygen. 1,200 km/h; faster than a ME 262 or a Spitfire."

Wolf: "How do you know all this?"

Protz: "I worked on the project with other German scientists at Nordhausen. Conversion of the Heinkels was the most difficult. In the end the project failed; we don't know why."

Wolf: "I do. I was there. Our mission was betrayed."

Protz: "If it had succeeded, Germany would have won the war."

Wolf: "Lots of maybes, Protz. They say at the end Hitler was mad. He'd rather have seen Berlin destroyed than give in to the Russians and the Allies. I'm glad I didn't see Berlin turned to rubble."

Protz: "I was captured in the end. That's why I'm here."

(Was there a hint Protz might be lying? Something in his tone: I was captured in the end.)

Wolf: "Oh? Where was that?"

Protz: "Nordhausen. Look, do you want to break? I am not bothered about tossing a coin or anything. But let's have a scotch, there's plenty of it."

Silence ...

Fox looked up from the transcript: "That's all there is, I'm afraid."

Alistair sighed in utter frustration: "This is the most important sequence, dammit. That's why we're here. At least he said Nordhausen, but I don't believe he was captured there."

Fox: "Sorry."

Freddie: "Is there more? Another recording which has been transcribed?"

Fox looked embarrassed: "No."

Freddie: "How can it just suddenly end? There must be more.

They were just about to break. The game hadn't even started."

Fox shook his head: "I don't know."

"And now Protz is dead. This isn't good enough." Alistair stood. "We'll need to see the Commandant."

Fox nodded, went over to his desk and picked up the phone.

*

Assistant Commandant (Intelligence) Lt. Col. Andrew Kirkpatrick should have sounded Scottish; instead, he spoke with a baritone voice, eloquent and educated. He was over six foot, imposing and wore full Army uniform, appropriate to his rank. He stood up from behind his desk as Alistair and Freddie walked in with David Fox. The brothers assumed he would remain, but instead he withdrew, quickly, after a sharp glance from the Commandant.

Kirkpatrick spoke without introduction: "We run a tight ship here, gentlemen. Policing and Collateral Security are our watchwords ... Please be seated." He gestured to a couple of chairs as if he were a headmaster addressing parents who were unable to settle their children's school fees.

"You may not question Harald Wolf about a conversation we have recorded and transcribed. It might possibly compromise the entire ... essence of what we do here ..." He eyed them both with cold blue-grey eyes and an uncompromising expression, holding out his hands as if making a point in Court.

"I interviewed Gertrud Wolf," Alistair said defensively. At once, knew it was a clumsy opening gambit to a man like Kirkpatrick.

"Indeed, you did, Mr. Valentine ..." He smiled very briefly and sat back down behind his desk ...

"And I have heard it. The rapport between you is concupiscent ..." He raised an eyebrow to demonstrate his disapproval ...

"The point is, you went to her with a specific question. Not one you had overheard from – or in relation to – one of our secret transcripts. No, I am afraid an interview with Wolf is out of the question."

Freddie: "It is a matter of national importance, Lt. Col. Kirkpatrick."

"National importance?" Kirkpatrick's tone was doubtful. Alistair and Freddie could see he was mulling the idea over in his mind. His gaze was severe:

"I hold Professor Brimblecombe in the highest esteem ... His department must make a formal request ... I'm sorry, gentlemen, but there it is."

There was no doubt. The discussion was over.

Alistair: "Sir, the fate of Dieter Protz seems untimely."

Kirkpatrick picked up his telephone and barked an order at his adjutant to the effect that his guests were leaving and should be shown to their car right away. And to make sure they did not stray. He rose from his desk to his full stature and addressed them both firmly:

"If one word of our operation here becomes known to the public, I will hold you and British Intelligence responsible ... is that clear?" His tone was brutal; a sharp rap on the door and two Infantry came in, at the double. There was no doubt.

Alistair and Freddie rose from their seats with a mutual 'Sir' and left the office. Kirkpatrick was consumed with rage, but like a lot of people in his position did not outwardly show it. That would be reserved for the appropriate rank. Alistair and Freddie were led out to their waiting Humber and the smiling face of Captain Clitheroe.

Alistair glanced up at the window where Gertrud had sat earlier, smoking a cigarette and watching them arrive. The curtains were drawn, and no one, it seemed, was there. Strange, he thought, and he hadn't mentioned what a terrible breach of security her view of the drive had been. Somebody must have realised.

Gertrud, the beautiful enigma. What Alistair didn't know was that somewhere behind the façade of the house she was watching him, with a great deal of interest.

"Come on, Freddie," Alistair said dismally, "let's get Clitheroe to drop us back into London. Find some lunch in the West End."

"Good idea. A pint of English beer and a Cornish Pastie. I know just the place. A stone's throw from the Baker Street safe house, the only benefit of being cooped up there."

Alistair nodded. He breathed in the country air but could still detect the fragrance of Gertrud's perfume on the lapel of his jacket. And for some reason, it made him smile.

Skindles

Skindles Hotel, Maidenhead, England.

BRIM ALWAYS SAID that Manfred was a man of a thousand faces. More accurately, he was a man of many expressions. Today he was composed. Still the bushy eyebrows and the air of the Sicilian underworld. Still the habitual practice of pinching his nose between thumb and forefinger when making a point or addressing a serious problem. His Loden-style wool duffle coat, hanging on the back of his chair, together with scarf and gloves. He claimed the climate in England was 'miserable.'

This morning's newspapers focused on the War Crimes Tribunal in Nuremberg; the first meeting of the United Nations to be held in London; Charles De Gaulle to resign as President of France and Prime Minister Clement Attlee to discuss the state of the nation.

Brim and Manfred sat in the 'Bridge Room' of Skindles Hotel

in Maidenhead; a place of which Brim was particularly fond. The two-storey former coaching inn was a fashionable rendezvous for assignations of all sorts: sexual, business and political. It enjoyed the added advantage of being near RAF Northolt, into which Manfred had flown an hour earlier, on-board a specially commissioned Lysander at the behest of British Intelligence.

Brim was dressed in a double-breasted dark blue blazer, grey trousers, cotton twill shirt and cravat. And, although in weekend attire, he looked immaculate, as always. Manfred's Alpine appearance didn't look out of place; even the heavy dark green cords and stout brogues were de rigueur.

It was the day after the Beaufort Lodge meetings; Saturday lunchtime. Alistair and Freddie walked into the room to find the two men poring over a large map of Germany. It was Military Ordnance. Berlin was ringed in red pen and marked where the Russians had invaded to the east, and the Allies to the west. The northern coastline of Germany was similarly marked at the port of Cuxhaven.

"Ah, gentlemen," said Brim. As if by magic, a uniformed waitress appeared, wheeling a tray of coffee pots, crockery and plates of delicious-looking sandwiches.

Manfred handed an envelope to Freddie and said: "From Astrid and Christina. Happy Birthday, Freddie."

Alistair tapped his forehead theatrically and said: "Of course. Sorry, completely forgot."

"So did I," said Freddie truthfully. "Too much else to think about and I didn't have Astrid and my daughter to remind me."

"How was yesterday?" asked Brim with a knowing look. He'd already had a phone call from Kirkpatrick, judging by his dour expression.

"Fraught," Alistair said, descending into an armchair, "but productive."

Freddie opened his card with an 'ah' sound which seemed to amuse Manfred and irritate Brim. Such domestic trivia didn't interest him:

"Shall we get on?" he said with a trace of impatience.

Manfred had whisked the German map away as soon as the waitress entered the room; a caution they all noted. She could mention it to a friend later, who might mention it to another. She poured their coffee; Brim handed her a folded ten-shilling note; she curtsied and scurried off producing a froufrou of stockings, petticoats and thighs. Alistair grinned, amused.

"Peter Braun has been revealing," said Manfred as soon as the Bridge Room door clicked shut with a 'Game in Progress' sign on the door. Brim's investment in the attractive waitress had paid off …

"Leo Hoffmann has questioned Braun at length. Nothing we do not already know, or have surmised, apart from the locations of two of Spengler's manufacturing facilities."

"All in Germany, by the look of your map, Manfred," said Alistair.

"Indeed. Nordhausen in the Unter-Harz. North of Barbarossahöle."

Alistair: "Where the Axis Powers invaded the Soviet Union, and where the RAF ..."

Brim finished the sentence for him, his tone grave: "Identified what turned out to be, during aerial reconnaissance, massive underground bunkers. Where the Vengeance weapons were reputedly made, according to American sources."

Manfred agreed and observed his colleagues:

"It is no coincidence Spengler built facilities – independent from the Nazis – but near to where identical technology was being developed. He needed their expertise and could call on it with the co-operation of Hermann Göring and Himmler. All part of the Präsidium of Nazis who had planned DAS SCHLOSS. To have it separate, as we have said before, was a clever bit of strategic planning on Spengler's part."

Manfred described how tens of thousands of prisoners were used as slave labour to dig out these massive underground facilities; hundreds of thousands of tons of concrete and steel were used for construction.

"Rocket technology expertise and materials were on hand for Spengler's people to take full advantage of," said Manfred.

"That ties in with what we heard yesterday, Manfred. Good intelligence," Alistair said.

"Yes." Manfred raised his bushy eyebrows and sipped his black coffee, pleased he was able to deliver such crucial information. He continued:

"He also has a facility at Cuxhaven and a factory in Berlin. Rosa is his second-in-command; unusual for a woman to hold such a prominent position, but he has no one else. She is, apparently, incredibly bright and a talented scientist."

Alistair and Freddie looked at one another; a million thoughts and unspoken ideas passed between them. Sometimes they did not have to verbalise, they were on a similar wavelength which Brim also picked up on:

"A complicated web," he said solemnly.

Manfred: "Braun also told Leo that Erich Spengler has around-the-clock protection, in a way mimicking Hitler's paranoia about security ... Rastenburg was a fortress."

"And yet there was an assassination attempt that was very nearly successful, according to the Americans ..." Alistair was keen to make a point. And with good reason; he had an idea in his mind.

"Do we know any more about Rosa?" Freddie asked, anxious to change the subject from the macabre to a topic more pertinent.

"That depends upon what you already know," Manfred responded, "which, I suspect, is precious little. Their private residence is not known. Father and daughter travel separately between their various operations throughout Germany. There is no confirmed timetable or agenda. Often one of them will arrive at a factory or port office, unannounced, usually by chauffeur-driven car. Or by air."

Brim pursed his lips – the way he did: "They must have meetings with their staff. They run a big company. Cuxhaven is a port. Surely they issue instructions to do with shipping and so forth."

"Chauffeurs can be replaced, can they not, Alistair?" said Manfred. "You could have asked your friend Admiral Canaris, if the butchers hadn't hanged him."

"We need to get someone into the core of Spengler GmBh," said Alistair, with a twinkle in his eye. "Deep cover. A 'ghost;' isn't that your euphemism, Brim?"

Yes, but who? was the common thought.

As if to address their unspoken question Alistair said simply: "Gertrud Wolf."

There was a collective sigh of disbelief.

"But she's a captured POW," said Brim, "detained at HM's convenience."

Freddie could see it at once: "She is now. But I'd bet she'd love to get out!"

Alistair grinned: "I bet she would too."

*

Later, in Skindles Cocktail Lounge, three stiff-looking gin and tonics stood on the counter. Franco, the bar manager, was pleased with his creation: crystal glasses, stirrers and paper coasters. It was very professional. As a concession to some senior

American Military Personnel staying at the hotel, they contained ice and a generous slice of lemon. Manfred was in his bedroom getting ready for dinner.

"Not sure about this," said Brim, gingerly supping the drink. "The ice waters it down."

"Drink it more quickly, then you can order another," put in Alistair.

"The thing is, Brim, if you live in California, as they might do, a long cool drink is pleasant after a game of tennis. Or a dip in a pool." Freddie finished his gin with a satisfied smack and watched the uniformed Americans. Not one of them was over thirty.

They were soon joined by a group of English girls, all dressed up in silk gowns, ready for a night on the town. In the background, the sound of Glenn Miller's 'In the Mood' trickled out of a hidden speaker. Franco was delighted with the ambience he had created for his American guests. One of the men did a 'thumbs up' to indicate his approval of the music. Lucky Strike and Chesterfield cigarettes were handed out and they all lit up.

Brim, still unconvinced about the ice in his drink, lowered his voice and drew closer to Alistair and Freddie:

"Kirkpatrick is being most unhelpful about the death of Dieter Protz."

"What a surprise." Alistair took a long pull on his G&T and watched the girls as they were being served exotic-looking cocktails. There were giggles and whoops of laughter. A good Saturday night was in the making.

"I suggest we leave well alone. Between Scheiderbauer, the Protz transcript and what Gertrud Wolf revealed, we have a great deal of information." Brim drank some gin, suddenly aware of the frivolity at the other end of the bar.

Alistair and Freddie knew that I suggest was a direct order and one they would not dare to transgress. Military Police would investigate, Brim explained. And, whatever the outcome, it was no longer in their hands. Kirkpatrick was proprietorial about internal affairs at Beaufort and his superior, the Commandant, would take control.

Brim went on to say that the detailed information Manfred had provided via Leo Hoffmann gave them a composite picture of Spengler's operations throughout Germany. All in all, a successful few days.

"What about Villa Languard? Pontresina?" Alistair saw Brim had finished his drink and was signalling the bar manager for another round.

"Nothing from your friend Leo Hoffmann, and again, I suggest we leave well alone. Any ramifications concerning those events ... Manfred and Nexus will deal with."

A second round of drinks arrived, and Brim seemed to be coming around to the idea of ice and lemon in a tall glass. Alistair and Freddie would later remark they had never seen Brim really relax. By the time 'Moonlight Serenade' was playing and the girls were dancing, the room was in full swing. Manfred arrived in the Cocktail Lounge looking very smart if not formal. A G&T was ordered for him; he was now three behind the others.

One of the girls pursed her lips at Alistair and he raised his glass in tribute at how wonderful she looked. She was blond with blue eyes, but lacked the appeal of Gertrud. As the music played, all he could think of was what he had to talk to her about the next day. He should have felt apprehensive, worried even. He would discuss the plan fully with Freddie and the others in the morning.

But no, he felt excited, and he could not decide why.

Gertrud

Beaufort Lodge, Middlesex, England.

YOU WANT ME TO WHAT?" asked Gertrud Wolf. Her sky-blue eyes regarded him with fervour; an intensity she could barely conceal. She was puzzled and then delighted he had chosen to visit her. It was a dark, rainy Sunday afternoon at Beaufort Lodge, and all was quiet. Captain Fox had admitted him after a discreet telephone call from Brim. It was an urgent and unofficial visit on behalf of British Intelligence, and he was happy to oblige.

There was no sign of Harald in the new quarters in which she had been billeted at the top of the house. It overlooked a vegetable garden and was more or less self-contained; he noticed a single bed in the tiny garret bedroom.

Alistair explained the plan to her in detail; one that had been discussed at length with Brim, Freddie and Manfred at Skindles that morning. At first, she was surprised at the idea, then delighted to have been asked. But there was nobody else who could carry out such an assignment. Alistair told her he would trust her; he would have to. Of course, she had plenty of questions – all of which they had anticipated – and he was able to answer as the rain beat down outside. It was risky, but she would do it. Better than being locked up here with nothing to do except read Dorothy L. Sayers and Agatha Christie paperbacks. He had taken a half bottle of Haig, which they sipped with a soupçon of cold water as he described the plan to her in minute detail. She was intrigued.

Alistair was sitting at one end of the four-seater settee. He had a map and loose pages beside him, and he was making notes for her. There were rail and ferry timetables: London, Amsterdam and ending in the far north of Holland.

Gertrud stood behind him, supposedly listening and studying maps of Holland and Germany. Suddenly she sat down on the arm of the settee:

"Are you in a hurry to go back to London?" She asked softly.

Watchers

Baker Street, London, England.

THE TWO WATCHERS sat in a downstairs room at the Baker Street Safe House. One was a demobbed RAF navigator who had flown Lancasters and Mosquitoes until the very end of the war, the other a retired Detective Sergeant from Scotland Yard. They had not met until two weeks before. Brim had a network of such contacts throughout London; people he could call on to do anything from surveillance to the odd break-in. Locksmiths, explosives experts, even museum curators such as Norma Smallbone were at his disposal. The two men sat in silence at the kitchen table, well aware of the possibility of being overheard. Even in a secure environment, the very nature of their work made them both naturally suspicious.

Freddie hadn't been back here since August '43 when he had flown back from Rangsdorf Airport to La Coruña in the north of Spain and finally to Northolt.

Brim and Freddie arrived in the Humber direct from

Skindles. Alistair decided Gertrud needed further briefing to prepare her for the assignment and Manfred Lochar had returned to his home in Baden.

"Fire away," said Brim to Watcher One after they had been served tea and toast by former FANY, Carole Benson. The First Aid Nursing Yeomanry had provided many such girls for the SOE and British Intelligence, their discretion and loyalty unquestioned.

"Clive Rowlands left Carter and Jackson in Weybridge mid-afternoon on the fifteenth and boarded the train to Waterloo. I followed.

"Yes, go on," said Brim.

"He met his contact at the Salmon and Ball Public House on Bethnal Green Road. It was too dark for a photograph and I didn't want to risk being spotted."

"Quite."

"They stayed an hour. Rowlands handed an envelope to his contact – a man dressed in a blue raincoat – he checked the content. It was obviously cash, a payment for something ... suspicious, I would say."

Watcher Two: "More about him later."

Brim and Freddie nodded. They had been thorough.

Watcher One: "Rowlands remained in the pub until ... over to you ..."

Watcher Two: "Thank you ... until he left it at closing time with the barmaid; spent the night with her at a B&B in Roman

Road. She left at 7.00am, and he, about ten past."

"You waited and watched all night?" asked Freddie.

"Yes, sir. And followed him back to a private address in Weybridge, which I took to be his home. I have the address noted; what estate agents might describe as a 'leafy suburb.' And, in that vein, detached, four bedrooms, 1920s."

"Our Mr. Rowlands is a bit of a philanderer then, not the old-school solicitor I took him to be," said Brim. "Carry on, sorry."

"Between us we watched Rowlands for another week, as you instructed in your cable from Zermatt. He met Blue Raincoat at Marks and Co., bookshop, 84 Charing Cross Road."

"How long were they in the bookshop?" asked Freddie.

"Oh, twenty minutes," said Watcher One, "but long enough outside it for me to get several decent photographs with my brother's Rolleiflex. I'll send some prints over."

"That would be most useful, thank you," said Brim.

"After which, I decided to follow Blue Raincoat to see where he went. He walked through Soho to Grosvenor Square."

"The American Embassy?" asked Brim with alarm.

"Macdonald House, yes. I have to say he took a circuitous route, looking over his shoulder all the time. The old shop window reflection trick," he said proudly.

"Did he realise you were tailing him?"

The Watcher permitted himself a chuckle: "No, sir. He was just being cautious, as I would. But I was wary of going any further than the corner of the Square. The Embassy might have their own surveillance. You know, Marines on the rooftops with high-powered binoculars, or sights. Rest assured; he didn't see me."

"Good job, both of you," said Brim, standing up.

Watcher One: "Do you want us to carry on, sir?"

"Yes. I would like to try and find out what the man at the Embassy does as a job. Your Blue Raincoat character. Is he English or American, for example?"

"I would say he was an American, maybe ex-military judging by his appearance and haircut. Probably in his thirties. The photographs will give you a clear idea, I hope."

"Thank you," Brim said, with a nod.

They left with a bundle of pound notes care of Central Funding/Miscellaneous Expenses, both looking pleased with what they had achieved.

"You were right to be cautious, Brim. Not telling Charles Foster where Joselyn spent Christmas '43," said Freddie. His mind flashed to Chalet Monte Rosa: Astrid and his precious Christina.

"Oh, it's nothing to do with Foster," said Brim, "but somebody close to him. We need to discover who Blue Raincoat is. What his role is at the Embassy. Certainly, he and Rowlands are crooks, traitors. And Rowlands knows a lot more about Peter Braun than he is letting on."

"He might even have a line into Spengler," Freddie suggested.

"That will be revealed as the new assignment develops," Brim said, glancing at his watch. "Speaking of which, I wonder how Alistair's getting on with Frau Wolf?"

"Yes, I was wondering that too."

"Let's get back to HQ on foot. He may have left a message with Miss Trueblood."

*

When they returned to Brim's office there was no sign of Miss Trueblood and the telephone was ringing. Brim answered it with a trace of impatience. It was Lt. Col. Andrew Kirkpatrick from Beaufort. Brim nodded a few times with the appropriate responses, not once looking at Freddie. Finally, he put the phone down and sat. He suddenly looked pale.

"What's up?" Freddie asked, thinking the call might have related to Alistair.

"It seems Harald Wolf has escaped. They believe he might have hidden in or under a bread delivery van. It was pouring with rain; a Saturday morning and the guards were 'slothful' according to Kirkpatrick. He's furious. He's talking about a court martial."

"I don't blame him."

"Neither do I. But Wolf's been missing for – what – thirty-six hours, and only now he chooses to tell us."

"I wonder if Alistair knows." Freddie mused aloud.

"We'll have to wait and find out," Brim said with a huff.

"Good God, a bread van. Whatever next?"

Visitor

Maria-Theresienstrasse, Innsbruck, Austria.

THREE MONTHS LATER, a tall Palestinian walked down Maria-Theresienstrasse in the heart of old Innsbruck. He turned into an elegant side street of typical Baroque houses. He walked slowly, but with purpose. He was holding a small hand-written map denoting landmarks: churches, statues, fountains. Ali Emran was used to the heat of his native Jerusalem and always walked with the same unhurried gait, no matter where he was in the world.

By the Spring of 1946, the American presence had mostly vanished from the streets: khaki-coloured jeeps, Army trucks and uniformed soldiers were gone. Today the mountains of the North Tyrolean Alps that surrounded the city gleamed with snow, the sky was blue and the air cool. Some shops were open, the aroma of coffee, roasted almonds and confectionery pervaded the air.

Emran found the house he was seeking and pulled the outside cord of an ornate-looking doorbell. The wood-panelled front door was substantial, the stucco façade of the building painted a pale yellow. Moments later a lady in her fifties answered. She wore a Hausfrau-style apron over black mourning clothes and regarded the visitor warily.

"Guten Tag. Herr Spengler, bitte," Emran said in the unaccented German he had been taught at the university of Munich in the late 1920s. Unusual for a Middle Eastern student to have been educated in such an esteemed seat of learning. But then, Emran was far from the norm. He came from a wealthy, powerful Palestinian family and his father recognised the value of a European education and familiarity with western culture.

"Moment," the lady said in a faltering voice and slightly closed the door, suggesting he wasn't welcome just yet. Emran stood on the doorstep and waited. He wore a three-piece suit, collar and tie, with an immaculate Cashmere overcoat draped over his broad shoulders. With his swarthy complexion he could easily have passed for Italian or Spanish. Five minutes later the lady returned and wordlessly beckoned him in. He followed her down a long marble-tiled corridor to a rear lounge with a high ceiling and massive windows. The morning sun shone into the room, casting intense rays of light through a haze of blue woodsmoke. A log fire burned in an open hearth and the sound of Mozart filled the room.

Erich Spengler sat in a leather armchair surrounded by newspapers. Der Jagdhund – as he was known – did not get up; merely glanced in the visitor's direction.

"How did you find me?" he asked without any pleasantries.

"As a representative of my People, it was my duty to find you, sir," Emran said solemnly.

"I know who you are, of course. And who you represent. Your picture has appeared in many newspapers. What do you want?" Spengler flexed his fingers as if he were about to perform surgery. Emran noticed the wiry old hands, perhaps a hint of arthritis at the knuckles. And his poise, even sitting, suggested a degree of infirmity. He knew about Spengler's injuries in the Great War. In fact there was little about him he didn't know. He'd done his research. Emran was thorough.

"You had ballistic weapons concealed at Boulogne, Calais, Dunkirk and Koksijde. Welded on to the hulls of Heinkels. Targeted on England in '43" ... Emran paused ...

"Where are they now?"

Spengler gave no sign of shock or fear that the man possessed such detailed knowledge of his affairs. He stood up from his chair, cleared a bundle of books and newspapers from another and bid Emran take a seat:

"So?"

Emran took off his overcoat, laid it meticulously on another chair and sat. There seemed to be documents and paraphernalia everywhere, as if Spengler had just moved in. Or was just moving out. He eyed Spengler carefully as he presented his offer:

"It is quite simple, sir. I wish to buy them. You must have salvaged them from the launch sites. You certainly wouldn't have let them fall into the hands of the British. Or the Americans. They took their share of the Vengeance Weapons after the war; and many of the German scientists."

Again, Spengler gave no reaction to the extent of Emran's knowledge: "How much?"

"We can afford one hundred thousand pounds. Fifty in cash to begin with; then fifty in gold on delivery. We can arrange transport, somehow. Possibly by sea. I am not sure of the cost and practicality, yet."

Spengler rotated his shoulders and neck as if he were in pain: "Why?"

Emran composed his thoughts and although he had anticipated this question on the train to Innsbruck, he didn't want to give away too much:

"The world is changing, Herr Spengler. The political geography of the Middle East will alter considerably. Plans are being made to settle a new state on our territory. It is the wish of the Americans and the British. There is a political will to settle the Hebrews on our doorstep. We predict problems. War between us is inevitable. We need to be prepared."

Spengler nodded, glancing at his collection of out-of-date newspapers. Emran knew he had probably read about such aspirations. Finally, Spengler conceded:

"How do you know about the Spengler weaponry? You are right, it was in Northern France and Belgium back in '43. Not anymore."

Emran wanted to smile: "Does the name Dieter Protz mean

anything?"

Spengler scratched his unshaven chin and frowned: "Protz? No."

He worked at your plant in Nordhausen ... rocket technology development and manufacture ... a fine achievement ... if I might be permitted to say."

Spengler shrugged, unflattered – so what? – he had employed hundreds of people at his facilities. He shook his head to confirm once more that he didn't know the man.

"He was liberated with thousands of others by one of the American armoured divisions – 104th Infantry, maybe – in April 1945. Many of Von Braun's scientists and yours went to the US, as we have said. Protz was arrested in Berlin by the British. I say arrested; he may well have defected."

"So?" Spengler regarded the visitor with heightened interest. His information was compelling.

"It was he who told my People you are still in possession of such weaponry."

"Where is this Dieter Protz now?"

"Dead. Murdered while in the custody of the British."

"How do you know this?" Spengler was suddenly on his guard. "He must be in prison somewhere in England. You did say in the custody of ..."

"A German national called Harald Wolf escaped from a detention centre near London. He killed Protz before he left to stop him talking. British Intelligence are on your tail, Herr

Spengler. Now, do we have a deal? One hundred thousand pounds?" He glanced at his Rolex Oyster Perpetual, suggesting time was now of the essence.

Spengler met his eyes:

"You know these weapons are lethal, particularly when launched from the air. Unlike V1s and V2s – the Spengler weapons are effective. The gyros work."

The Palestinian returned eye-contact:

"My mission is to protect our People. War is war."

Spengler smiled for the first time: "Then yes, you have a deal. We can decide. I have to travel to the North of Germany tomorrow: Cuxhaven. Contact me there; I will give you the number. It is a port, so we can arrange shipping. We do business all over North Africa and the Mediterranean. We have a office in Port Said." Spengler wrote several numbers on a piece of headed notepaper and handed it to his visitor.

The tall Palestinian stood, slung his immaculate overcoat around his shoulders and inclined his head into a vague bow:

"Thank you, Herr Spengler. It has been an honour to meet you at long last." He glanced at the paper. "I will telephone in a week or so."

"Good."

After Emran left the house Spengler picked up the telephone: "Get me a line through to Rosa. Tell her it's urgent."

Rosa

The Port of Cuxhaven, Germany.

ROSA SPENGLER was in many ways a humble person. She lived in the town of Nordenham in the Wesermarsch district of Lower Saxony. It was within easy reach of her father's premises and the port of Bremerhaven, which she often had to visit for business. She was an academic who lived in the shadow of her tyrannical father Erich. It was a strange relationship; she loved him, but certainly didn't like him. She didn't even really admire him; he lacked ethics and had no conscience whatsoever. She had seen him kill people who had crossed him, and it troubled her greatly. Captain Richard Lambert – Wax Jacket – of the FV Clarissa was a prime example; a cold kill with no second thought whatsoever. She had thought then, back in October '43, she could no longer tolerate his unscrupulousness. But here she was two and a half years later, still at his beck and call. She was forty-five years old and had nothing except the possibility of an inheritance she didn't really want. Knowing her father, he'd probably leave it to someone else anyway. Some raunchy young nurse down in Salzburg where he was allegedly relieved of a lot more than just hard cash.

Rosa lost her mother when she was ten years old and spent most of her childhood either with relatives in Stuttgart or a puritanical boarding school near Heidelberg. It was a lonely upbringing with all the trappings of family wealth, but little affection. Her father barely spoke to her until she was in her late teens and more interesting, as he had put it in a speech on her twenty-first birthday. He thought it was highly amusing. She was devastated and humiliated in front of friends and her late mother's family.

Finally came her years at Dublin University, where she studied for her Doctorate in Chemistry. And it was here she met Giles Walcott. Suddenly her world changed. He was adventurous, amusing, well-travelled and exciting to be with. It was many months before she discovered he was a fanatical Irish Republican with an intense hatred for the British. For her it was a dilemma; she had only ever lived in Germany and Ireland and held no opinion of the British or their culture. Only what she had gleaned from her highly prejudiced father who had been injured in the Great War. In a way her relationship with Giles was such that it didn't matter. She tolerated his ideals because they were suited in so many other ways and she certainly wouldn't have visited the United States had it not been for him. Several trips to New York and Boston in the early 1930s had opened her eyes. She met the infamous Donoghue family; their world was of corruption and organised crime. They controlled most of the state of Massachusetts. It was a milieu she couldn't accept. Her life was of academia, not illegality. Then Giles Walcott met 'the woman of his dreams' in Joselyn, his 'raven-haired American Princess' and their romance was over. Rosa returned to Germany – heartbroken – and fell headlong into working for her father and a man called Peter Braun. He was a lawyer and Spengler's right-hand man, involved in all matters to do with corporate finance and the expansion of Spengler GmBh. And, if she thought Walcott was corrupt and lacking moral fibre, Braun and her father were another league altogether. A phrase often sprung to her mind when she was out sailing: dancing with demons. And the Nazis whom her father had sponsored were certainly that.

Today Rosa Spengler sat in her office in a building adjacent to the port in Cuxhaven. The same place as where she'd had the meeting with Patrick Devlin and his bodyguard in December 1945. She shivered at the thought, unaware that today, a spring morning in April 1946, that same scenario would come back to haunt her.

"There's a lady downstairs to see you," said her secretary Gisela. She had climbed the stairs and come up to the office so quietly that Rosa was startled.

"Tell her ... I'm in a conference and can't be disturbed," Rosa said, removing her spectacles and looking out over the harbour. It was late afternoon and getting dark. But the view of the sea never failed to thrill her.

"She says it's urgent, Dr. Spengler."

"Who is she?"

"She represents Lloyd's of London," Gisela said, consulting her notepad. "She said she is looking for a Dr. Karl Schwarz."

Rosa's heart sank; she cursed her father and all she had unwittingly got involved with.

"Alright, show her in. But come and disturb us after ten minutes. You know the drill, Gisela."

*

The visitor was a complete stranger to Rosa. She was attractive: sky-blue eyes, high cheek bones, blond hair, the haughty look of a professional. She was immaculately dressed, introduced herself in perfect English as Caroline Montgomery. There was no preamble; she re-emphasized what she had told the secretary. Keep it simple, Alistair, Freddie and Manfred had said. We want her curiosity piqued, not her suspicions aroused. This was a hook, not a sinker. Not yet.

"I don't know a Dr. Karl Schwarz," Rosa said, keeping her expression calm.

Caroline carried on: "It concerns an explosion at Villa Languard, Pontresina, Switzerland, December 1945; about four months ago."

"There must be a mistake," Rosa said with growing anxiety.

Caroline consulted a legal notepad and what appeared to be official-looking documents:

"No mistake. Schwarz GmBh belongs to the Spengler group. Your father's company. Although it was very cunningly concealed in Swiss beauacracy. I must say ..." Caroline removed a pair of ornamental spectacles which Alistair had said 'made her look studious.' "Yes, I must say, it took a lot of digging. But that's what Lloyd's of London do. One of the things." She chuckled in a self-deprecating way to demonstrate how proud she was of her position as a broker. Or perhaps an underwriter. In any event, she was very convincing. Rosa flinched, sensing doom: Braun had not done that good a job at concealment.

Gisela came into the office after a discreet knock, with the excuse that Rosa was needed for a meeting; had she overlooked it? Rosa waved her away with an 'it can wait' dismissal. Gisela retired gracefully. Only the heavy footfalls down the stairs betrayed her irritation.

"If you are busy, I can return," said Caroline helpfully. "I'm staying in a guest house in Nordenham. Do you know it? Very pretty, affluent."

There is no point in lying, thought Rosa: "Yes, I have a house there."

"How nice," said Caroline. "Now, where were we?"

"You were telling me my father owns a company I know absolutely nothing about. I think this is a matter for our lawyers," she said with blustering sincerity.

Caroline permitted herself a dainty chuckle: "And Police. Possibly the British Army."

"What?"

"Oh, goodness, didn't I say? Three people were killed at the villa." Caroline fixed Rosa with a serious expression.

"I – I don't think ..."

Caroline put her fake documents into her legal document case. The Lloyds motif on the lid was a convincing addition to the deception.

"Swiss Police are trying to discover if it was an accident ... or murder. In any event, Lloyd's feel they can subpoena your father to London. This is not a matter for the occupying powers. It is the law. One of the deceased is an American civilian and her family are insured with Lloyd's of London." She paused for effect ... "Any questions?"

Rosa was speechless: "No."

"Is your father in Cuxhaven? I'd like to speak with him before the Authorities are involved. He might like to make a preliminary statement. The sooner he does, the better, I am sure."

Rosa summoned words that were not easily forthcoming. She took a breath: "Do you know who my father is Miss ...?"

"Montgomery. Yes, he's a suspect. In fact," another little in-joke chuckle, "he's the prime suspect."

"I see. I don't know where he is."

"I think, Dr. Spengler, with respect, my question really merits an honest answer."

Rosa took a breath: "Very well. He's away, but he will be back soon."

Rosa thought of the telephone call she'd had from her father that morning, telling her about the visit from the Palestinian and his dire plans for the Middle East. She hoped her face did not betray the fear she felt.

"We urgently need to speak to him." Caroline emphasised the word 'we'.

She handed Rosa a printed business card with an attractive motif of a typical Saxon building and the words: Gästehaus Flora – with an address in the centre of Nordenham – a small guest house run by a very respectable German family.

"This is where we will be ... for the foreseeable. Good evening."

Caroline turned without another word and descended the wooden staircase, her legs like jelly and her breaths fast. A taxi waited outside the reception office. She nodded politely at Gisela and left the building. Caroline Montgomery smiled at her performance.

Now she could become Gertrud again and meet Alistair at a bar in town. Gästehaus Flora had been a red herring, but pleased to assist Caroline. They were all staying somewhere else. The taxi driver asked where and she told him.

Upstairs, Rosa was petrified. Her shaking hand hovered over the telephone cradle and stopped. Her father would have left

Innsbruck by now and was probably on the way to his special Klinik in Salzburg, which he thought she didn't know about. What the hell would he say when she told him about her unexpected visitor from London?

Rosa picked up the Gästehaus Flora business card, dialled the number and asked the landlady if she could speak to Caroline Montgomery, the Lloyd's of London guest.

"No," said the voice politely, "She's not here, but I will happily take a message for her."

*

Rosa let herself out of the reception office just after six pm and locked the front door. Gisela had gone home, and all the other staff had finished for the day too. It was dark and quiet; all the cars in the car park had gone apart from hers and one she didn't recognise.

A well-built man in his fifties appeared to be waiting for someone. He glanced at his watch and looked around expectantly. He had bushy eyebrows and the look of a Sicilian. He wore a Loden-style duffle coat and a deerstalker hat which he raised politely as Rosa came over to him.

"Oh, excuse me," he said appearing highly embarrassed, "I'm looking for Caroline Montgomery. I am dreadfully late. Missed my train connection." He spoke German, but with a heavy accent and held out an ID card for her to inspect. The light was failing, and she had to squint to read it:

"Detective Heinz Johner, Graubünden Canton Police ... Switzerland?" She read the card out with incredulity. He picked up on her surprise.

"Yes, a long journey."

"You've missed her I'm afraid," said Rosa. "I believe she is staying at the Gästehaus Flora in Nordenham ... although she is not there at the moment. I just tried phoning her as a matter of fact."

"I see." Johner looked bewildered.

"I can give you a lift," Rosa offered, "I'm going to Nordenham myself."

Johner attempted a smile: "It's alright. I have a hire car," he said pointing at the other car. "Another reason why I am so late. The hire company had lost my booking." He raised his hat again and walked towards the car as Rosa got into hers and left.

Once inside, Manfred Lochar laughed. He couldn't wait to hear how Gertrud had fared with her deception as Caroline. He started the engine and turned:

"Are you ok in the back?"

"Yeah, I guess," said a muffled voice, a trace of Massachusetts.

"You can sit up now, Joselyn. We're on our way to meet Alistair ... I have the address here somewhere."

Paradise

Die Paradise Klinik, Königsee, Austria.

ERICH SPENGLER LAY face down naked on a doctor's-style treatment couch. Strong fingers and thumbs eased down on to the base of his neck and shoulders. They massaged hemp oil, lavender and rosemary extract deep into the pores of his skin and muscle. The pressure was intense, almost torture. He felt like screaming, forced into a wall of pain. Next the fingers ran down his spinal cord, selecting vertebrae, pushing, manipulating. He felt fit to die and then a sudden euphoria as endorphins and cannabis oil took control. The chiropractor Ernst stopped, quietly withdrew. Spengler heard Mozart ... but he couldn't identify the piece.

The Paradise Klinik at Königsee, south-west of Salzburg, was exclusive and expensive. Not far from Berchtesgaden, it offered its clients relief from corporeal aches and pains. And a number of other services too, if they were deemed appropriate by the Klinik's director, known only as Fräulein Stefanie.

Spengler didn't know how long he'd lain there; his sense of time had become distorted. Then a female voice and familiar phial of sanctuary under his left nostril, then his right. He sniffed the benison of pure cocaine deep into his system. Two nurses turned him over on his back: deft, skilful hands which knew every sinew of his body. A hot moist flannel of rosemary-scented water was placed over his face to drive the cocktail into his bloodstream. It was bliss ... Mozart played ...

The two nurses applied warm massage oils on to his tense, twisted frame. He felt a tinge of arousal in his loins. He knew they were topless, but couldn't see their bodies, his vision obscured. It was all part of the tantalising thrill. He felt their breasts brushing against his face, chest, stomach, thighs as they leant over him and massaged his tissue and muscle. Then euphoria as the cocaine also took over and his world fell away. His sensations drifted amid the fragrance of menthol and eucalyptus; he felt fingers lightly dancing around his groin, complementing his testosterone. The room was warm; he floated like a foetus in its mother's womb. He could not move; he did not want to. All he felt was relief from the pain that tortured him day and night.

He rid his mind of his company, Peter Braun and Ali Emran. He purged all thoughts of Rosa, the daughter of whom he was ashamed, who hated both him and his methods. Money couldn't buy him love or contentment. But what it could buy was temporary solace and make him forget the agony of failing Germany. At some stage he felt the sharpness of a needle as it pierced his cephalic vein.

Then, finally, blessed sleep.

Rowlands

Weybridge, Surrey, England.

BRIM MADE HIMSELF comfortable in the waiting room of Carter and Jackson Solicitors. Beside him sat Brian Cummins, retired DI Scotland Yard, another member of his network of contacts. Brim had fully briefed Cummins on the background of the case: Walcott, Spengler and Braun; the attempted murder of Joselyn, Alistair and Freddie. He was a positive asset. Cummins had played a significant role in the Windsor operation Windsor and Brim trusted him without question.

Rowlands came into the room, hand outstretched. He had the build of a boxer, but that soft, incongruous voice. Introductions were made – Brim clear in his description of Cummins as a retired Detective Inspector – and they followed him into his busy office. Brim reminded Rowlands of their previous encounter and thanked him for seeing them at short notice.

"Joselyn Walcott was murdered," was Brim's opening gambit.

Rowlands's eyelids fluttered nervously: "Really? I understood

…”

“Understood what, Mr. Rowlands?” Brim asked, poker-faced.

Rowlands’s hand shot up to his thin lips nervously. He said nothing.

“In fact, how would you understand anything, since you are, as you claimed, merely an intermediary? …

Peter Braun, your Swiss contact, is in prison awaiting trial.” Brim paused again and watched the well-fed face flicker with guilt.

Rowlands attempted some court-room charm: “Who did you say you were exactly, Professor Brimblecombe?” He glanced at Cummins as if he might provide an answer.

“You know precisely who I am, Mr. Rowlands.”

Rowlands: “There is a client confidentiality issue here, I believe.”

“Not when your client conspired in a murder, Mr. Rowlands. Braun has made a comprehensive statement to the Graubünden Police.”

Rowlands felt the ice start to crack beneath him; slow, menacing and unstoppable, as Brim continued:

“Your client is Erich Spengler.”

Rowlands shook his head: “Braun said this? I’ve never met him.” His denial sounded hollow and untrue.

“What puzzles me is how,” said Brim, “how you – a parochial solicitor – come to represent a man like Spengler. How did you get involved?”

Rowlands affected his most self-deprecating expression:

"Professor Brimblecombe, I am, was, Giles Walcott's parochial solicitor." He cast Brim a stare to show how hurt he was. "I dealt with the Needle's Eye paperwork, as you know. My client wanted his money back. Braun, I assumed, was their lawyer. That is how I got involved. Simple."

"No, Mr. Rowlands. Your client didn't want his money back. You both created a trap and lured a young woman to her death." There was no doubt in Brim's tone.

"I didn't know she'd die," he said in a timorous little voice.

"Oh, really? When I came to see you here in December, with my colleague Bill Pickering, you asked me twice where Joselyn was. Do you recall that conversation?"

"Spengler wanted to know."

"Why?"

A deep breath: "He believed Joselyn walked away from the villa unharmed. With two men." A globule of perspiration formed on Rowlands's shiny left temple.

"Alright. But how would he have known that? The incident happened in Pontresina. Spengler, I assume, lives in Germany. The matter was investigated by the Graubünden Police and was not publicised."

"I don't know. That's why he sent me £1,000 to try and find out what I could."

"That's quite an inducement," said Brim.

There was a knock on the door and a man looked in: well-coiffured, Oxford tie. He looked at Brim and Cummins with a perplexed expression.

"Oh, can't it wait, Nigel? I'm busy," said Rowlands in a huffy voice.

"No, it can't!" equally huffy. "We have an appointment with the Maxwells ..." He glanced at his watch ... "ten minutes ago. They go to trial on Friday."

"I'll be there," Rowlands snapped and wiped his temple with a pressed handkerchief. The man left, muttering his displeasure.

Brim pursed his lips: "We'll not detain you too much longer ..." Brim paused and regarded Rowlands's face. He was a man under pressure. Then the bombshell:

"Who is your contact at the American Embassy?"

Rowlands's mouth dropped open as if he could not believe what he'd heard:

"Are you having me followed?"

Brim waited ten seconds for him to calm down and then repeated the question.

"He's a contact of Erich Spengler. Not mine."

"And what did he tell you? What did you pay him for?"

Rowlands was almost in tears; the ice had cracked, he was about to fall: "He told me Joselyn's maiden name was Foster ... and her father is ... Charles Foster, the Deputy Chief of Mission at Macdonald House."

"Go on."

"She'd told Giles she was orphaned, her parents killed in a

train crash. Joselyn fabricated her life story to, to mislead him." Again, his little pink tongue darted out and brushed his lips nervously. He thought about Blue Raincoat and the enormity of his treachery and the inevitable consequence.

"What exactly did Spengler want to know?" Brim asked him softly, his voice persuasive – seven words delivered ever so slowly – as if he was asking a close friend to betray a marital indiscretion.

Rowlands swallowed noisily: "Whether or not Joselyn worked for, for British Intelligence." A whisper and at once Rowlands definitely knew who Brim was.

Brim: "And?"

"How she was recruited, being an American."

"But why would he ask the question? How would he know to ask it?" Brim phrased the question carefully and waited ten seconds for Rowlands to reply. He was cornered:

"Spengler assumed Joselyn worked for British Intelligence because she had identified Walcott as a threat to British Security with his connections to the Irish and the Germans."

Brim raised his voice: "What else?"

"He also told me Foster has a luxury apartment on the top floor of Macdonald House. That's where Joselyn stays when she is in England. Protected by American Marines. All her personal details – travel arrangements, everything - are – classified."

"Something else?" Brim persisted.

"I asked him to, to, break into Foster's apartment to try and find out as much as he could. When, if, she was meeting her father. To confirm whether she was alive or not. Spengler wanted absolute certainty, that's what the money was for."

"Good God," said Brian Cummins. He looked at Rowlands with utter contempt. But noticed Brim didn't display any anger.

Brim altered his tone to matter of fact: "When are you meeting your contact next?"

Rowlands consulted his diary, meticulously flicking pages: "Three days' time."

"The Salmon and Ball public house? Perhaps a little R&R in Roman Road afterwards?" Brim could not resist the jibe. It sounded more like an insult.

Rowlands's head slumped forward; the brink of tears: "Are you going to arrest me?" he sniffed. "Will you tell my wife about ... Lucy. I have family. Two young daughters. They must not know about this; they'd never forgive me."

The price of treachery: they will never forgive him.

Brim said nothing; let him stew.

The desperation on Rowlands's face was overwhelming as he realised the hopelessness of his predicament. He had lied to HM Government, his law firm; worse still, his family.

"Mr. Rowlands. Where are you meeting this person?"

"Burlington Arcade. The Vigo Street end. Five in the evening." He blurted the treacherous words out. "What do you want me to do?"

"Nothing," said Brim standing. "Meet him and see what

confidential information he sells you concerning my dead agent, Joselyn. Good day."

Brim and Cummins left without another word.

Foster

Grosvenor Square, London, England.

"THIS IS AN UNEXPECTED PLEASURE, BRIM," said Charles Foster. The tall New Englander greeted him warmly at his office on the sixth floor of Macdonald House. Still the elegant Savile Row suit, pressed white shirt, Stamford tie, weather-beaten features and carefully styled silver-grey hair. He could have easily stepped off a Hollywood film set or out of a Beverly Hills golf club.

"Can I organise some coffee?" said Foster. He grinned; his face exuded charm; his voice deep and mellifluous. It was not difficult to see how he had climbed the political ladder with such ease. And probably still only in his mid-forties.

"If it's Puerto Rican, as last time, then yes please."

Foster picked up the phone and called his secretary with the order: "Yes and I've no idea where Barbara buys it from. I do not ask. Probably brings it back from NY on a ship. Her husband is in the Navy ... please sit. Make yourself at home."

Brim sat down in a superbly comfortable leather armchair and admired the spectacular view of Grosvenor Square below. The park area was green, people were out and about and the daffodils in flower. Barbara served their coffee – 'no cream, sorry' – and Foster joined him on the visitor side of his busy desk. Brim noticed a 10x8" portrait of his late wife Maria. Of Italian descent, she gazed confidently into the photographer's lens with a serene, almost regal nobility. Neither sad, nor smiling, but natural. And utterly beguiling, as was her daughter. There was no doubt this was Joselyn's mother: the hair, the eyes, the shape of her face.

"I think of her every day, you know," said Foster, following his gaze, "She was quite something."

"I'm sure. Joselyn certainly inherits her beauty."

"Thank you, she does." Foster nodded; his craggy features creased into a smile: deep laughter lines formed around his blue-grey eyes. "Now, what can I do? I sense this is not just a social visit."

Brim produced a photograph of Clive Rowlands which one of the Watchers had taken outside Marks Bookshop, 84 Charing Cross Road. It had been shot on a Rolleiflex Twin Lens professional camera – the sort wedding photographers use – the quality was perfect.

"This man," said Brim, "is meeting a member of your Embassy staff at five o'clock this Friday afternoon, top end of Burlington Arcade. An informant of some kind."

"A traitor, here at the Embassy? You sure?" Foster was

stunned, all humour wiped from his face.

"Yes. And it concerns Joselyn. That's why I've been so cagey about exactly where she is staying in Switzerland. We had an instinct about this, particularly Alistair. Sixth sense."

"Good God! Tell me."

Brim relayed the conversation he'd had with Rowlands at the office in Weybridge, not omitting a single detail. Foster's face melted from shock to anger.

"What do you want us to do, Brim?"

"Arrest them. I suspect Rowlands will pay his contact a substantial amount of money for any information relating to Joselyn. The money comes from Spengler GmBh – the people behind the attempt to murder Joselyn, Alistair and Freddie in Switzerland. You know the story, Charles, as well as I do."

Foster's expression was dark. He said nothing. He did know the story, only too well.

"And rest assured, we are working on that now. Alistair, Freddie and Manfred are in Germany, concocting a plan. Revenge will be sweet, believe me."

"Consider it done," he said finally. "Is Joss alright? I haven't heard from her for the best part of a week. That's not unusual for her."

"She's fine. Once Rowlands is in the custody of the US Embassy, he is under your jurisdiction. He waives any rights to protection under UK law. This is the way I want it done, without any publicity."

"From what you've just told me, the bastard's already waived his rights."

"How true. Keep the photo, your MPs will need it," said Brim and finished his coffee with relish. He would be happy when Rowlands and his treacherous contact were under lock and key and unable to contact Erich Spengler.

Let him sweat.

Contacts

The Port of Cuxhaven, Germany.

ROSA SPENGLER WEARILY climbed the stairs to her first-floor office, which overlooked the port and marina. The day was bright and clear, gulls swooping down to the water in search of a morsel of food.

The SS Solveig cargo ship was being unloaded of vital supplies to help fulfil the growing demand after the war. Germany, like the rest of Europe, was bereft of even the barest essentials. Cranes were hoisting solid-wooden pallets from the ship's five holds on to the dockside: food, medical supplies and clothing. Solveig was one of a fleet of three Spengler vessels carrying out such philanthropic assignments.

Rosa could vaguely hear shouting and instructions being barked out by crew to waiting dockers. Captain Edvard Langerhans, Solveig's flamboyant skipper, caught her eye as she looked out of the window. She returned his greeting, sapped of energy.

She looked terrible. There were dark rings around her eyes from lack of sleep, like livid bruises. She'd drunk whisky the night before – unusual for her – hoping it might relax her. It hadn't. She'd taken her black Labrador Fritz for a long walk by the river, read, listened to the gramophone; nothing would settle her. Too much on her mind. When she did finally succumb to sleep, her dreams turned to nightmares and she was awake again by 5.00am.

Gisela brought her a coffee and placed it on her desk along with the morning's mail and 'Die Welt' newspaper. If she noticed how drained her boss looked, she gave no sign. Rosa glanced at the headlines:

Leading Nazi officials indicted for war crimes –Hermann Goering, Rudolph Hess. IMT wants to indict key German industrialists ... IG Farben ...allied with Nazi Party ... Nuremberg Trials are –

She didn't want to read anymore; the trials had taken on a high profile and, understandably, caught the imagination of the world's media. A number of Nazi officials had either been executed or taken their own lives.

"Any news from my father, Gisela?"

"No, Dr. Spengler. Although a man did phone earlier but didn't leave his name or a message."

Rosa's face flashed with alarm: "When was this?"

"An hour ago, while you were at the bank."

"Hm. What did he sound like, this man?"

"Sound like? Normal, I would say."

"No trace of an accent?" Rosa was thinking of Detective Heinz Johner, the Swiss policeman she had encountered in the firm's car park the previous evening.

"Not that I noticed, Dr. Spengler," Gisela sounded puzzled. "Oh, what's this?" She picked up the card which Caroline Montgomery had left on her desk and passed it to Rosa.

"I'll leave you be, Dr. Spengler." She descended the stairs to her reception office.

Rosa, curious, glanced at the card and wondered why she had not noticed it the previous evening when she was packing up to leave ...

Caroline Montgomery, Senior Underwriter, Lloyd's of London, 12 Leadenhall Street, EC3.

She picked up the phone and asked the Cuxhaven operator to connect her with the Overseas Telephone Exchange in London and the 'City' number embossed on the card. It took twenty minutes to establish the connection and she could imagine rows of ladies with headphones pushing plugs into sockets ... hundreds of miles away. Finally, they answered:

"Good morning, Lloyd's of London. How may we help?"

"I'm looking for a Caroline Montgomery, Senior Underwriter," Rosa asked in her very best English.

"Hold the line," the female voice said in a clipped BBC accent

Rosa had heard on the World Service. Oxford? Cambridge? Where was she from? There was a series of clicks and hollow static, then: “Claims.” Brusque, to the point.

“Oh,” said Rosa, not sure what to say when finally confronted, “Is-is Miss Montgomery there, please?”

“I’m afraid not. May I take a message?”

“No, that’s alright,” Rosa replied, completely flustered. “I’ll call another time.” Rosa put the phone down. Damn! She should have left a message when she had the chance. She stared at the card. Where the hell are you, Miss Montgomery?

*

Brim took out his familiar battered silver cigarette case and lit a Senior Service. He was down to ten a day now and his Physician, Dr. Patrick Heron, had been adamant he should adhere to the new regime. He was finding it a challenge because he knew he would have to give up completely.

“Bravo, Miss Trueblood! That was pure theatre,” he said, glancing at his secretary and another lady, “worthy of Bristol Old Vic.” He exhaled smoke with pleasure, not a trace of guilt.

FCO/MI6 Signals Intelligence had rigged up a mobile telephone exchange in Brim’s office, with five lines in, one of which had been the number on ‘Caroline Montgomery’s’ phoney business card from Lloyd’s. Colonel John Penfold – another member of his network - had also lent him Jean Morgan, an experienced telephone operator from Churchill's 'toyshop' in Whitchurch, Buckinghamshire.

The secret laboratory Military Defence (MD1) was originally based at 35 Portland Place, but after their building had been badly bombed by the Luftwaffe was forced to evacuate. 'The Firs', as it was known, had staff experienced in all matters concerning COMMS and Official Secrets. Within twenty-four hours Penfold's technicians had built the exchange from scratch using components borrowed from the GPO and RAF at Brize Norton. Now, the two ladies sat there, headphones clamped to their heads, with their scripts in front of them.

Alistair, Freddie and Brim decided not to give too much away to Rosa Spengler when the call inevitably came. To tell her 'Caroline' was away on business in Germany would be overkill. And it only needed one call from Rosa to 'the London office' to establish 'Caroline's' credibility; they also had a telegram facility at their disposal if need be. Even so, Brim ordered the exchange to be manned around the clock until further notice.

Puzzles

Pontresina Police Station, Switzerland.

DETECTIVE LEO HOFFMANN was sitting in the smoky canteen of the police station in Pontresina when the call from Germany came through. He was busily attempting to solve the multi-language crosswords, but his instructions to the switchboard had been absolutely clear: he was not to be disturbed, unless it was his third wife, Elisa, to whom he was physically devoted. He lit a cigar, sipped Italian coffee and was delighted he had solved a clue in a battered copy of the 'Times': lachrymose adj., tearful, sad.

Hoffmann looked perplexed; he had plenty of other puzzles on his mind, but few solutions.

The Graubünden switchboard operator told the caller:

"Detective Hoffmann is on his lunchbreak at the moment and I don't know where he is. He can call you back; he won't be long."

The caller said:

"No, I will call him back myself. One hour. Please tell him."

It was curious, the switchboard operator said to Hoffmann

when he returned, that the lady wouldn't leave her name or a message. The call had originated from Cuxhaven. It had been put through to her from the exchange at St. Moritz.

'No,' Hoffmann had said when she finally asked him, 'I'd have been surprised if she had."

Hoffmann took the call exactly one hour later. He knew who it was, of course, because Manfred Lochar had warned him. He'd contacted Rosa Spengler, posing as Hoffmann's own officer, Heinz Johner. This was Nexus – the Swiss Network – acting at its most stealthy:

"Good afternoon," said Hoffmann politely. The real Johner and his team sat opposite him, wide-eyed with anticipation, their note pads at the ready.

"Hello, Detective Hoffmann. Do you have an officer in Cuxhaven by the name of Heinz Johner?" The voice was female, German and formal. There was a slight time delay:

"Yes, we do. We are conducting a murder investigation here in Pontresina, Switzerland. December 1945," said Hoffmann.

The two sentences were delivered in perfect German. Most of the team spoke in their local Schweizerdeutsch dialect, not formal German.

"Thank you." The line went dead. Johner and the team regarded their boss with renewed respect.

Hoffmann stretched back in his chair, closed his eyes and rubbed his bare scalp:

"Outside of the department only two people know Joselyn

Walcott and the Valentine brothers survived that explosion at the villa." Hoffmann sat forward ...

"Peter Braun and Wolfgang Koch, the carriage driver from Silvaplana. I advised the concierge at Badrutt's Palace that their three guests had to leave St. Moritz urgently for medical reasons ..." He paused again ...

"Spengler's two hired killers, Dieter Schmidt and Werner Kocher – we have both identified from Braun - were, shall we say, dispatched at the scene ..."

There was a little snigger from the team; Braun had shot one with a telescopic rifle and Alistair Valentine had killed the other by brute force in self-defence. Hoffmann continued, looking at Heinz:

"We must keep it that way, Heinz. We have absolutely no proof Erich Spengler was involved. The Divisional Commander has insisted we don't approach him without concrete evidence; a prejudiced statement from Braun is not enough. Cuxhaven, where that call came from, is a long way from here. But I don't think we'll hear from Dr. Rosa Spengler again. She has now established two bona fides: you, Heinz, and a lady called Caroline Montgomery. I think we can let this go."

Heinz: "What about Frau Monika Gessler at the town hall in Pontresina. We dragged her way from her anniversary dinner that night. Do you recall?"

Hoffmann laughed: "Good point, Heinz. But all she established was that Villa Languard was owned by Schwarz

GmBh, an inactive company that only exists on paper. It has no office or employees, just a bank account to pay bills."

"Yes."

"It doesn't trade, and she can't find out who owns it. And just a simple name does not help us discover who caused the explosion there. It's as simple as that, I'm afraid."

"Of course," said Heinz, "I understand, sir."

Hoffmann laughed again and thought of his meeting with Manfred Lochar when he handed the uniform of Heinz Johner and Police ID over to him:

"Alistair and Freddie are on the case. Who knows what the hell will happen next?"

*

A few hours later in London, Miss Trueblood was about to go home for the evening when the telephone rang. She looked over at Professor Brimblecombe to see if she should answer. He nodded; she picked up the receiver and listened for a moment:

"The American Embassy, sir," she said, holding her hand over the mouthpiece. He nodded once more and she put him through. She made a departing gesture, picked up her handbag and left for the evening.

"Hello, Brim, Charles Foster. Look, I will be brief. Two plainclothes MPs picked up our two friends at Burlington Arcade as agreed ..."

“Yes,” said Brim, lighting a Senior Service.

“Our guy is in temporary detention; the man you call Blue Raincoat. He is an Irish American by the name of Samuel Donoghue. Part of a Boston crime syndicate.”

Brim blew smoke and repeated the words: Crime syndicate? I’ve never heard of such an expression.”

“No? Probably an Americanism. But yes, he is,” Foster said with resignation. “Trouble is, he’s protected by diplomatic immunity.”

“I see. Is treason against the UK in wartime not an exception?” Brim’s tone was grim.

“No. But our lawyers are looking into it. There is one piece of information you might be interested in ... Donoghue told us Giles Walcott was also part of their syndicate and Braun’s on their payroll too.”

Brim considered the implications: “That is interesting, Charles.”

“By the way, Mr. Rowlands fate was not good. He threw himself in front of a taxi on New Bond Street. Died at the scene.”

“That is unfortunate,” Brim replied sarcastically. “Listen, Charles, please keep me informed about Donoghue’s legal status. And I’ll make some enquiries with the Home Office. I have a senior contact there. And he owes me a favour.”

“Will do. But I wouldn’t hold up too much hope. We’ve been faced with this before.”

“You’re right. But thanks for letting me know anyway.”

"Not a problem, Brim." The line went dead.

Brim stood up from his desk, wandered over to the window and looked at the fading beauty of St. James's Park. He poured a large single malt into a crystal glass and held it up to the evening light and the view outside. He pursed his lips – the way he did – and drank half the malt in one go. It felt immensely satisfying. And well deserved.

He picked up the still warm telephone receiver and dialled his team at their hotel in Mitte-Nord. Diplomatic immunity: Spengler has been resourceful, he thought. Time to up our game. He finished his drink. It was Alistair he finally spoke to when reception put him through.

"Hello, Brim," he answered cheerfully. "I had a feeling you might call. Any news?"

Spengler

Rosa's Office, Cuxhaven, Germany.

"DON'T BE SO NAÏVE, Rosa. The Joselyn bitch is still alive and so are her two accomplices." Spengler spat the words out with such spite that she flinched with fear.

She had told him about the visits from 'Caroline Montgomery' and 'Heinz Johner'. Spengler was sitting in Rosa's neat and tidy office, on the other side of her desk and snarled at her stupidity. How could she be so gullible? And he wasn't finished with her yet:

"Why do you think the two former Wehrmacht I hired failed to return to Berlin to collect their bounty? Enough money to comfortably retire on. Why?"

Rosa shook her head, unable to move, confused, frightened. Worse, humiliated. And Gisela could no doubt hear every word in her office below. Didn't he realise? Or maybe he did.

"Because the Brits killed them. That's why, Rosa. Get it into your head." The old man sat there in a black leather jacket, black shirt and trousers. She noticed his jaw muscles. It was called Bruxism; he ground his teeth and clenched his jaw muscles with tension. The look on his face bordered on hate. She had to fight back:

"So, these two former Wehrmacht were outwitted by two civilians and a woman?" Again, there was a hint of sneaking regard for Joselyn's continued resourcefulness.

Spengler ignored her sarcasm: "Peter Braun is most probably dead, or worse, in prison. My two men certainly dead. Anyway, we have bigger things to attend to now."

They seem real enough, she thought to herself. But it was pointless pursuing the matter; arguing with a man who refused to listen. Spengler was always right.

"What about Samuel Donoghue at the Embassy in London?" asked Spengler. "Have you heard anything? I haven't."

Rosa was too embarrassed to admit she had not heard from Donoghue or Rowlands for over a week and feared the worst. She decided to lie.

It was easier than facing another tirade:

"Nothing exceptional, father." She could tell he was suspicious of an indirect answer; she had known that since she was in her teens. He always said he could smell her lies on the rare visits he made to her boarding school near Heidelberg: boyfriends, going to dances, anything that displeased him.

"How was your trip to Innsbruck?" she asked, changing the subject.

The old man's face lit up: "Ah, good. I am glad you asked. I will require the SS Solveig within five days. Loaded and ready to sail. An exceptionally long voyage."

He told her about the visit from the tall Palestinian, Ali Emran, and his wish to buy ten missiles, but neglected to tell her at what price. As he described the conversation he'd had, her expression altered from concealment to horror:

"Isn't it dangerous to try and transport those weapons by sea? Surely they might be unstable after the long journey from France?"

"I thought you'd be appreciative of the offer, Rosa. Clearly I was wrong." His tone always made her feel inferior, that everything was her fault. Such was his manipulation of her and his mastery of twisting the facts to his advantage.

Before she could reply Spengler stood, about to explode. Always ready for confrontation. He looked stiff and in pain; she thought he had aged considerably in the last few months he'd been away. Again, he wasn't finished with her:

"Devlin failed because of Joselyn Walcott and her Merry Men from British Intelligence," Spengler said sarcastically, annunciating the last five words in English. "At least now we can get some of our money back." His eyes sparkled at the thought, any notion of political principle a thing of the past.

"Surely many innocent refugees would die," she said feebly, "if those weapons were ever used against a small country."

His nostrils flared: "A lot of English would have died if those missiles had been deployed from France. The Royal Household at Windsor would not exist now if your former lover Giles Walcott hadn't totally fucked things up. That didn't bother you, did it, Rosa? Not then. Your morals are very selective all of a sudden."

For a moment she thought of Giles: "That was different. Germany was at war. We were supporting the interests of the country ... the Reich."

Spengler slammed her desk with such force that the whole office shook, and a table lamp fell to the floor, the bulb shattered.

"Spengler is always at war, Rosa. Never forget it. I'm going to my apartment for a rest. See that Solveig, her captain and crew are ready. On standby. I will make sure the hold is adapted to facilitate the missiles. You speak to the foreman landside. Is that clear?"

"Yes, father. It is clear."

"By the way," Spengler's eyes twinkled, "this Caroline Montgomery woman. What did she look like?"

Rosa was perplexed but described her as best as she could remember. Spengler absorbed the information and nodded without comment.

"The foreman, don't forget."

Rosa merely nodded, shocked at what her father and this Palestinian militant planned for the Middle East. But what could she do? Who could she tell?

He left without saying goodbye and clumped down the stairs to the reception office. Gisela said 'goodbye' to Spengler, but he ignored her and went out to a waiting car.

*

Alistair and Freddie were sitting in the front of their hire car, with Manfred in the back. Their binoculars were trained on the front entrance of the Spengler building and the reception office. They could see the secretary Gisela stand up, her hand at her mouth, pale-faced for some reason.

"That's him alright," said Freddie, "the great Erich Spengler. In person."

"And he doesn't look very happy," Alistair agreed. "God, he looks an evil bastard!"

"He looks like Rudolph Hess," said Freddie, "with those bushy eyebrows and the thick neck."

"And with two goons in tow," put in Manfred. "The driver looks ex-military and so does the man beside him. I bet they're former SS."

The three of them focused on the black Mercedes-Benz saloon as it pulled out of the company car park. Spengler sat in the back behind what was probably bullet-proof glass. Several onlookers – possibly employees – watched the shiny car crunch gravel.

"I will relieve Gertrud at 2.00pm," said Manfred precisely. "Rosa probably won't go back home until close of business anyway. 6.00pm, if the last three nights are anything to go by."

"Good plan," said Alistair.

"Surveillance is a stock-in-trade for us spies. Tedious, but establishing behaviour patterns is central to what we do. I don't have to tell you two that. You are the masters." Manfred sounded very serious and Germanic.

Alistair: "Yes. But don't forget the element of surprise."

Manfred chuckled: "Never."

They followed the black Mercedes, keeping well back. There were few cars about as they drove out on to the main road.

"Where do you think he's going now? Home? I wonder if he's been away somewhere," Manfred speculated.

Alistair said: "Spengler looks in bad physical shape. Did you see the trouble he had getting into the back of that car?"

"It's a First World War injury," said Freddie. "He fell from a horse in combat. Brim told me about it years ago. God knows how he knew."

"Brim is a mine of information," Alistair quipped.

The black Mercedes suddenly pulled off the main road and turned left. Alistair slowed to crawling, Manfred leapt out and darted after it as fast as he was able. He kept to the inside of the pavement, out of sight.

Up ahead, the car swung into the front driveway of a block of 1930's-style apartments. The passenger opened the rear door – searching with his eyes, left and right – while Spengler awkwardly got out. The man practically stood to attention as

Spengler grabbed his suitcase from him and entered the lobby. Manfred stood back in the shadows and raised his glasses; there seemed to be a desk and an elevator. That suggested a concierge, and that meant security.

He made a mental note to tell the others.

*

Just outside the pretty town of Nordenham in the wide boulevard where Rosa lived, Gertrud stood across the road. The house was pretty, with a vegetable patch out front, a neat lawn and trimmed borders. A lady stood at the bus stop, with a headscarf, gaberdine and a push chair. She cooed the baby with a quaint German lullaby; it was quiet, snuggled up in its little cocoon of warmth.

Gertrud watched the house and wondered what it was like inside, thinking of her encounter with Rosa yesterday ...

The stocky man came out of nowhere, twisted her right arm into a painful half-Nelson. She yelped in pain.

"Caroline Montgomery?" The words came out with a heavy Berlinisch accent, tinged with tobacco and too much schnapps.

"Let go of me!" Gertrud found herself answering in English. She would later ask herself why the hell she had done that.

"Who wants to know?" The female voice also spoke in English, tinged with something else. The man did not know who that voice belonged to, but Gertrud did, immediately.

As the man turned, the woman flat-palmed the tip of his nose with the heel of her hand, a swift, powerful upward thrust. In seconds it had twisted into a gushing retroussé, a brutal close combat technique Alistair had taught her. And she was a good student. The second move, following victim bewilderment, was a blow to the right temple – ledge of the bunched fist – 'No point in breaking your knuckles, Joss,' he had said. Good lesson: the man dropped. She danced like a lightweight, considering another strike. There was no need.

Gertrud was astonished; not only seeing Joselyn out of the blue, her but seeing her fight with such ferocity. Last time they'd met Joselyn had been Walcott's 'trophy' wife at Needle's Eye. Now she was a dangerous street fighter and probably a lot more besides.

"You?"

"Yeah, let's get the hell out of here."

Alistair and Freddie's hire car powered down the wide boulevard and pulled to a sharp stop.

"Get in," Freddie yelled, as the rear doors swung open. Joselyn folded the push chair and hurled it into the footwell. And they were gone, leaving the assailant groaning on the pavement.

Plan

Hotel Landaus, Mitte-Nord, Germany.

JOSELYN WAS NOT HAPPY, and the atmosphere felt tense: "Did you bed Gertrud, Alistair? That's all I want to know."

"I told you, no."

"You had the opportunity that Sunday afternoon, you told me. You almost joked about it. I was actually hurt," Joselyn persisted.

Alistair chose to ignore her.

"I hope I can believe you," she said softly.

"I hope you can too, because it is true." Alistair was starting to get irritated.

"Alright."

But he could see she was not placated, and it was out of character for her to be so obstinate. But he shouldn't have joked:

"Joselyn. Listen to me. I had to persuade Gertrud Wolf to carry out a dangerous mission. Effectively to work for us ..."

Joselyn unwisely cut in: "But ..."

"No 'buts'. I had to persuade her to work for her former

enemy – us."

"You had to persuade her to leave prison – enjoy freedom – come home to Germany and play one simple role. I wouldn't call that dangerous."

"I would."

"And now, oh what a surprise, she's vanished."

Alistair and Joselyn were in the bedroom of the Hotel Landaus. Outside, the sea crashed against the promenade. She was sitting on the double bed and he gazed out of the bedroom window. Downstairs, Freddie and Manfred were in the bar playing chess. But no Gertrud. She had disappeared along with Manfred's hire car, apparently without any explanation.

"She may return," Alistair suggested calmly.

"Gertrud couldn't take her eyes off you all through dinner. Didn't you notice? And me as well for that matter."

"Can you blame her, Joss? The last time she saw you, you were Walcott's wife ..."

"Stop!"

"No. Now she can see you are one of us. A spy, all along. Think about it."

Joselyn remained quiet, mulling his words over.

He gave her ten seconds and continued, his tone firm and persuasive:

"Don't you see? One minute she sees you pouring Chablis, the perfect hostess at a country house, the next you are beating the living daylights out of one of Spengler's thugs. And from what you have told me, using a combat technique I taught you in Switzerland."

Finally, Joselyn flashed a reluctant, involuntary smile, trying to hide her amusement at what he'd said.

"Correct?" He asked firmly.

"Yes."

"I would never betray you, Joselyn. That is the end of this conversation."

"I'm sorry."

He moved on: "Anyway, it appears Gertrud has gone. Probably to meet Harald who escaped from a secure facility you won't have heard about."

"I see."

Alistair searched her face, trying to decide what to reveal. If he should reveal anything. In truth, he hated confrontation. And, in truth, he could have slept with Gertrud that afternoon, but chose not to. She had given him ample opportunity.

Suddenly he thought of Pontresina and how close he had been to death. To losing her. And Freddie. He made up his mind:

"Yes, Harald escaped. He killed a man called Dieter Protz, an inmate at the facility, knowledgeable about Spengler's manufacturing operations at Nordhausen. Freddie and I heard a transcript. Protz and Harald playing snooker. Well, they were just about to break, actually."

"And?" Joselyn asked, intrigued.

"The transcript cut off inexplicably. And suspiciously."

Joselyn stood up from the bed and came over to Alistair, who was still standing watching the crashing surf outside: "I'm so delighted you would never betray me, because ..."

Alistair suddenly turned around, as if he hadn't heard her.

"I'm going to tell you something I shouldn't ... but I really need to ... nothing to do with us, Joss. I love you and nothing in the world will ever change that."

"What is it?" she asked, concerned.

His tone was deadly serious:

"We know there were ten missiles trained on the UK. To annihilate London, Windsor, and the south. Utter destruction, Joss. The obliteration of everything we know." He paused and she still held his gaze.

"Yes?"

"You prevented it, Joss, by killing Devlin."

"Uh-hu. So?"

"So, where are they now? Ten high-speed ballistic missiles, each with an explosive warhead and a gyroscopically stabilised fin. I told you the whole story that evening at Chalet Monte Rosa."

"Ah, The Valentines Cup," she said softly. She could be incredibly demure and loving when she chose to.

"Yes, Joss."

Now she was deadly serious: "This is what we are talking about? Not just killing Spengler and taking off home?"

Alistair ignored her quip:

"The British Army scoured the coast of Northern France. They found some V1 and V2 launching ramps, nothing else. The V1s and V2s were taken to America after the War, along with Von Braun and his team of scientists. That is classified, for now."

"But Spengler's were never found?"

"No. His men must have recovered them. And brought them back here to Germany. Somewhere. Conceivably anywhere he has a facility. If only we knew where they all were, we could start searching. And set about a plan to destroy them."

Joselyn could see the horrendous possibility: "What could Spengler possibly do with them now, in peacetime?"

"Sell them. There is always a nutcase who wants to start a war somewhere. Someone with money and a damn great motive."

"Who?

"That's the question," Alistair said and took her in his arms. "What were you going to say when I interrupted you a moment ago?"

"It really doesn't matter now, does it?"

He held her even tighter: "No."

*

Rosa knew at once something was wrong as she sat in her little kitchen, sipping her third whisky. The gramophone played; her book still lay unread. The confrontation with her father had physically exhausted her; but it was more than that; he was a bully. And he treated her badly. She was more hurt than angry.

Then, that sound again. And where was Fritz? He hadn't barked for ages. She stood, opened the screen and kitchen door, and stepped out into her meticulously manicured garden. It was dark; she could hear the sea in the distance. Someone was sitting on one of the sun loungers. Who could it be: one of her father's bodyguards? God, she was sick of being watched. And followed. The figure stood and wandered over to her, into the light cast by the open kitchen door. Confident. Sky-blue eyes, high cheek bones, blond hair, a look of haughty superiority. Rosa could not believe her eyes.

Caroline Montgomery spoke perfect German: "My name is not Caroline, Fräulein Doktor Spengler. It is Gertrud Wolf. I am as German as you. I'm sorry if I startled you ..."

But Rosa was unable to speak. She waited.

"I worked indirectly for your father. My husband Harald and I were the London sleeper spies who delivered the Tabun gas cylinders from Poole Harbour ... to your friend Giles Walcott at Needle's Eye House."

Rosa fell back against the kitchen door, wheezing, the symptoms of an asthma attack. The second time that day she had been utterly paralysed with fear. She controlled her breaths:

"What-what do you want? Where is my dog? Where's Fritz?"

"Asleep in his kennel, with the help of a sniff of chloroform." Wolf held up a cloth, to show how she had anaesthetised Rosa's beloved dog.

"Will he be alright?"

"I wouldn't hurt him; we had a Labrador when I was a girl growing up in Hannover." Still the fluent German continued.

"What do you want?" Rosa's voice was shaky.

"To talk."

"About what, Frau Wolf – if that really is your name."

"I think you know."

"My father?"

"Partly, yes."

Rosa took a deep breath to try and regain composure:

"Where did I go to University, Frau Wolf?"

The question did not shock Gertrud, because she was prepared for it:

"Dublin. You studied Chemistry for your Doctorate and you were successful. It was there you met Walcott and fell in love with him. At some stage you discovered he was an Irish fanatic and then, he met Joselyn. You returned here to Germany and started working for your father and Braun, whom you hated. And he was the man who organised the murder of Joselyn and ..."

"Alright! Stop!" Rosa shouted, "wait here." She walked down to Fritz's kennel at the lower end of the garden near an immaculately kept greenhouse. She knelt down, listened to his chest and stroked him affectionately.

Rosa wandered back and held the door open for Gertrud: "You'd better come in."

"Thank you."

Rosa closed the door firmly.

At Landaus Hotel the following morning, Manfred dashed into the breakfast room in search of Alistair and Freddie. He wanted to tell them his hire car had finally turned up. Then he saw her as large as life.

Gertrud Wolf was sitting at a table by the window, a Frühstück platter in front of her: fresh bread, cheese, ham, soft boiled eggs, salami, coffee and a selection of juices. The waitresses wore traditional outfits, blouses with puffy sleeves and black skirts. It was like a scene from Oktoberfest, but the wrong month. And no steins of beer.

"Good morning, Manfred," she said as if nothing had happened. "Your keys are on the table here. I think the clutch is slipping. Tell the hire car company."

Manfred poured coffee as Alistair, Freddie and Joselyn walked in. Joselyn was the only one who seemed surprised:

"Good morning, Gertrud," said Freddie taking the lead. "How was Doktor Spengler?"

"You won't believe what that evil old man has got planned." Gertrud nodded at Alistair and Joselyn. If there was any awkwardness nobody showed it.

"Tell us," said Freddie.

"After Frühstück," said Gertrud. "This is the first German breakfast I've had since Harald and I left ... and that was a long time ago."

"Guten Appetit," said Freddie.

*

Later at Cuxhaven, Alistair walked into the Post Office and sent a telegram. To Professor Nicholas Brimblecombe, Minister of State for Agriculture, Fisheries and Food. BI Dept. Whitehall, London, England.

Once the Post Room girls at the Ministry in England recognised Brim's full name, his title and the initials 'BI Dept.' it would be immediately re-directed to British Intelligence. The telegram read as follows:

START* NEED TO PERSUE LOAN OF ITEM SUGGESTED* STAYING AT HOTEL LANDAUS, MITTE-NORD* BREMERHAVEN* TELEPHONE NUMBER FOLLOWS* PLEASE CONTACT SQUIRES* SURPRISE FOR TAURUS* TKS* STOP AV*

Alistair walked out into the sunshine with a grin. But what would Freddie think when he eventually discovered that Brim had visited his old CO at RAF Northolt – Squadron Leader David Squires? He got into the hire car and drove back to the Landaus. On the way he thought about breakfast and the chemistry between Joselyn and Gertrud. The dynamic had worked out well despite Joselyn's cynicism in the hotel bedroom the previous night. He caught his expression in the rear-view mirror: he loved Joselyn, but she could be bloody difficult sometimes.

Squires

RAF Northolt, Ruislip, England.

"HOW WAS YOUR ANNIVERSARY evening, Captain Clitheroe?" Brim asked his driver with genuine concern.

"Oh, very nice, ta, Professor. Took the Missus to Lyons Corner House in Piccadilly – cor, some of them 'Nippies' is pretty in their little black skirts and stockings – same age as our daughter probably! Then up the Odeon Leicester Square and a light ale on the way 'ome. Don't get any better really. She's a treasure, my Sheila. Puts up with me, so she's got to be!" He laughed at his little joke and Brim wondered what exactly she had to put up with. Perhaps it was his penchant for black skirts and stockings?

He was studying the MOD report about the Tabun cylinders retrieved from Windsor Castle. It didn't make good reading; none of the components were branded Spengler GmBh and therefore, they had no evidence against its owner. It was a major blow to British Intelligence and to Brim in particular. Another tactic was needed if they were going to nail Spengler once and for all.

"Go the Bayswater Road route, Captain. Such a lovely day."

Brim was being driven in the trusty Humber from St. James's out to RAF Northolt on the A40 Oxford Road. Clitheroe drove up Park Lane, round Marble Arch and turned west towards Notting Hill Gate. Hyde Park was an area Brim loved and as they drove down Bayswater Road, he noticed the buildings which had been spared bomb damage. And the ones that hadn't. Londoners were out and about: shopping; going to work; children back at school. Life was starting to return to normal just over a year after the German surrender. At the traffic lights near Paddington Station, he saw a newspaper vendor. The Nuremberg Trials were still headlining. He went back to his report.

Squadron Leader David Squires resembled the actor Robert Donat. And often the girls at RAF Attlebridge, Freddie's former base, would mimic him. But Freddie's uncanny impersonation was legendary to everyone throughout the Airforce apart from Squires.

After Freddie's accident in the Tiger Moth over the Fens, he had been disqualified from flying Spitfires, following a lower limb amputation and subsequent prosthetic. Freddie had been an 'Ace' in 1942 – six kills in action – and suddenly he was unable to fly. At first, he had been devastated. But his convalescence at East Grinstead and a feisty romance with Sally Brooke had given him time to take stock.

Ironically, it was Sally who had recommended Freddie to

Brim in the first place; they were distantly related and always looking for recruits. Neither Alistair nor Freddie had ever been aware of this.

David Squires had always felt a sense of guilt about the crash, because he was the one who had asked Freddie to deliver the TM trainer in the first place.

Squires met Brim at the West End Road perimeter gate and escorted him on to the airbase. Squires was saluted by a number of RAF ground staff as they crossed to his office. There was an open hangar and Brim noticed a De Havilland DH93 and a Vickers Wellington inside, like two monsters waiting to pounce. They climbed stone steps up into an open-plan area near the control tower.

On the map table was a chart depicting the east coast of England, the North Sea, Holland and the North of Germany. Tracking east from Northolt was a line of red cotton pinned to Den Helder, Groningen, over the Deutsche Bucht and finally on to Cuxhaven.

"Colonel Alistair Valentine has been in touch, as you know, Professor, with a request concerning his brother, Group Captain Alfred Valentine," Squires said formally.

"Freddie, yes," said Brim. "We can skip formalities if you don't mind. I see you've been busy," Brim said, pointing at the chart.

"Oh, right-ho then. There are two issues, uhm, Brim. A suitable aircraft and the choice of navigational course. Over sea or land. It's about five hundred miles, give or take, depending upon the option taken."

"Which is preferable?"

"Looking at the chart, I would ignore the sea option depicted and take this route ..." He grabbed the top half of a snooker cue and tapped the route with its tip ... "alright, from here, over the North Sea – over the Port of Rotterdam – due east – Utrecht – Apeldoorn – north- east up to Emden – change course to - Bremen and approach Cuxhaven from the east. Other side of the River Weser. We have identified five airfields suitable to put down in, between Bremerhaven and Cuxhaven on the north coast. High altitude over land."

"Why this route?"

Squires chuckled: "Quite simple, really. If you took the sea route over the Wadden Islands, to the north of Holland, the aircraft would be seen approaching. I take it, surprise is of the essence." He carefully placed the cue on to the table.

"Yes," said Brim.

"Now, I have to ask, do you think Freddie could be persuaded to, uhm, fly again? It might do him good."

"What did Alistair say?" Brim asked warily. He was not sure if he'd even spoken to Freddie yet.

"He was cagey, I have to say."

"Could he fly?" Brim put in, "I mean physically? With his prosthetic?"

"Oh! I've no doubt he could fly. But would he want to? His

injury was the only reason he was relieved of operational duty, after all. Bloody unfortunate." Squires sounded uncomfortable and Brim knew why.

"But that was as a fighter pilot in the war, surely? Dogfights over the Channel and so forth?"

"True," admitted Squires, considering options.

Brim tapped the chart: "Good work with this, David. This is a classified British Intelligence mission which has the sanction of the DG of MI5 and, of course, the PM."

Squires nodded: "Understood. Come to think of it, I've just had an idea about Freddie."

"The course you've just described to me seems to make sense. But I am not a pilot or a navigator. In the end the decision is up to you and the aircrew."

"There was one other detail before you go, Professor."

"Fire away," said Brim.

"Exactly. The aircraft. Possibly a Mosquito. She will need to be armed, I presume."

Brim put his overcoat on: "To the hilt. I'll contact Alistair and Freddie and tell them we're on. Good day to you, David. And thank you."

*

In the back of the Humber on the way back, Brim made some sketches of the Abyssinian Crimson Wing. It is a small olive-coloured finch with bright crimson wings and perfect for a mission name and emblem. Brim smiled and thought to himself: this will amuse Alistair and Freddie when they see the Mosquito land in Germany. He must remember to telephone David the moment he arrived back at the office. The ground staff at Northolt could surely paint the Crimson Wing image on the tail.

He made a further note as an aide-mémoire: what did David mean: I've just had an idea about Freddie?

"Straight back to St. James's, Professor?" asked Captain Clitheroe, "or would you like a little detour round by the river?"

Brim glanced at his sketches and notes: "No, straight back today, thank you. Lots to do before end of play. But thank you anyway, Clitheroe. A kind thought."

"Sir."

Garden

Hotel Landaus, Mitte-Nord, Germany.

ALISTAIR WALKED OUT of the hotel into the rear garden. Freddie, Joselyn, Manfred and Gertrud were playing croquet on a freshly mown lawn. A pot of coffee and cups stood on a wrought iron table. It was all very civilised.

He noticed a newspaper half-folded on the hotel tray. Someone had been catching up:

GOERING SUICIDE – Nazi Chief cheats the gallows.

Alistair smiled at the irony of Goering's death. They all turned as he stepped out into the sunlight:

"That was Rosa Spengler on the phone," he said slowly, almost as if he didn't believe it himself. There was a collective look of incredulity.

"How did she get this number? How did she know where we

are staying?" It was Manfred, immediately alarmed.

"She dialled the number on 'Caroline Montgomery's' business card – Lloyd's. Spoke to Miss Trueblood and she passed it on."

"Very enterprising," Gertrud said.

"Not really. She called the number before, didn't she? Anyway, she said her name was Rosa Spengler and wanted to leave a message for Gertrud Wolf."

"What was the message?" Gertrud asked, sensing trouble. She bit her lip.

"She wants a meeting with you, Gertrud – and 'the woman who killed my father's bodyguard with two blows.'"

"Did I hit him that hard?" said Joselyn. She gave Alistair a rueful look.

Alistair ignored her: "But this is the clincher. She said – 'I believe her name is Joselyn Foster - Devlin's killer.'"

Joselyn exploded: "How the hell does she know my name? Christ!"

"Easy, Joss."

"No, I won't easy Joss. How does she know my maiden name? No one knows that outside Daddy's office."

Freddie looked at Alistair who nodded imperceptibly.

He said: "We know from Brim that Spengler had a spy at the American Embassy."

"Had a spy?" Joselyn was anxious.

"An unidentified male – Blue Raincoat as he was known - is being temporarily held in London at the Embassy. His name is

Donoghue, part of an Irish American crime syndicate based in Boston. Walcott was part of it and Braun is on the syndicate's payroll."

"Braun, really?"

"Yes. Donoghue was passing classified information to Clive Rowlands, the lawyer. Rowlands committed suicide."

"Convenient."

"Yes. The trouble is your father's people at the Embassy have a problem. Donoghue is protected by diplomatic immunity. He is free to return to the US."

"Great."

"But Rowlands obviously spoke to Spengler before he threw himself in front of a taxi. New Bond Street."

"It would be nice to have been told," Joselyn said. "And don't say you didn't want to worry me ..." She paused, to take a breath ... "Anyway, it's a trick. It has to be."

"Not necessarily," said Manfred, looking around the garden, up into the trees. Alistair thought of his comment about surveillance the other day.

Alistair: "I agree. From what Rosa told Gertrud the other night, she's not that close to her father ... in fact, 'ängstlich' was the word you used – fearful. Isn't that right, Gertrud?"

Gertrud nodded. Said nothing.

"But how did Rosa know it was me who decked that thug?" Joslyn said. "She's never met me."

"I didn't tell her, Joselyn." Gertrud looked at Joselyn.

"Simple, really," said Manfred. "Deduction. Who else could it have been?"

Alistair went over and stood beside Joselyn and took her hand. Their affection was obvious and there was no point in concealing it. Everyone knew they shared a bedroom.

"What do you think, Joss?" Alistair said.

"I'm not sure." There was a hint of something in those famous blue eyes.

Gertrud wandered over closer and joined them: "Is it a trick? A meeting?"

"To do what, though?" Freddie put in, "You've spent time with her, Gertrud."

Joselyn was on fire again: "To hand us over to goddam Spengler, that's what, Freddie. He wants my guts. You might as well gift wrap me."

Manfred, ever serious, ever practical: "The tactic would be to meet her somewhere neutral – and then move on to somewhere else with her – so Spengler and his goons can't follow. Or, if they did, we would see them. There are three of us to protect you."

Joselyn looked at Gertrud, raised her eyebrows as if to say: what do you think?

Gertrud actually laughed: "I don't think you need protecting, Joselyn. What's there to lose? I'd say yes."

Joselyn rallied: "Yeah, what the hell."

Meeting

Schloss Ritzebüttel, Cuxhaven, Germany.

ALISTAIR THOUGHT ROSA was a beautiful woman. Even through high-powered binoculars he could see that she emanated class and had a sense of presence. Despite her German heritage she had that Russian appearance present in old photographs of the Romanovs, with her slender neck and finely etched features.

He was perched in a roof turret of the Ringelnatz Museum with Manfred, looking out of an open window. Freddie meanwhile had a vigilant eye on the scene from the parked car. Manfred and Freddie had spent two days scouting the area for the ideal location for a meeting. And Ritzebüttel Castle near Cuxhaven was the final place. The ancient edifice was surrounded on all four sides by inner and outer gardens. They were effectively enclosed. While Alistair's binoculars were trained on the three women, Manfred clutched a high-powered rifle in classic sniper's pose, the barrel pushed out through the open window. The breech of the gun was pushed into his shoulder, eyes fixed on the sights. His finger gripped the trigger. The vantage point was ideal, and they had an ex- Swiss Army field telephone to keep in contact with Freddie, if the need arose.

After Joselyn and Gertrud initially met Rosa at the Port of Cuxhaven Customs Office, they quickly relocated to the castle gardens. Rosa parked her car beside the museum. At the hotel before the meeting Manfred had been instructive: 'Once inside the castle gardens, keep moving. We'll be watching.' The advice was based on experience.

Rosa was not as Joselyn had imagined. Perhaps mid-forties, quietly mannered, not particularly confident. Attractive and apparently willing to confide.

'Don't cause friction,' Manfred had also said. 'She wants the meeting, let her speak.'

The only concession to this tactic was the question of Patrick Devlin. Rosa explained – convincingly - it was he who wanted Joselyn 'out of the way'. But it was definitely Peter Braun and her father who had been responsible for the failed attempt in Pontresina. She explained about the Irish Republican angle and the arrangement Walcott established with Germany.

The three women had walked around the perimeter three times and, so far, only Rosa had spoken. It was as if she wanted to confess; concede the truth before the ultimate betrayal.

Rosa suddenly slowed her pace, she turned to Joselyn: "I

admit I hated you because of what happened – but any rational man would choose you over me. You are a ..."

Joselyn stopped: "Please don't, Dr. Spengler."

Rosa ignored her: "Allow me, I beg you. You are a beautiful woman, but, more importantly, incredibly brave. We have no ..."

Again, Joselyn tried to interrupt; again, Rosa prevented her: "We will never have the opportunity to discuss this again ..." She gave Joselyn a look of intense sensitivity, no matter their past differences.

Joselyn nodded.

"We have no idea how you prevented Michael Devlin from sending that signal – and I don't need to know how – but you did. And I am delighted you did, believe me. Humanity would have changed if my father and that monster Himmler had got away with it."

Joselyn, for a change, was speechless. It was Gertrud who urged Rosa to explain why she had wanted to meet. Was there an edge of concern in her tone? Joselyn sensed something and she wished Alistair was with them.

For a moment the three women walked in companionable silence. Then Rosa described everything her father had told her about the tall Palestinian and his radical ambition. They knew nothing about the situation in the Middle East or the formation of a Jewish State. And even less about the notorious Ali Emran ...

From the roof turret of the museum Alistair and Manfred

watched in frustrated silence, unable to hear the conversation, but relieved it had lasted so long. Twice the field phone squawked, but no sound of a Mayday – the decided signal – if trouble approached. 'Freddie is probably bored,' Alistair had said, after an hour had passed. Joselyn was to drop her shoulder bag if there was any sign of trouble whatsoever; or evidence of Spengler's goons hiding in the bushes.

Rosa said: "That is the reason I asked for this meeting. My father will sell the ballistic missiles to Ali Emran. I am telling you because I think he is crazy. The firepower he will have at his disposal is deadly."

"There is something else, isn't there?" Joselyn said with growing concern.

"Yes, there is. Because the man who brokered this arms deal, Gertrud, was your husband Harald. But then, you knew that didn't you?" Rosa said calmly. She eyed the two women. And their growing discomfort.

Joselyn recalled what Alistair had told her that night at the Landaus: Harald killed a man called Dieter Protz, an inmate of Beaufort. Harald escaped under or in a bread van. He was very knowledgeable about Spengler's operations in Nordhausen.

Rosa continued: "And you knew the reason why Harald escaped from prison – or wherever – was specifically to meet Ali Emran somewhere in England. You knew all along."

Gertrud said nothing.

From the window of the museum Alistair watched through binoculars. He saw Joselyn drop her shoulder bag. The signal. Gertrud viciously kicked Joselyn in the shin with her walking boot and tried to punch Rosa in the face. Joselyn collapsed to the ground, evidently screaming, clutching her leg. Gertrud ran. Manfred also saw the scene unfold through his telescopic sight. Mein Gott!

Joselyn was shouting at Gertrud, pleading with her to come back.

Manfred: "I have her in my sights ... what shall I do?"

Alistair grabbed the field telephone, desperately trying to call Freddie:

"Freddie! Hello! Hello! Come in! Fucking battery's flat. Freddie!!!" Nothing.

Manfred: "I've got ten seconds before she's out of range."

Alistair waited, counting seconds He had to decide. She was an enemy of the state; running away. He could not let her escape.

Manfred, now shouting: "Alistair! Quick!"

"Shoot, damn it! Shoot!"

The single shot resounded in the small turret of the museum lookout but missed its target. Manfred quickly reloaded - stock, action, bullet.

Alistair put the binoculars back to his eyes again. Gertrud was running with incredible strength and power.

Crack: the second shot.

The running figure's white summer dress exploded blood red as the round tore through her spine and out through her stomach. Her legs seem to carry on for a few paces, then she fell flat. He turned the binoculars to Rosa, both hands at her mouth, shocked. Down to Joselyn still on the grass. Her face; disbelief, shock.

Ten seconds.

Alistair, despite his instruction, was shocked. In the background he could hear Manfred dismantling the weapon, sliding the telescopic sight off its mount, wrapping it quickly in chamois, placing the gun in its case, clicking the locks. He felt Manfred's strong hand clutch his shoulder:

"Get the field phone," he said firmly. "Pull yourself together ... quickly." Only Herr Seiler had ever spoken to him like that. But Manfred was right. Alistair's hands were shaking as he folded the apparatus into its field-issue canvas bag. Manfred was already halfway down the winding steps to the entrance. Alistair followed.

No matter the reason, he had ordered Gertrud's execution.

Outside in the castle garden, Joselyn and Rosa had gone over to Gertrud's body. Her bare arms were splayed out in front of her in surrender, legs twisted, the white dress soaked in blood. The wound was extraordinary, as if someone had punched a hole through her. Freddie came hobbling over from the car park with a camping rug, desperate to meet the others. He shook his head, saying: "What happened? What happened?"

He threw the rug over Gertrud's body, relieved it had, for a moment, disappeared from sight.

Rosa turned away, leant over and retched noisily. It was oddly out of character for one so composed. She was pale: "What next?"

She could not face the bundle under the rug and looked away.

Manfred took control: "You get out of here, Dr. Spengler and we'll deal with this."

"How do I contact you?" she said.

Manfred: "We will contact you."

Rosa looked down at Joselyn: "You still don't trust me despite all I have confided?"

Joselyn shook her head, confused, not knowing what to say. No, she didn't trust her. Not for a minute.

"There's no time," Manfred said. "We will contact you. You can be sure of that."

"Very well." She nodded at the group in farewell and walked off across the castle gardens to the side of the museum where her car was parked. She did not look back.

"I'll get the car," Alistair said and ran toward the car park.

Manfred placed Gertrud's body into the rug, properly covering her and lifted her on to his shoulder. Freddie helped Joselyn up from the grass and steadied her as she tried to walk. She was shaking like a leaf. Her shinbone was badly bruised and swollen.

None of them could see Alistair's face and the sorrow he felt as he ran for the car. Despite everything, he had never killed a woman before.

Blood Stains

Spengler GmBh, Cuxhaven, Germany.

ERICH SPENGLER WALKED into the reception office of his shipping facility in Cuxhaven. Gisela stood sharply, almost to attention, as he entered. He was accompanied by another man, a stranger. He was tall, three days' worth of stubble, well dressed, of Mediterranean appearance. The man said nothing; didn't even acknowledge her.

"Is my daughter not here? I can't see her car." Spengler asked bluntly.

"No, sir." A hesitation.

"Where is she?" Slightly louder. He marched towards the desk, eyed her face carefully, trying to detect a lie.

"I'm, I'm not sure," Gisela answered nervously. "The bank, perhaps?"

Spengler shot his cuff, glanced at his Rolex: "At this time of day? Surely not."

Gisela shook her head, petrified of saying the wrong thing.

She knew Rosa was concerned about something but dared not breathe a word to this despicable man.

"Tell her to telephone me at the Schilthorn Apartment the moment she returns." It was an order. Not a request.

Spengler and the tall visitor left without another word, leaving Gisela trembling with fear as she dropped back into her chair. Who was the man? she wondered.

*

Half an hour later Rosa Spengler returned from Ritzebüttel, looking drained. Gisela thought she had visibly aged in the last week. She knew there was escalating friction with her father because she had overheard the awful row.

"Your father was here, Dr. Spengler," she said respectfully, "with another gentleman. He asked if you could call him – at the Schilthorn Apartment – when it is convenient to you, please."

"Thank you, Gisela," Rosa said with a wry smile. "I will."

Rosa turned to climb the stairs up to her office and, as she did, Gisela noticed that the back of her dress was splattered with what, red ink? Dye? Gisela cleared her throat judiciously and pointed it out.

Rosa turned around to look, shocked at the sight of the blood, making light of the stains with a quip:

"Goodness me, yes. I must have leant on a container in the yard. Most probably rust. Or paint. How clumsy! Thanks, anyway. Lucky I've got a spare upstairs."

Once in her office Rosa ran into her tiny en-suite bathroom, switched on the light and looked in the mirror. She closed her eyes and remembered the awful moment:

Crack. The instant the second round had torn through Gertrud's flesh, her dropping down to the summer grass, the checking of her pulses; the evidence of death.

Rosa slipped off the blood-splattered cotton dress, folded it and dropped it into her waste bin.

Schaffer

Schilthorn Apartment, Cuxhaven, Germany.

ERICH SPENGLER LIVED SPARTANLY. His apartment was austere: no ornaments or trivia. No feminine touches: photographs, flowers, cushions, frills; the furniture cheap and ordinary. The only concession to his fortune was a number of priceless works of art: Raphael, Degas, Canaletto. But then, only as an investment, because the German economy had been in ruins. And still was. Nobody dared question the provenance of his collection and Spengler barely looked at them.

Spengler and his visitor, Ali Emran, listened to one of the hired minions. Peter Schaffer, a former SS Obersturmführer - Lieutenant in the British Army - wasn't particularly tall, but he had the stocky build of a wrestler. A man used to his own way, particularly with women. He fancied himself as God's gift to females.

Harald Wolf, another visitor, sat in the corner of the room, taking it all in.

Spengler had asked Schaffer what he had observed whilst spying on his daughter; he was keen to please:

"Fräulein Doktor Spengler met two women at Cuxhaven Port and then the three of them drove round, in her car, to the Ringelnatz Museum. It's ..."

"I know where the Museum is, damn you. What next?"

"The three women walked round the gardens of Schloss Ritzebüttel for at least an hour. They looked as if they were making casual conversation. Of course, I couldn't hear ..."

"Were you seen?" Spengler snapped rudely.

"No, Herr Spengler. But I took some photographs. The film is still in my camera. I will develop it tonight. I have a darkroom ..."

"I don't care about your fucking darkroom. What next? What did they look like?"

Schaffer took a breath, not familiar with being the subject of interrogation: "One was mid-forties, the victim I mean. The other, younger, I couldn't see her face properly, she wore a headscarf, you see." He paused, waiting for a reaction. There was none. Spengler snapped his fingers irritably ...

"Suddenly there was a gunshot – high-powered rifle – then another. The second round hit the victim in the back, and she fell. Flat on her face. Blood everywhere."

"An execution? Like your good old days at number 8 Prinz-Albrecht Strasse, eh, Schaffer?" Spengler said with a twisted smile.

The address referred to the Sicherheitspolizei – Security

Police in Berlin - known for inflicting extreme cruelty on its prisoners by interrogators like Schaffer. Schaffer didn't acknowledge Spengler's sick humour. Emran was visibly sickened.

"Then two men came running from the direction of the Schloss towards the scene. By now Fräulein Doktor Spengler had joined the victim. She checked the victim's wrist and neck for the sign of a pulse, but I don't think ..."

Spengler interrupted again: "Fuck her damn pulse. Tell me about the three men you saw."

"One of them was Sicilian-looking; he was carrying a gun case."

"The others?"

"The other two were well-built, fair-haired, athletic. I reckon they could be brothers. The one who came from the car park, with a rug, had a pronounced limp. The other carried what looked like an Army field telephone ..."

"British?" Spengler spat the word out.

Schaffer shook his head.

Harald Wolf spoke for the first time. He was a stocky little man, with a pock-marked face and bald head. The antithesis of his late wife. Together they had operated as Walcott's sleeper spies in London.

"British Intelligence. They were at Windsor Castle in September '43. One arrested Gertrud and Cynthia. The other killed Giles Walcott in a dazzling display of street combat. They prevented the gas cylinders from exploding ... I am not quite sure how ... I was out of earshot to hear the exact words uttered."

Spengler's eyes narrowed: "Yes, while the Joselyn bitch was killing Devlin in Southampton, Harald. The details of the failure are chiselled on my brain, believe me."

Harald could not make eye contact with Spengler – the failure had been his as well. Spengler revelled in his obvious discomfort:

"And who is Walcott's killer? Do you have a name, Harald?"

"Alistair Valentine. He looks a vain bastard. He came to see Gertrud at the detention centre where we were being held in England."

"What did he want with her?"

"She never had the chance to tell me," Harald said. "I had escaped by then. Gertrud was going to try too. But so far, she has failed to show at any of the three towns we had agreed upon. She knew my last stop was here. My guess is either she hasn't escaped or worse, was killed while trying to. I have no way of finding out what happened to her."

Spengler sounded unconvinced: "You are telling me these three men work for British Intelligence? What are they doing executing an unidentified woman in Cuxhaven? Who is she? None of this makes any sense. Tell me."

Schaffer looked uncomfortable:

"The only person who can tell you that, sir, with respect, is Fräulein Doktor Spengler," said Schaffer. "She might also tell you who killed 'the Doberman' the other day outside her house."

“I realise that,” Spengler said, “but I don’t want Rosa to know we are on to her. She’s bound to meet these brothers again and possibly the woman with the headscarf.”

Ali Emran, looking majestic and regal, who had followed the conversation between them with growing alarm, suddenly spoke:

“I do not like the sound of what I have heard, Herr Spengler. I have forwarded your bank a substantial sum of money as a deposit for these weapons. And now I am hearing about an execution in a park; and your daughter appearing to be a traitor to our cause. This is unacceptable to me. And my People at home. What do you say?”

Spengler forced a smile of civility. Instinctively, he wanted to kill this bloody Palestinian; tear the shine off his fucking countenance. But he couldn’t. Or could he? He had half the money, all he really needed. He could take off to the Paradise Klinik at Königsee and while away his twilight years in the hands of Fräulein Stefanie: sex, drugs and Mozart. What could be better? Her hands, her soft moist lips. Utter bliss ... Was he in love with her or was it just lust?

“Herr Spengler?” Emran interrupted his daydream.

“Yes, sorry. I was merely considering logistics. Your weapons will arrive here in two days. From the far reaches of Eastern Germany. By road. My ship Solveig is ready with the cargo holds adapted so the missiles can be loaded on board and stored safely for the voyage to Port Said. All is arranged.”

Emran’s noble features creased into a smile; he clapped his

hands together as if he were summoning his harem to commence a belly dance:

"That is all I wished to hear, Herr Spengler."

"Good."

*

Rosa knew once again something was wrong as she sat in her little kitchen enjoying the effects of her third whisky. The gramophone played; her book lay, still unread.

It was Fritz's bark and then silence which alerted her. She looked out of her kitchen window; her trusty dog was devouring a large piece of bloody meat. Again, someone was sitting on one of her sun loungers. He was stocky, with the build of a wrestler and she knew at once who it was: Peter Schaffer. She opened the screen and kitchen door and stepped out into her neat garden.

"What do you want?" She put her hand to her forehead to shield her eyes from the glare of the early evening sun. "I don't need protecting. And certainly not by you."

Schaffer stood and walked towards her, holding a fan of black and white photographs, like a croupier in a casino. He gave her a lopsided grin, the sort he had copied from an American cowboy film star:

"I thought you might like to see these, Dr. Spengler, before your father does. They were taken at Schloss Ritzebüttel yesterday." He held one up; it was clearly Rosa, Joselyn and

Gertrud together. Rosa swallowed with fear.

"What do you want?" she said again.

"Oh, I think a little chat, a little trade. Because I could accidentally expose this film and destroy the evidence of your meeting. If you see what I mean?" He allowed himself a little chuckle so she could see how easy it was.

She shook her head.

"You look very pretty tonight, Dr. Spengler. Why don't you invite me in for a drink and we can come to an arrangement? I can explain how easy it is to open the camera and ... bang ... the film is exposed to light ... ruined. Whisky, I think, is your favourite tipple. And it's mine too."

Schaffer walked towards her, thinking, believing he was charm itself. And he'd attempted to impress her: collar and tie, perhaps too much Eau de Cologne.

She glanced down the garden at Fritz: "Have you hurt my dog?"

He laughed: "My dog loves steak and so does Fritz, you see? That piece of beef cost me a small fortune, but I believe it was a wise investment."

"Alright, come in." She held the two doors open.

"Oh, this is homely. And you have a gramophone. And whisky, how fortunate."

"Let me see the photographs."

Schaffer handed them over to her and helped himself to a large tumbler of her expensive whisky. He sank half of it in one gulp; took off his jacket, loosened his tie. Made himself at home. He looked over her shoulder to share the experience:

"A colleague of your father's believes this one here is Alistair Valentine. But we do not know who the dead woman is, or the one with the headscarf ..."

"You don't know much."

He moved closer to her, breathing hot whisky on the back of her neck:

"Your father and I think the one with the rifle case, this Sicilian - is the shooter - that makes sense, but who is the one with the rug? The man with the limp. They are brothers, according to Harald Wolf."

Rosa flinched. Wolf.

"Ah, I see I have struck a chord." He finished his whisky and poured himself another. "Are you going to join me?"

"I'm not thirsty."

He emitted a filthy laugh: "My brother says: 'the three great pleasures for a man are a drink before and a cigarette after.' He was SS too. A lower rank than me, of course."

"Before what?"

He suddenly started caressing her breasts from behind, squeezing, and tried to kiss the back of her neck: "Sex, of course."

She recoiled, repulsed and tore the photos into fragments, on the verge of tears.

"Copies at your office, Frau Doktor. Negatives hidden, locked in my safe at home." He took off his tie, "I wouldn't bring all my aces, would I?"

"When my father hears about this, he'll kill you."

"Oh no. When your father sees these, he'll kill you!" Schaffer laughed, grabbed the bottle of whisky and swigged it from the neck: "You're far better off having sex with me than British Intelligence. Take your clothes off, let me see ..."

It was the creak of the pantry door which gave Alistair away. But it didn't matter. Schaffer was too shocked:

"I believe the lady said she wasn't thirsty." Alistair's elbow caught Schaffer's left ribcage with such force that he heaved. The bone may have punctured his lung; it sounded like it. The second, final blow caught him on the left side of his face and shattered his jaw. Schaffer dropped headfirst on to the stone floor and smashed his face into it.

The two moves took a little over eight seconds. Rosa was shocked and looked down at the body. It had been alive ten seconds before.

"Are you alright?" Alistair asked her quietly.

She nodded, caught her breath. The sudden violence shocking: "I think so."

Alistair attempted to lighten the mood: "Our friend here was right about one thing though?"

Rosa, dropped the fragments of torn photographs and fell into his arms:

"What?"

There was a sudden sharp knock on the other side of the kitchen window; Manfred was pressing his face against the glass. Alistair signalled for him to come in. He glanced down at Schaffer's body:

"At this rate we'll have to open an account with the mortuary at Cuxhaven." Manfred shook his head at Alistair, a look of admonishment. He continued:

"Dr. Spengler, you have to leave here now. They're on to you."

"Rosa, please."

"He's right, Rosa."

"But my father won't have seen these photographs yet," she said naively.

"They are already on his desk," Alistair said quietly.

"But ..." Rosa pointed at Schaffer's body and the torn fragments.

"He'll already have betrayed you, Rosa," said Manfred. "Typical SS tactics. It's what they call 'perks' – seduce the target into a false sense of security – gain their trust – then stab them in the back."

Rosa looked crestfallen at her own gullibility, then turned to Alistair: "Thank God you were here."

He took her hand: "Just one suitcase. We'll wait and take you somewhere safe."

She picked up the torn fragments and left the room. The evidence removed.

Manfred bent down, turned Schaffer's crushed face slightly: "This man was at the Schloss Gardens. I saw him with a camera, supposedly taking pictures of the flowers."

"That makes sense."

Rosa appeared moments later. Her suitcase must have already been packed. She avoided the corpse and looked at Alistair.

Manfred said to them both: "You take Rosa to the Landaus and I'll deal with him. With luck we'll be in time for dinner."

"Something on your mind, Rosa?" Alistair said, picking up on her expression.

"Gertrud came to see me the other night, as you know. She told me her name wasn't Caroline Montgomery, but Gertrud Wolf."

Alistair: "Go on."

Rosa took a breath: "She also told me she was a double agent, working for you."

"Really?"

"That bit may be partly true. But I fear you might have been played, Mr. Valentine."

"How so?"

"Gertrud knew an awful lot more than she let on."

"Such as?"

"I confronted her in the castle park. Joselyn was there; she can confirm this. I know Harald escaped from wherever you were holding him and went to meet Ali Emran, the Palestinian terrorist. It was Harald who brokered the deal with my father for the purchase of the weapons."

"How do you know this?" Manfred asked; the pieces of the jigsaw were slotting into place.

Rosa: "I overheard them talking at the shipyard.

"Are you saying Harald Wolf is in town? Now?"

Rosa nodded. She turned to the garden, to look down towards Fritz's kennel, her slender neck and finely etched features in profile; elegantly feminine: "Yes he is. And so is Emran."

Alistair: "We already know what they're planning."

"Yes. But Gertrud knew too. That is the point. She knew Harald had arranged to come to Cuxhaven right from the start. And she knew Harald killed Dieter Protz to shut him up. Harald will make a lot of money, probably already has. Gertrud knew that too."

Alistair suddenly felt illogically betrayed and Rosa could see it.

"I don't blame you," she said with a look of collusion, "and I will tell you exactly what my father and Emran plan tonight, in more detail than you can know, even from Gertrud. When we are somewhere safe ..." She picked up her suitcase and handed Alistair her door key... "then you'll know I'm not trying to play you, or anyone else."

The last three words were directed at Manfred; she walked out of the house into her garden towards the kennel.

"Komm, Fritz! Zum Auto! Guter Junge!" she shouted and

patted her thighs: “I hope this safe house doesn’t mind dogs.”

“Only one way to find out,” said Alistair. He winked at Manfred, who merely shook his head again and glanced down at Schaffer.

Langerhans

Spengler GmBh dock, Cuxhaven, Germany.

THE SS SOLVEIG was a type C3-P cargo ship designed by the US Maritime Commission. Built in the late 1930's, she was one hundred and fifty metres from stem to stern. At 8286 gross tonnage, she could carry 12 passengers, with two luxury State Rooms for the privileged. Named after the old Norse expression 'daughter of the sun' she had an impressive orange solar image painted on her hull. Above the bridge, the company flag fluttered in the breeze. It was black, white and red; boldly Germanic. And, at the stern, the German home flag looked equally striking.

Captain Edvard Langerhans from Malmo was her skipper. He had nine children scattered all over Scandinavia, care of four ex-wives. Rosa had nearly made it ten a few years previously after an ill-advised, self-indulgent fling. He was 6'4" tall, lean, with a shock of blond hair and blue eyes. Today he wore a black polo neck sweater under his navy-blue uniform jacket and grey flannels. The gold band and star insignia at his cuff was the emblem of captain.

He stood on the bridge, at the wheel, binoculars at his eyes. Behind him on the chart table, a chart depicted the sea route from Cuxhaven to Port Said. In well-used leather cases were the tools of his trade: compass, dividers and sextant. Also, on the table was a copy of the Swedish newspaper 'Sydsvenskam.'

A copy of 'The Times' also bore the same front-page headlines. They were both dramatic and significant:

British Mandatory Government of Palestine
Arrest 100 leaders of Yushnuv ...
Black Sabbath Brits arrest 2,700 Jews in
Palestine as alleged terrorists ...

The port-side bridge door slid open; Spengler and Emran entered. The headlines of the paper immediately caught Emran's eyes, but he made no comment. Spengler was at his most charming:

"Good morning, Captain Langerhans. I'd like you to meet Dr. Emran from the hospital in Cairo. It is his oxygen cylinders you will be shipping to the Middle East."

Langerhans wasn't sure if he should offer his hand or bow to this tall enigmatic-looking Palestinian. In the end, he removed his cap and saluted: "Welcome aboard, sir. Good morning, Herr Spengler."

Spengler said nothing but walked over to the wheel and

looked out of the bridge window, his back turned. His tone was concern:

"Have you seen my daughter, Edvard? I thought she might come aboard to see you ... since you are her favourite captain in the Spengler fleet."

Langerhans's handsome features melted into a smile of embarrassment: "No, sir, not yet. But you are correct, as always. Dr. Spengler normally comes aboard to see the charts and discuss the voyage details."

Spengler turned and faced him: "Nonsense. It is you she comes to see. And don't think I am not aware of the little relationship you had ... in Malmo."

Langerhans started to protest his innocence. Sleeping with the boss's daughter was not the best idea. Surely a recipe for disaster. But Spengler was uncharacteristically avuncular and friendly:

"No need to look so bashful, Edvard. I would have encouraged such a union. A merchant Captain; with your good looks and future prospects with my Company."

"Well ..."

"And Rosa's an attractive woman, if I say so myself. My grandchildren would have been most appealing ..." Spengler smiled, a rare occurrence. "Tell us about the cargo, Edvard. I see I have embarrassed you in front of our esteemed visitor ... but what I said is true. Remember that. Future prospects."

Langerhans eyed the two men cautiously: "Sir, there are

twelve wooden crates in the lower hold, secured with webbing and rope on to steel loops. They are welded to the tank top; they will not move. In case you were concerned."

Emran spoke for the first time, but only one word: "Good."

"You would be welcome to go down and inspect them, Herr Spengler."

Spengler looked at Emran, who shook his head, uninterested in the practicalities of shipping his weapons three thousand miles. He had achieved what he wanted; the rest was academic.

"That won't be necessary, Edvard. But there is one small change." Spengler relished last minute changes of plan. It kept staff on their toes.

Langerhans looked worried; had he done something wrong?

"I shall be accompanying Dr. Emran on the voyage, so we will need another cabin prepared. I take it the State Room is ready for Dr. Emran?"

"Yes, sir. Gisela from the office and another lady saw to it."

Spengler nodded: "Then we will leave you. Please inform me when, if, my daughter deigns herself to come aboard. I would have thought she would have overseen all the voyage accommodation."

"Maybe she already did, sir, and I simply wasn't aware of it," Langerhans said, always the diplomat.

Spengler sighed doubtfully. He had not seen Rosa for twenty-four hours and Peter Schaffer was inexplicably missing. To add to his annoyance, the photographs he had discovered on his office desk clearly depicted Rosa with two other women. He was convinced one of them was Joselyn Walcott.

"Come, Dr. Emran," said Spengler, "let's go for lunch."

Langerhans turned back to the wheel. He picked up his notepad and found the letter concealed within; the feminine hand of the writer was direct:

'Dear Edvard – the news is I am definitely pregnant – I cannot hide it from my husband for long. Please come and see me as soon as you are able to in Malmo. At least you assured me you are not going away for a while. I love you, Anna.'

Langerhans brushed the scented letter against his lips and nose. Anna was a twenty-two-year-old teacher from the south of Sweden. He thought about her long blond hair, brown eyes and curvaceous hips. He slid the letter back into its flimsy envelope, put on his cap and headed for Rosa's office.

'I love you too, Anna,' he thought to himself. But he loved so many other women, in other ports. Particularly this one: Rosa was a passionate woman.

What did old man Spengler say? Future prospects.

Gisela

Spengler GmBh, Cuxhaven, Germany.

GISELA REPLACED THE TELEPHONE receiver, a very worried woman. She went up to Dr. Spengler's office and into her tiny en-suite bathroom. There in the waste bin was the folded dress, where Rosa had just told her it was. The fabric was dry and stiff. She unfolded it slightly; the splatters of blood had congealed. She refolded it and made her way softly down the stairs to the reception office.

"What have you there?" Spengler said out of the blue.

She screamed and dropped the dress, petrified. She hadn't heard the office door open, too intent on her purpose.

"Pick it up," Spengler barked.

Gisela bent down, not taking her eyes off him, convinced he would kick her in the face if she did.

"What is it?"

She handed the bundle across to him and he tore it viciously out of her grip. He felt the texture of the material between his fingers, opened the dress out onto her desk; the bloody stains, the colour of rust. The smell of iron.

"This is Rosa's dress." A statement.

Gisela could not answer; she could feel her teeth chattering with fear.

"Isn't it?" he screamed.

"Y-y-yes." A whisper.

"Where is she?"

"I don't know, sir."

"Is she injured? Is this her blood?" He tossed the dress on her desk.

"I ..."

Spengler raised his gnarled fist to hit her when the office door suddenly opened. The tall figure with the Cashmere overcoat appeared, his fierce brown eyes challenging:

"Spengler, what's going on?" Emran said, alarmed. He looked at the dress. Saw Gisela's petrified face.

Captain Langerhans came bounding in next, unaware of the tension in the room. Gisela grabbed the dress and dropped it down to the floor out of sight.

"Oh, sorry," he said lightly. "Am I disturbing something?"

Spengler lent over and whispered into Gisela's ear: "I don't know what game you are playing, young lady. But you see Rosa contacts me. Do you understand?" He was so close she could smell his rank breath and knew she had narrowly escaped a beating.

"Yes, Herr Spengler."

The old man painfully straightened himself up, having controlled his temper, and turned to Emran:

"A private medical matter of no consequence; let's go."

Emran looked doubtful, shook his head and followed Spengler out of the office door, leaving Gisela and Langerhans breathless.

"What's going on?" he asked anxiously.

Gisela darted around her desk and collapsed into his arms, panting with tears of fear. He held her until she had calmed down. Finally, she looked up into his handsome features:

"Edvard, I don't know what to do. I'm so frightened for Rosa."

He wiped her tears: "Just tell me what you know ... don't worry." His reassuring words had the desired effect on the desperate woman. He was like that.

Crimson Wing

Seefliegehorst Weddewarden airfield, Germany.

IT WAS SIX forty-five am. Alistair and Freddie were waiting in a large, deserted aircraft hangar near the Port of Wesermünde. The long grass airfield was deserted, its surface riddled with potholes from Allied air raids.

Early morning, blue sky and sunshine. Alistair had been checking his watch every ten minutes; Freddie was curious. Finally, they heard the throb of two supercharged Rolls- Royce Merlin engines, way off in the distance. Freddie, who should have looked baffled at this moment, did not. He merely smiled at his older brother.

"Let's go out and take a look, shall we?" Alistair said, clutching hold of his high-powered binoculars.

On the horizon, in the morning haze, a Mosquito FB V1was losing altitude as it neared the airfield. It appeared to hover, looking motionless as it made its final approach. Then lower, ready to land, the sun glinting on the canopy windscreen. It looked magnificent. An old Luftwaffe windsock blew in the breeze beside the runway.

The noise of the powerful bomber grew louder as it touched down on the grass with a skid and taxied toward the hangar. The engines were switched off and suddenly the air was still; the aircraft hot from its 400-mile journey. She had been painted an anonymous grey. And, forward of the cabin door, three words had been stencilled in black:

Freddie 'Ace' Valentine.

"It was your friend Squires's idea, according to Brim," said Alistair. Freddie was touched and clasped his brother's arm in appreciation all the same. A thoughtful gesture.

"I knew you were up to something when you asked me the question at Christmas in Zermatt ..." Freddie grinned.

"Thought I'd done rather well, you know, discretion?"

"Did you speak to Squires then?"

"Didn't have to."

Freddie walked over. The hatch door on the side of the aircraft opened and the navigator pulled out the telescopic ladder secured inside it. He clipped it on the lip of the hatch and carefully climbed down. The pilot was next. They simultaneously removed their goggles, flying gloves and looked around the airfield.

"Compliments from RAF Northolt. Now, let me guess, Group

Captain Valentine?" asked the pilot. He chose correctly and shook Freddie's hand. They exchanged introductions.

"Charlie Morris," he said beaming with pleasure, "and navigator David Swift. This is an in-and-out, so I hope you've got some coffee and sandwiches."

"Over there." Alistair pointed at a rattan picnic basket.

"Thank God for bennies," said Swift. "I need a piss!"

Alistair: "Forgive me for asking, Charlie, but why is there – what looks like – a small olive finch painted on your aircraft's tail?"

"Ah," said Charlie", scratching his chin, "well observed. It's actually an Abyssinian Crimson Wing finch ... very colourful as you can see."

"Yes, but ..."

"This mission is codenamed Crimson Wing, the idea of somebody in London called Brimblecombe, a colleague of Squadron Leader Squires."

Alistair and Freddie chuckled with an it had to be him feeling.

"Our call sign is GOLF – Tango – Charlie – Romeo – Whisky. Although we've kept radio silence as much as possible over Holland to Bremen. We are not officially here, you see."

"Understood. GOLF - TCRW", said Freddie. "I'll get your hamper."

Swift returned from his micturition: "We'll need bearings for the Port at Cuxhaven and the location of the SS Solveig."

Alistair and Freddie nodded.

Charlie said to Freddie: "Squires said you might like to pilot her, Group Captain."

Freddie was shocked: "Serious?"

"Never more so. She has your name on the side after all. Rather a nice touch, don't you think?"

"Good old Squires." Freddie couldn't hide his jubilation.

"Right," said Charlie, "let's get your fixed up. There's a spare of everything in the Mossie. I'd like to get her airborne again in ten minutes, say 7.00am? Oh, and you'll need to find a ladder or something to climb on board ... tricky, with that leg of yours."

*

Simultaneously at the Port of Cuxhaven Joselyn was waiting to board Solveig. She was not in good spirits. Not in good spirits at all. It was Spengler and Braun who had tried to kill her at the villa. Them and Devlin. Thank God Alistair and Freddie had also survived. But it was she who had been the target of Spengler's bitter crusade for revenge. What was it Brim had said so decisively at Chalet Monte Rosa back in December?

'What we need is evidence. Get the evidence and we can nail Erich Spengler for War Crimes.'

'Well then, I'll get it for you,' she thought bitterly. She had no idea where Alistair had disappeared to so early that morning. He'd slipped out of bed, dressed, pecked her on the cheek with a see you later expression. It irritated the hell out of her. Where had he gone? Why didn't he tell her? Why couldn't he share it? And she wasn't sure about Rosa now either. Friend or foe? She had, though, given them a lot of information about her father. Only one way to satisfy her curiosity completely: go to the ship and find those damn weapons.

'Headstrong, like your mother,' is what Grizzly always said. Maybe he was right.

She waited for the quartermaster at the top of the gangway to leave his post. Then she boarded Solveig, up the gangway to the main deck, into the mast house for number three hold and climbed down the steel ladder to the lower cargo hold. Rosa had told her exactly where the crates would be stowed for the voyage to Port Said. The only source of light in the hold was from the open hatch, so she kept close to the bulkheads. She was wearing dark clothing and her black headscarf.

At the bottom of the hold she found the twelve crates, secured to the tank top. On the top of each was a Customs declaration note. Presumably fake. The tops of the crates consisted of slats of wood – narrow strips of tongue- and- groove – just over a metre in length. She found a crowbar, presumably discarded by the stevedores after securing the crates. And with it, she levered open one of the slats. Inside she found an oxygen cylinder nestling in straw packaging. The cylinder was strapped in securely with rope. The valve was covered with thick wax paper.

Mystified, she replaced the slat and moved on to the next

crate, repeating the procedure. As soon as the panel opened, she could see the gyro fin of a ballistic missile. She took out her flashlight and held it inside. Once illuminated in the dullness, it looked surprisingly innocuous: silver-grey, with a dull matt surface. She swallowed, knowing what was within the pressurised missiles. She flicked out the light.

"Looking for something, Frau Walcott?" It was Harald Wolf, the familiar voice from Needle's Eye.

The shock of hearing a voice so close unnerved her. She stepped forward, tripping over one of the crate's lashings and fell ... hitting her head sharply on the steel tank top ... and then, black.

When she finally came round, she found she was tied down on a bunk in a pitch-black cabin. It was dry and airless. She tried to sit up but could not. She sensed the slight pitch and roll of a ship at sea. She heard the sound, felt the throbbing of a powerful marine engine. She felt dehydrated and delirious. Her head swam in confusion ...

She would be alright, wouldn't she? Surely, she was safely aboard the Orca with her Uncle Mark sailing off the coast of Martha's Vineyard. They were fishing, having fun. Soon they would head back to Edgartown for a fish supper and plenty of wine! Joselyn smiled in her delirium:

'Shall I pour?'

‘Nah, let it breathe. I need a shower. Back in ten.’

‘You’d better or I’ll drink it.’

Spengler opened the cabin door and a shaft of light caught Joselyn’s face. He could not resist a smile:

“Got you.”

*

At the Hotel Landaus Manfred dashed into the breakfast room in search of Joselyn. It was 7.00am. He knew Alistair and Freddie were at Seefliegehorst Weddewarden airfield waiting for the Mosquito to land.

Rosa was sitting at a table by the window, an uneaten Frühstück platter in front of her. The scene was identical to the setting with Gertrud only a few days earlier. Manfred swallowed, fearing the worst:

“Where’s Joselyn?”

Rosa was anxious: “She went to the port. She was desperate to know if the missiles were on board Solveig. I couldn’t stop her. She was adamant. And no sign of Alistair or Freddie either ... I thought I’d wait here ... for you.”

“When does she sail?” Manfred was fraught: God, Joselyn.

“I don’t know. I haven’t been back to the port since you grabbed me from home.”

“Shit! I’ll need your car keys, Rosa. Hell! Why did she go

alone?"

Manfred darted out of the breakfast room, to the car park. He didn't hear Rosa say under her breath:

"Because I told her one would be safer than two."

*

As predicted, the most difficult procedure for Freddie was boarding the Mossie. They had found an old wooden ladder in the hangar and that was a blessing. He had to climb the steps and then twist himself up into the cockpit. It was extremely problematic manoeuvre with his leg because the cabin was so cramped and tight. As narrow as a small car, with additional instruments both left and right.

Once finally settled in the uncomfortable seat, he re-acquainted himself with the controls and instruments. He had flown several Mosquitos before and was well aware of their capability and versatility. Elevator trim indicator, throttle, prop lever, air speed indicator, artificial horizon, altimeter, compass, landing gear indicator, brake pressure, radio and magneto. Swift strapped himself in behind Freddie's right shoulder; he was clutching a chart and an RAF-issue compass. The clock read 7.00am.

"Bomb selection, fusing and release all correct, Group Captain Valentine." Swift called out, strapping his mouthpiece under his chin. "The cine-camera master switch is to the left of the fuel contents gauges – inner wing tanks."

Freddie found the switch and looked over his right shoulder: "Understood," he said, "and please call me Freddie. Everyone does, including our friend Squires."

He started the port engine, then the starboard. A cautious look at the gauges: oil temperature, and radiator temperature. Everything was fine: 'Good to go'. He heard a distant voice in his memory.

Freddie's body was pushed back into his seat as the Mosquito gathered speed. The tailwheel lifted, followed by the main wheels and she was airborne. He gently lifted the nose and felt the familiar sensations, the old thrill of take-off. All the memories flooded back as the airfield below became the size of a postage stamp. He felt Swift tap him on the shoulder. She was a delight to fly and could climb at a rate of 2,850 feet per minute and achieve a speed of more than 400 mph, fully laden.

Freddie's headphones crackled into life: "Suggest a ceiling altitude of one thousand feet. Reconnaissance due east, keep the airspeed low; we'll do a sweep over the port and see what's what."

"Wilco," Freddie said and immediately knew something was wrong. The Port of Cuxhaven was directly ahead of them now; the wharf where Solveig should have been moored was empty. The quayside was deserted, Spengler's car park unoccupied.

The headphones again: "According to my bearings ..."

"She's not there." Freddie tapped the stick. "Bugger, what do we do?"

"Back to Seefliegehorst or fly on. It's not ideal to land armed, but it's been done many times before ... and the bombs aren't dangerous, not at the moment."

*

Less than a thousand feet below Crimson Wing, Rosa's car screeched to a halt. Manfred shot out of the driver's seat and looked up into the sky. He shielded his eyes from the sun. The Mosquito appeared to be descending. Alistair had told him the ultimate mission was clear: locate and destroy SS Solveig and get out fast. She was carrying ten missiles with a payload of Tabun gas. And a Palestinian terrorist.

And Joselyn was probably aboard her now; she might even be a hostage. God! What the hell should he do?

He felt powerless. The clock was ticking ...

Sea

Deutsche Bucht; the SS Solveig – heading west.

EIGHT AM. Captain Edvard Langerhans powered down the steps from the bridge to his cabin. His Second Mate Anders was on watch. He found his cabin door open and knew he'd closed it earlier; second nature on any ship. Could Spengler or his curious companion Harald be snooping around? Surely not and why would they? And Dr. Imran he knew was safely tucked away in his State Room. He cautiously pushed the door open.

A dark-haired woman with striking blue eyes was sitting in his chair. She was fiddling with a Swiss Army knife, a gift from Manfred. It had saved her life more than once and had done so once again today.

"Who on earth are you?" he asked tentatively, not concerned. A beautiful woman in his quarters was never a cause for concern.

She met his eyes: "I work for British Intelligence."

He could hear she wasn't British even in those five words: American. He found himself saying: "You're joking."

But she was serious: “No, I’m not. You must be Captain Langerhans.”

“Yes. How do you know my name?”

“You are not German,” she said, ignoring his perfectly reasonable question. She stood, tucking the folded penknife into a discreet pocket on the waistband of her black riding trousers. If she’d been searched earlier, it had been badly.

“Swedish. Malmo. Look, what are you doing here?”

He took a cautious step back. She had a look about her, not dangerous or threatening. He had known enough women who possessed both traits. But there was a driving vitality in those piercing blue eyes ... could be of Italian descent ... he thought to himself. He had known a few over the years. Fiery, irascible, redheads like Sophia from Napoli.

Her face broke into a sudden smile that was at once magnificent and captivating, but her tone remained serious, at odds with her expression:

“The crates in the cargo holds below us ...” she moved half a pace nearer ... “contain ballistic missiles primed with Tabun gas. They are headed for Palestine.”

Edvard laughed at the idea: “No! They are O2 cylinders bound for Port Said. An Egyptian family are gifting them to the,” he paused to remember, “Qasr El Eyni Hospital in Cairo.”

The woman said nothing, giving him the opportunity to explain further. Silence was a good tactic. Grizzly had taught her that years ago. So had Brim.

“I checked them myself,” Edvard continued.

“Did you?” Those famous blue eyes; smouldering, provoking, arousing.

“Yes, well no, actually. Not all of them. Herr Spengler opened one of the crates for me to see inside it, for Customs purposes. As Captain, I’m obliged to sign the declaration.”

“Yeah, I bet you are.”

Edvard found his mouth was dry.

“Just inside the one crate, right?”

“Yes.”

She caught him off-guard: “Emran is a Palestinian terrorist about to wage war in the Middle-East.”

“No,” he said again. But even as he uttered the word, a shadow of doubt crossed his mind and he couldn’t fathom why.

She produced her trump card: “Ask Rosa.”

“Rosa?” The sound of her name punched a hole in his conscience, and she could see it all over his handsome face.

Once again, the mystery woman said nothing for ten seconds: “Your former lover, Rosa, yes. I had coffee with her this morning ... you two had a lucky break, right? She told me the story. Once Mother Nature intervened ... and another baby captain was avoided.” She gave a little chuckle which suggested: Oh, things we girls chat about over morning coffee!

Edvard stumbled and tried to say – how – but it wasn’t forthcoming.

“Oh, and Rosa told Gisela to get the blood-stained dress out of the waste bin in her office. What happened? Did Spengler catch her with it? Rosa didn't know. But you were there, weren't you? Rosa thought you might have, what, comforted Gisela? Huh? She might have been upset if that old bastard had confronted her. Sound familiar?"

Edvard chewed his lip, desperately weighing possibilities. If this woman – whoever the hell she was - knew all this detail she must be a friend of Rosa's. And genuine.

"Edvard!" barked Spengler from somewhere outside. "Are you in there?"

"You must trust me," she whispered. She held up her wrists so he could see where she'd been tied. Her face, her eyes imploring ... "Where can I hide?"

"The shower," he said quickly. "Get in."

"Thought you'd fallen overboard." the old man said with a slur. He'd been drinking, Edvard thought, but not with the abstemious, pious Emran. Harald probably, that German idiot – beer and schnapps – no doubt.

"No," Edvard said, producing his reading glasses, "I'll need these later when the light fades. How was your lunch? I know Chef was preparing something special for you and your guest, sir." Edvard put on his glasses for effect and brushed hurriedly past Spengler. "I must get back to the bridge and see Anders."

"If you like lamb cooked that way, with rice, it was fine. Not a German dish, with potatoes." Spengler looked around the

Captain's cabin and, seeing nothing of interest, closed the door and made his way painfully toward his State Room.

In the shower cubicle, Joselyn sank to her haunches, rubbing the rope burns on her wrists. As her Uncle Mark always said: How many lives does this little pussy cat have?

When Edvard reached the bridge, he could see Anders out on the port bridge wing, binoculars in hand. He quickly checked their heading to ensure they were still on course. An excited Anders dashed back inside with a boyish grin:

"You'll never guess what I saw earlier, Captain. A British bomber! Really!" Anders said, barely able to contain his excitement.

"Are you sure?"

"It was unmarked, but I'd recognise most aircraft and I'm sure it was a British Mosquito. What is it doing here? The war is over!" Anders laughed at his little joke.

"I'll be damned." He thought of the girl hiding in his shower. She'd said: 'British Intelligence.' However unlikely it was, the two had to be connected.

If only he could speak to Rosa. She would know what to do.

"Anders don't mention it to Mr. Spengler. Unless he brings it up, alright?"

"Aye-aye, Captain."

Air

Deutsche Bucht; Mosquito – altitude 800feet.

AT SEVEN-FIFTEEN AM, Freddie yelled into his mouthpiece: "I think we should turn back to base."

The noise of the engines was punishing, although the FB V1 was not uncomfortable at low level. Indeed, she had been built specifically for low level work, such as ground attack and anti-shipping strikes. Freddie could see the target but was uncertain about what to do. And any doubt should be considered seriously.

"Solveig's in clear sight," Swift replied.

"I know. I can see her," Freddie snapped more sharply than he'd intended.

He pulled back the stick and made a sharp starboard turn. He knew something wasn't right. It was a Saturday and Solveig had left early. The man on the bridge wing had seen them; examined them through binoculars. Thank God they weren't flying any colours; shrewd move of Squires to have the Mossie painted grey. It was the right decision, to fly back to Seefliegehorst and consult with the others. If Charlie Morris wanted to take over as pilot, then so be it. At least he'd had some 'airtime' and for that he'd be eternally grateful to Squires.

And Alistair, of course.

"Mission aborted," Freddie said into his mouthpiece and headed back to the airfield.

"Check," said Swift, confused at Freddie's change of heart.

Land

Seefliegehorst Weddewarden airfield, Germany.

SEVEN-TWENTY AM. On the ground, eight hundred feet below them, Alistair had his binoculars trained on the approaching Mosquito.

"There she is," he said anxiously, "but is the bomb bay empty?"

"Let's pray not," Manfred said.

He had driven from the Landaus to the airfield, stopping only once to see Crimson Wing headed west to destroy Solveig – the Mosquito was descending, preparing to attack -but had she? He told Alistair and Charlie exactly what Rosa had explained. Joselyn must be on board Solveig because she wasn't anywhere else. Alistair had been at first annoyed she'd taken matters into her own hands and then concerned for her safety. Her life was in the balance.

In less than ten minutes the Mossie had touched down, once again, on the Seefliegehorst airfield. Alistair, Manfred, and

Charlie bounded over to her as the engines were killed and the propellers stopped turning.

The suspense was agonising. Had his brother inadvertently killed the woman he loved? Finally, Charlie gave them permission to approach the aircraft. The hatch door opened, and Swift was out first. He pulled off his goggles shaking his head:

"Mission abort," he said to the group, with a trace of irritation. He knew nothing about Joselyn and could not understand their collective relief.

Alistair desperately dashed over to the hatch with the wooden ladder and Freddie twisted out of the cramped opening, climbed down and removed his head gear too.

"You didn't attack. Thank God!"

Freddie blinked into the sunlight: "What?"

"We are pretty sure Joselyn is aboard Solveig." Alistair was panting with relief. He explained to Freddie and Swift exactly what they knew. Freddie was shocked. They walked back toward Charlie, who stood outside the hangar.

"As a matter of interest," Charlie said casually, "why didn't you attack her?"

"Is there any of that coffee left?" Freddie asked. Manfred dashed into the hangar and retrieved the hamper ...

"As we were approaching the port and the Spengler buildings, I could see Solveig had already set sail. I just sensed something was not right. I saw a crew member watching us through binoculars and made a decision."

Manfred unscrewed the lid of the flask, poured coffee into it and handed it to Freddie.

"What next?" Charlie asked. "Do you still need us?"

It was Alistair who took the lead and asked if they could stand down for a couple of hours while they worked out a new plan of action. They would return to the Landaus and see Rosa. She knew the area and knew the options. In any event, they had to destroy Solveig and find a way of getting Joselyn off her alive. They assumed Spengler and Ali Emran were aboard, but who else? Both had a considerable motive to want her dead. They could take her by surprise and throw her overboard ... no one would know.

Colt

Deutsche Bucht; SS Solveig – heading west.

A LITTLE AFTER nine-thirty am, Edvard Langerhans made his way down to his cabin. He was cautious, now deeply concerned about Spengler and the Palestinian. His reputation counted for everything among the German and Scandinavian maritime communities.

Joselyn was asleep on his bunk, hair dishevelled, her black clothing in disarray as she had tried to make herself comfortable in strange surroundings. She stirred the moment he came in. He closed the cabin door quietly, forefinger to his lips.

"I've checked one of the other crates," he whispered, pulling his chair over to the bunk beside her. "You were right. I apologise." There was a slight singsong in his Swedish accent she hadn't noticed before; she found it charming.

Instinctively she clutched the forearm of his uniform jacket, as if to express a don't worry about it sentiment. She looked sleepy.

"I ordered the release of one of the lifeboats, discharged most of the crew about twenty minutes ago. It's well out of sight now. I checked."

She sat up surprised, suddenly reassured, a flicker of a smile.

"It might buy us some time," he continued. She noticed the use of the word us but said nothing.

"A strange thing happened. My Second Mate Anders is sure he saw a British bomber – an unmarked Mosquito – flying to the stern of us. It is unlike him to make a mistake about such a thing."

"Freddie." She stifled a heartfelt sob because she felt it had to be him. Who else? Edvard brushed her hand and rose.

She rubbed her eyes: "Tell me, who would Rosa contact once she realises I am missing and that her father's vessel departed early?"

He nodded: "The Harbourmaster at Cuxhaven is the obvious choice."

"On a Saturday? At this hour?"

"Somebody will be on duty because there is always traffic. And a lifeboat, with a crew on call. It could be my friend Lucas. Or Commodore Jansen."

She swung her legs off the bunk and sat forward: "Could you get a message to them? A short one?"

"Yes. We have a Morse transmitter."

She thought for a moment; how brief? "Joss onboard Solveig. That's me by the way. Joselyn."

“Hello, Joselyn. Pleasure to meet you!” He smiled and his blue eyes shone. She could see why Rosa had fallen for him. He looked like a tennis pro or perhaps a golfer. “My name is Edvard, with a ‘v’.”

“Where can I hide?” she said suddenly, back to reality.

“Here?” he suggested playfully.

“Other than here,” she responded. “I’m thinking if Spengler decided to play hide-and-seek. Or that idiot Harald Wolf.”

Edvard thought of the possibilities: “The other lifeboat. Under the tarpaulin. It’s as good a place as any. The cargo holds are dark and dangerous, as you discovered.”

She looked at him questioningly; she was sure she hadn’t mentioned where she’d fallen.

“You have a nasty bruise,” he touched above his left temple, “just here. You must have tripped.”

She gingerly touched her head: “Ow! You’re right, I did!”

“I will go to the radio room and send a signal to the Harbourmaster.”

“Thank you. I will feel happy once I know a message can be sent to Rosa. And I have some friends who will be worried too.”

He nodded; so many questions to ask her; such as who is Freddie? But decided to say nothing. The thought of the missiles down below and the death they would cause was enough to motivate him to help her.

“Can you slow the ship down, without alerting old man Spengler or the Palestinian?”

“Yes. Just stay here, Joselyn ... Listen, there is a semi-automatic Colt M1911 pistol under the bunk ... it’s loaded. Do you know how to – “

“Yes,” she said with lovely smile, “I do.”

He turned to leave: “I thought you might.”

There was a lot more to Joselyn than met the eye.

*

At nine forty-five am, Edvard went to the radio room and tapped out the signal just as Joselyn suggested, pre-fixed ‘urgent’ for the attention of the Harbourmaster. He glanced at the newspaper headlines once more: British Mandatory Government of Palestine arrest 100 leaders of Yushnuv.

It didn’t really mean much in itself. However, much of what Joselyn had told him about the Middle East threat now made sense. He was just about to pick the paper up ...

“Where is the woman? Where is Joselyn Walcott?” It was Wolf, with his pock-marked face and bald head.

“What woman?” Edvard grabbed an old Swedish newspaper and casually covered the Morse transmitter.

“I have searched the ship. Your cabin first, of course, cargo holds ... even the spare lifeboat,” Wolf’s piggy eyes bore into his brain. Edvard could imagine him in a Gestapo uniform like that idiot Peter Schaffer.

“I don’t know of any woman.”

"You can't fool me. Do you think I believe she escaped in the other lifeboat? A clumsy effort, Captain."

Edvard turned away from him, walked out of the radio room and on to the bridge. Wolf followed him and, from behind, grasped hold of his uniform jacket.

At 6'4" Edvard was at least a foot taller than Wolf: "I would let go if I were you, Herr Wolf. No matter who or what you are to Spengler, you don't frighten me. So, get off my bridge and let me get on."

Wolf turned to leave: "Very well. If you choose not to cooperate, I will inform Herr Spengler. But be warned, I will find her and kill her."

As he left, Edvard shook his head and muttered under his breath: "Not while I'm Captain you won't."

Wolf hadn't noticed Anders standing by the starboard exit: "What exactly is going on, Edvard? And who is that man?" The Second Mate spoke Swedish, which added an air of confidentiality to their conversation.

Edvard replied:

"It's time I explained everything. As of today, Solveig is a pirate vessel. And we have to stop it reaching Port Said. The lady in question works for British Intelligence. We must extend her every courtesy." He gestured with his chin toward the door through which Wolf had just walked. "And watch him. He's trouble."

"Understood."

"I am going to reduce ship's speed, then I'll tell you what I know."

*

Wolf entered his cabin; it was not dissimilar in layout to normal crew quarters: bunk bed, fitted wardrobe, small bathroom with a shower, a chair. And it was in the latter that Joselyn was sitting with the Colt M1911 trained on the doorway. The last place Wolf would have thought of looking. He cursed his own stupidity and envied her nerve.

"Gertrud ist tot," she said with as much brutality as she could summon to those fateful few words. Hearing them in his native tongue made an immediate impact upon Wolf. She had to take control of the situation even though it was she who was holding the weapon.

He looked bewildered, believed her: "Dead, how?"

"Ironic. She made it all the way from London to Cuxhaven and then ..." Joselyn stood "... Bang! She has a hole blown through her the size of a dinner plate in the gardens of Ritzebüttel."

Wolf fell against his cabin door – Gertrud.

"An execution. I saw it happen."

Wolf mulled it over. In one way he believed Gertrud had come to Cuxhaven, but how had she got there? She had no money or passport. Unlike him. He thought of Beaufort Lodge; why had

Alistair Valentine come to interview her? Twice. Why?

Despite the balance of power, he had nothing to lose:

"Alistair Valentine killed her, that vain bastard. I saw him kill Walcott in Windsor. He and his crippled brother prevented our plan ... annihilation of the Royals and their pitiful household ... the Valentines are a pair of bastards."

Hearing their name took the wind out of her sails, but only for a split second.

Despite the balance of power, she had nothing to lose. She powered ahead with verbal viciousness:

"Has Spengler paid you a finder's fee yet? Or is that why you are here? On some kind of a promise? He's a Nazi pig, just like you and Gertrud. Nothing else."

"Screw you!" The pock-marked face was riled.

"He'll double cross you. Have you killed somewhere in the Middle East. Or thrown over the side at sea. Face it, he doesn't need you anymore. You are dead. It's what Spengler does."

Wolf laughed: "What the hell do you know? It was us who deceived the dumb Brits right under their pompous noses. We know all about British Intelligence, Brimblecombe, the Valentines and particularly you."

"No, you don't." She tested the trigger gently.

"Oh, we do ... the Yankee bitch who Walcott talked into bed ... Devlin was impressed that Walcott seduced you into marriage."

"Was he really? Devlin, huh?" Even now Wolf could not fathom the truth.

"Yes, the yankee bitch." Wolf laughed.

Three spiteful, vindictive words and she felt she was back in that filthy Republican safe house. Devlin's uncouth, insulting manner, mocking her, challenging her to use the weapon pointed at him.

The enemy.

She quickly grabbed hold of the bunk's pillow and stuffed the pistol deep inside the spongey material. Automatic, unplanned. The round sounded blunt, but at virtually point blank, it hit him squarely in the chest. The sheer velocity of the forty-five smacked him against the cabin door and then seemed to hold him in suspended animation, almost balletic, and he dropped to the deck with a final thump.

Joselyn sank back on the chair; Wolf's insult hit home – Oh, we do – but who was we? Had they discussed her? Is that what they thought? Not that it mattered now. But the shadow of having to kill Devlin at close range had suddenly reappeared with Wolf. But it was the insult which had really hurt, despite everything. The truth was that she was under orders from Brim: get to Walcott. And she had; and fooled everyone.

She took the Colt out of the blackened pillow and flicked on the safety. She realised the tiny cabin was thick with smoky cordite. Suddenly she wanted to retch. There was a loud knock on the door:

"Wolf. Captain Langerhans ... Herr Spengler and Dr Emran wish to see you. They say it's urgent."

Joselyn stared at the cabin door praying it would open.

Commodore Jansen

Commodore's Office, Cuxhaven, Germany.

AT SEVEN-THIRTY AM, Alistair and Manfred drove Rosa's car from Seefliegehorst airfield back to the Landaus at Mitte-Nord. They left Freddie with Charlie, Swift and the Mossie, just in case.

Before they left Swift had handed Alistair half a dozen emergency distress flares, wrapped in oilskin: 'These are hand-held maritime spec,' he had told them, 'luminosity of 15,000 candelas – that's the technical spec – three white, three red. According to the instructions they have a burn time of at least one minute.'

'So, if you need us,' Charlie had added, 'either colour will do.'

'Good thought.' Alistair had taken the flares and placed them carefully into the picnic hamper.

Charlie: 'We'll keep a look out and assume any signal from you is an instruction to fly, locate Solveig and attack."

It was nine-thirty am when Alistair and Manfred arrived at

the Landaus and Monika Bauer, the hotel's owner, was there at the door to meet them. She must have been watching out for the car.

"Dr. Spengler has gone to the Harbourmaster's Office. She left you this message with the address and the directions from here."

"How long ago?" Alistair said, taking the note and reading it.

Frau Bauer consulted her watch and said vaguely: "An hour. Maybe more."

Alistair and Manfred were back in the car within five minutes of arriving at the Landaus. Their mood was sombre, and little was said. Manfred sensed Alistair was unhappy at leaving his brother at the airfield. But logistically the decision was sound.

*

Alistair and Manfred arrived at the Harbourmaster's Office a little after ten-thirty am to meet the ebullient Commodore Folker Jansen. There was no doubt in his mind about the timing of the communication from Solveig:

"I received an 'urgent' Morse signal at nine-forty-five am in English – 'Joss on board Solveig' – it was from the hand of Captain Langerhans; I would bet my career on it."

"Less than an hour ago," said Alistair. "At least we now know she's on board. And alive."

Rosa saw he was shaken at this confirmation, but not surprised. She took his hand and squeezed it in an almost maternal way.

Jansen was the epitome of a senior naval officer. In his late fifties, a veteran of the oceans, with a bearded face and ruddy complexion. His unruly hair was steel grey and he wore a monocle which seemed to be permanently clamped to his right eye socket.

Everything in his maritime domain was polished mahogany, oak and brass, right down to the antique ship's compass inlaid into a vast desk. A magnificent telescope stood on a tripod and focused on the panoramic view of the harbour and marina. Alistair always took in his surroundings and these, inevitably, reminded him of Herr Seiler and Monte Rosa.

"Can you tell us what happened?" asked Manfred.

They were speaking German, but the Commodore was from the East Frisian islands, a chain in the North Sea, off the coast of Lower Saxony. Borkum was his birthplace. He spoke with a strong accent; Alistair and Manfred, despite their linguistic skills, found it challenging to follow.

"As I explained to Rosa, Erich came to see me and said he wanted to leave port a few hours earlier than he had originally intended. There was no reason, except, I suppose, the prospect of a long distance to cover."

Jansen went on to explain that Solveig had taken on her crew, fuel, water, supplies and there was no reason to delay. They were transporting important medical cargo and, as I said, had a long voyage ahead of them. He saw no reason to decline the request.

No other significant shipping was due to arrive or leave the port that weekend.

"What time did she leave?" asked Alistair.

"She slipped her moorings at seven this morning. I stood Spengler's harbour staff down, soon after that, on Erich's instruction."

The old sea dog took out a chamois tobacco pouch and went about filling an elaborate pipe, tamping down the sweet-smelling tobacco.

"What speed could she make?" Manfred asked, wary of the onslaught of tobacco which was about to fill the room.

Jansen consulted a large naval chart which covered a tiltable architect's drafting table. He beckoned Rosa, Alistair and Manfred to join him as he rubbed his large hand over the crinkled surface of the paper. His finger finally rested on the port.

"Solveig is what, seven years old, Rosa?" There was a familiarity between the two of them; she had probably known him since she was a child.

"About that, yes."

"She's fairly light. I gather Spengler's commission was to transport only the twelve O2 cylinders from here to Port Said."

'Oxygen cylinders' thought Alistair wryly. 'That's a good one.'

"Solveig could make good 16 knots, depending on tide and weather conditions. It's rough north of the East Frisian islands, but at this time of year ... who can say?" His hand plotted out a route. "She'll be maybe ninety nautical miles out by now."

Rosa, Alistair and Manfred looked at the chart and then each other with a mutual unspoken thought: this is not going to be easy.

Jansen wandered back to his leather armchair and finally lit his pipe. It took four matches to get the contraption going:

"Tell me," he said through a blue haze. "How ill is this Joss person?"

"Why do you ask?"

"The normal reason for such an urgent Morse signal ... is some kind of medical emergency." He puffed on his pipe and waited for an answer.

"Commodore, do you know of any fast boats we can quickly lay our hands on?" Alistair asked and looked out of the window. "We need to get after Joss as soon as we possibly can."

The old sea dog had a twinkle in his eye: "I can do better than fast ... if it will help my lovely Rosa."

Rosa demurred at the compliment; but said nothing.

"Because I sense this is much more than a medical emergency. Would I be right?"

Rosa: "You would, Folker."

Cabin

SS Solveig. North Sea.

EDVARD EASED Wolf's cabin door open, unaware of the nature of the resistance behind it. He waved his hand in front of him to clear the smoke, pushed forward and smelt cordite. Joselyn was still sitting on the chair, staring at the door, transfixed.

"Joselyn!" He was shocked at what he encountered; Wolf's dead body and a beautiful British agent clutching his Colt.

She met his gaze: "I'd like to say it was self-defence, but it wasn't."

He opened the cabin door wider in an attempt to clear the air and waited for her to explain herself.

"Wolf was part of a Nazi enclave in London. Hired by Heinrich Himmler to kill the British Royal family and thousands of other innocent people. September 1943 ..."

Edvard was spellbound: "I've never heard of such a thing. And I read newspapers."

"It was covered up by the British and the Americans. My

father was part of it and so was I, working undercover for MI6. There's a lot more to it, but that's the crux."

"God!" was all he could say.

"Wolf killed a German scientist and escaped from a British detention centre. He approached Emran first to broker an arms deal. And then Emran went to see Spengler in Innsbruck to buy them. Half the cash up front. The rest you know."

For a few moments Edvard said nothing, absorbing information completely alien to him. He was a sailor from Malmo. The father of nine children, ex-husband of four wives and lover of countless women all over the globe.

This one was different. Stunningly beautiful but cold, dangerous, professional. For the first time in his forty years, he was petrified. Finally, he broke silence in a whisper. The only thing he could think of saying that might interest her:

"I've sent the signal – exactly as you said – and reduced ship's speed."

"Thank you. I thought I felt the engine had slowed a little." The beautiful blue eyes sparkled, pupils dilated. For a moment she looked utterly beguiling; sensuous.

His mouth was dry with fear. He could barely speak:

"Spengler and Emran want to see ... Wolf ..." He gazed down at the dead body; he had clearly never seen one before. The .45 calibre slug had made a mess. He slowly and carefully closed the cabin door and looked at Joselyn.

Joselyn stood, seized control: "We have to get rid of him, over the side. Spengler must not see him."

"You can't hide anything from Spengler. There are no secrets. The ship is not big enough." He looked genuinely frightened.

Joselyn picked up the Colt: "Edvard. We have this, and we have the element of surprise."

Edvard shook his head, out of his depth: "Spengler has a small arsenal in his State Room; I have seen it. Rosa also knew about it: guns, grenades, God knows what else. Old weapons from the war."

"What about your friend Anders? Your Second Mate?"

"What about him?"

Joselyn put the gun back on the bunk and walked the two paces over to him: "Can we depend on him? Does he have a weapon?"

"Yes, to both questions."

"We need to act now, Edvard. Get rid of Wolf and confront Spengler. Surprisingly, I am more concerned about Emran."

The cabin door suddenly shot open and Edvard was propelled forward into Joselyn's unprepared body:

"So you should be," said the tall Palestinian. He wasn't clutching his Cashmere coat this time; he was holding a machine gun and he looked like he knew how to use it.

Joselyn made a grab for the Colt, but the weight and size of Edvard's body made it impossible.

"No, no, no." Emran raised the gun, as if to shoot: "I would kill you both without a second thought, believe me. Your Second

Officer is at the wheel."

Edvard lurched forward: "You have no right on the bridge without my say so."

But the Palestinian was quick. He swiftly inverted the gun, caught Edvard on the chin with the butt. Agonizingly painful, brutally efficient:

"I am now in command of this ship." Emran deftly took out a handkerchief and passed it to Edvard. The cut on his chin was bleeding profusely and his teeth and lips were gory.

"But you are still her Captain." The dark supercilious eyes looked down his long, pointed nose at Joselyn, "and you are, what is the expression, a hostage to fortune. Just in case your employers attempt anything ... unwise."

Joselyn pushed Edvard ruthlessly out of her way; it did not bother Emran. He gazed at her with contempt. Women were not high in the pecking order where he came from:

"What about Spengler?" she asked.

He sighed: "Ah, Spengler ... he was surplus to requirements. I suppose the blood money I paid him Rosa will inherit. Poor Rosa. She won't have the courage to spend it."

"I wanted to fucking kill him, you piece of ..."

Emran stepped into the cabin, pointed the gun at Edvard, as if he had not heard her:

"On the bridge, Captain ... where you belong ... you'll find the Morse key, is, out of action. Are there any weapons or tools in this cabin?"

"I doubt it," Edvard said, a defeated man. He was now outside the cabin and walking away, to the bridge.

Emran hadn't taken his eyes off Joselyn: "Pass me the gun. Try anything and I'll kill you."

He pointed the barrel of the machine gun at her. She had no choice but to pass him the Colt, which he took with his left hand:

"Your filthy American language offends me ... you offend me ... Wolf told me all about you ... Thank you by the way for killing him, he was next on my list. But you will make a good price in Port Said, or Alex. White prostitutes are extremely popular with some Egyptian men, but particularly American women. Watch out for gonorrhoea, though. I am told it's excruciatingly painful. I am sure you can imagine what I mean."

Emran pulled the cabin door to close it.

"What are you doing?" Joselyn said anxiously.

"I'm going to persuade Captain Langerhans to increase the ship's speed, after he slowed it down earlier." The door was nearly closed.

"You can keep Herr Wolf company. And don't expect any help from Rosa. Or your friends at Cuxhaven. Nothing in the world can catch us now."

The door clunked shut with finality, key turned. Joselyn glanced at her watch: it was ten-thirty am. They had been at sea for three and a half hours. She tore the top sheet off the bunk and covered Wolf's inert form. She sat back in the chair and felt the reassuring contours of the Swiss Army knife in the waistband of her black riding trousers. Once again, she found herself looking at the cabin door, praying it would open.

She thought of her Uncle Mark in Martha's Vineyard and smiled: How many lives does this little pussy cat have?

Joselyn stood, pulled out the pocketknife, resolute. Plenty.

Boatyard

Cuxhaven Boatyard, Germany.

ALISTAIR, MANFRED AND ROSA waited with bated breath; it was as if Folker Jansen was trying to keep them in suspense:

"You can do better than fast, how?" asked Alistair just a little cynically.

"A decommissioned Kriegsmarine S130 (Schnellboot) ... there's one in this very port."

Alistair laughed: "You're joking?"

Jansen placed his pipe in a large ashtray piled high with spent matches and ambled back over to the chart table:

"No. As I just said, I sense this is more than a medical emergency."

Rosa joined him: "More of an international emergency. These gentlemen work for British Intelligence. And Joss, the lady in question, has been kidnapped by my father and a Palestinian terrorist called Ali Emran."

The name Emran registered with Jansen: "She's a hostage

then?"

"Yes."

"And Captain Langerhans?" The old face crinkled questioningly.

"Edvard doesn't or didn't know anything about this situation," said Rosa. "He believes his passenger is an Egyptian doctor."

Jansen considered: "I see. My Schnellboot can make 45 knots. If we leave now, we can catch Solveig within say, two to three hours."

He went over to a hat stand and retrieved a leather binoculars case.

"Your Schnellboot?" asked Alistair.

Jansen nodded and hung the case around his neck.

Manfred went over and joined them: "But who would take command of her?"

Jansen grinned: "You didn't ask me what I did in the war."

*

They were walking toward the boatyard; Alistair, Manfred, Rosa and Commodore Jansen; a brisk walk that turned into more of a trot.

"What have you got in your picnic hamper?" Jansen asked. "Sandwiches? Rum? English tea?"

Alistair opened the rattan basket – on the move – and showed him the distress flares.

"Ha! You'll need a lot more than those kids toys when we get up to speed ... Who are you proposing to signal, anyway?"

Alistair slowed his pace: "You'd better know who's on standby at Seefliegehorst Weddewarden."

"Tell me," the old sea dog said warily; they stopped walking.

Alistair explained about Freddie, the RAF aircrew, the Mossie and the finer details of the operation designated Crimson Wing. Manfred and Rosa quickly supplied specifics. Jansen took it all in and showed no reaction when he heard about Spengler, the missiles and the tall Palestinian. He picked up his pace and the others followed:

"A Mosquito, eh? I think we'll be able to send her an adequate signal. It's called an anti-aircraft cannon."

Alistair looked at Manfred and Rosa, not sure if he was joking or not.

Deadlock

SS Solveig, North Sea.

JOSELYN REALISED she wasn't looking at the cabin door, praying it would open. No, she was staring at the lock, calculating how to pick it. Captain Cullum at Sgian Dubh in Scotland had taught his class how to pick a lock with a paperclip or hairgrip and a pair of pliers. That had been an English lock and the one she was looking at was presumably German. But the principle must be the same.

She knelt down so the lock was at eye level, took a hairgrip from the corner of her headscarf, opened her Swiss Army knife, and selected a toothpick. She used the toothpick as a tension wrench, inserting it carefully into the aperture of the cylinder. Next, the hairgrip, pushed into the barrel until she felt the first pin, then she pushed down. After less than twenty seconds, five pins were depressed. But there was a resistance. She rotated the toothpick and grip 360 degrees. Nothing. She tried again. The same result. What to do?

She sat back on the bunk and considered her options. The sheet under which Wolf's body lay was stained with blood and she fancied she could smell the onset of putrefaction.

Maybe searching for the missiles on her own had been a mistake; she should have listened to Rosa earlier at the Landaus.

Her mind flicked to Alistair. Where had he disappeared to so early in the morning? And what was it Edvard said about a British bomber? A mistake, surely. She was about to try picking the lock again when the handle moved up and down and into a vertical position. She selected the longest blade and held it ready …

The cabin door opened, and a man took one pace inside. He was tall like Edvard; she had seen him before. But where?

"Wer bist du? ... eine Freudin von Edvard?" the man said.

Joselyn shot to her feet, trying to translate: "Do you speak English?"

"English -no."

Her brain rattled with the words to translate – Who are you? a friend of Edvard? – God, the man thinks I'm a girlfriend stowed away for a voyage romance. Or copious amounts of voyage sex? What had he told him? The man came in a little further and saw the bundle under the bloodstained sheet. He put his hand to his nose, repulsed by the smell. She had got used to it. Olfactory fatigue: your senses become accustomed.

"Wer bist du?" Joselyn said, mimicking his question. Because I am a hostage care of a Palestinian terrorist and a dead Nazi.

She tried to the form words. She thought of Manfred and Ingrid and their language lessons at Monte Rosa. But the German words were not forthcoming.

“Quartiersmeister Martin Zimmer. Komm!” He beckoned her to follow him with his open hand.

Of course. Quartermaster. He was the man she had avoided just before she boarded the ship to check the hold for the weapons. Did he work for Spengler?

“To see Edvard?” she asked with growing concern.

“Edvard, ja. Käpitan!” He smiled and held the door open for her. Whoever he was, she was no longer a hostage. But for how long?

Deutsche Bucht

Cuxhaven boatyard, Germany.

FOLKER JANSEN had a wicked sense of humour. And, in his younger days, was a practical joker. So Rosa had explained to them as they approached the Fast Attack Craft. Jansen had gone to 'rustle up some crew' and Alistair, Manfred and she were admiring the Schnellboot. He had no intention of using an anti-aircraft cannon against the Mosquito, but they would need to send a signal when the time came.

The boat was a small, fast, warship, normally armed with cannon and torpedoes, as Jansen had explained to them earlier. Better than anything the British or Americans had and, in fact, the 'envy of the international maritime community'. So much so that many countries had bought others from the remnants of the Kriegsmarine after the German surrender more than a year earlier.

"What about this one?" Manfred had asked the wily old man.

'This one, I have liberated for my own personal museum,

“Jansen had replied. ‘Liberated’ seemed to imply stolen. But she was fuelled, with full water tanks and minimal weapons. And, as they looked across the boatyard, they could see Jansen with three crafty-looking characters in old naval uniforms. They were laughing and joking. Jansen’s mischievous face was beaming.

“Oh my God,” said Rosa, “Folker thinks it’s 1940. I hope he has not been on the rum with those three reprobates. I was sure the one in the middle went to prison. Not sure why.”

“Well, if he did,” said Alistair, “it looks like he’s out now.”

*

The prow of the boat cut through the choppy waters of the Deutsche Bucht, the sea to the north of Germany and the west of Denmark. Alistair, Manfred and Jansen stood on the exposed bridge above the wheelhouse, sea spray beating against their faces. To the casual observer, the monochrome grey of the powerful vessel gave it a sinister, lethal appearance. Somebody had painted the face of a shark on her hull, with an exaggerated image of the fish’s teeth and the word Achtung.

She was hardly ‘decommissioned,’ as Jansen had first described her. The idea of a mothballed relic was far from the truth and Alistair wondered what he had really planned for the boat in the future. Nevertheless, the deck armament still consisted of a forward 20mm anti-aircraft cannon and a torpedo ‘in the tube’. Jansen stared ahead through his high-power Zeiss binoculars:

"Ahead of us now is the first of four islands, Wangerooge. To the port side is the headland of Minsen. Have a look, get a feel for the waters here." Jansen passed his binoculars to Alistair and he scanned the coastline as suggested.

Jansen consulted his folded chart with Spengler's supposed course plotted on it. The watery onslaught from the sea made it difficult to talk. He shouted above the noise:

"According to what Erich told me, the idea is for Solveig to hug the coast over there at Minsen, then west to Norddeich, off the coast of Ostfriesland. Here, look ..." He pointed at the map so they could both see. "But I don't believe him."

Manfred: "Why?"

"Too shallow ... so now we have a choice."

"Go by your experience, "Alistair yelled. He handed the glasses back.

Jansen cupped his hand around his mouth: "Solveig's been at sea for about four hours now. At 16 knots they cannot be further than the last island – Borkum – my home, north of the Dutch coast at Groningen. I know these waters. The weather is good, visibility clear, but the sea state is force four/five. Maybe she's not as far away as that."

Jansen ordered a turn to starboard, headed north of the Friesian islands on full speed. The wind and spray were overpowering now, beating on their faces. Alistair shouted again:

"Why would Spengler specify a route he didn't intend to

take?"

"Because he is Erich Spengler and always does the unexpected. All Captain Langerhans would have known when they slipped moorings this morning was their destination."

"Is this Captain Langerhans a good man?" Alistair shouted.

"The best. Go below and see Rosa. She suffers from seasickness. She has done since she was a child. I'm surprised she came today ... By the way, don't mention Langerhans to her unless she brings him up." Jansen grinned.

Alistair stepped down into the wheelhouse. It was dry, warm, and as he slid the portside door closed, relatively quiet. Rosa sat calmly, seemingly lost in her own world. She looked up with an off-colour smile. Was it the sea's motion or something else?

"What have you two been talking about?"

Alistair said nothing; unscrewed the lid of a coffee flask and took a swig: black coffee and rum. Fifty-fifty. Rosa was right – Folker Jansen did have a wicked sense of humour.

*

On Solveig Joselyn was on the bridge. All was normal. No sign of Emran. She had followed Quartermaster Zimmer from Wolf's cabin to the bridge in silence. Edvard was at the wheel, not surprised to see her. She felt in the waistband of her trousers for the reassuring contours of her Swiss Army knife. Anders discreetly handed her his Colt, knowing she might need it.

Joselyn left the bridge and made her way to Spengler's State Room. On arrival, she found the door was ajar. She cautiously pushed it fully open. She quickly scanned the room. Her first impression was the size of it compared to the normal cabins. The suite was furnished like the lounge of a comfortable house, but spartan, almost austere in its simplicity. She crept stealthily around the carpeted area. The door to Spengler's bedroom was open; his inert form lay partially covered by a blanket, eyes closed, face impassive. She wondered how Emran had killed him. There was no sign of violence or blood stains. Poison perhaps?

She looked out of one of the portholes: no sight of land now. She wondered where they were as the ship rolled from side to side on the open sea. Back in the lounge area was a large old French bureau. She pulled out the wooden desk section. It was packed with papers and a fortune in German currency.

"What are you looking for?" It was Spengler, large as life, holding a stick hand grenade, a type issued widely in the Wehrmacht during the war. His face was a picture of complacent superiority.

"Weapons," she said feebly, manifestly irritated at how easily she had been deceived by Emran and this devious old man.

"Joselyn Walcott," he smiled and perched on the arm of a leather Chesterfield: "I wondered what you'd look like ... awake. Giles described you as beautiful; but then, as you know, he was prone to exaggerate," he paused, "but not on this occasion."

Joselyn was stunned, said nothing.

"Do you know what this is?" He held up the grenade.

"I'd rather not."

Spengler laughed: "Put the gun on the table, please, the one tucked into your waistband. A present from Anders? I must remember that when the time comes."

She pulled the gun out carefully and placed it on the table. Spengler was composed. He resembled the file photos she had seen of Rudolph Hess: bushy eyebrows, thick neck. Despite his age, a man not to be crossed. Joselyn said:

"Did you ask Mr. Zimmer to free me?"

Spengler nodded: "Please sit."

Joselyn perched herself on the other arm, so they were equal in height. Although she appeared relaxed, she was immensely wary of this man people called der Jagdhund.

"Why did you kill Harald Wolf?"

"He insulted me."

Another laugh, tinged with an edge of irony: "A tough price to pay for an insult, don't you think?"

"He called me the Yankee bitch." As soon as she uttered the words, they sounded innocuous, hollow.

"I've heard worse."

"What exactly do you want with me, Mr. Spengler? You lured me into a trap and tried to have me murdered in Switzerland."

He regarded her carefully, narrowed his eyes and examined her in profile. He wanted desperately to interrogate her but knew he would not have to. His tone became suddenly solemn:

"How did you get from Needle's Eye to the Republican safe house in Southampton?" He paused a moment ...

"The question has perplexed me."

She waited, let him burn: "Why should I tell you?"

Spengler stood painfully from his perch and wandered around to face her: "Why should you tell me, hum ...?

I think because you want to. You are not sure if you will walk out of here alive. Because you believe I am an unstable old man who has nothing to lose. And I might just kill you for the hell of it."

"That's three very good arguments, Mr. Spengler."

Yet another laugh; surely a world record: "What I have heard about you is true. Giles was infatuated with you and I can see why. He dumped my Rosa for you, and I don't blame him."

Once again she waited, not wanting to play that particular card:

"I hid in the back of Devlin's car while he emptied his bladder on Giles's flowerbed. Given his intake of alcohol that night, I'm surprised he was able to drive."

"Devlin enjoyed a drink, it is true."

"Yeah he sure did." She emphasised the last world.

Spengler shook his head, impressed by the simplicity of what she had done; astounded at the sheer bravery. But he would not tell her that.

"I won't insult you by asking how you discovered who and

what Giles Walcott was. You were or are a British agent. It was your job."

This time Joselyn stood, not wanting to be tricked into any admission: "What do you want with me, Mr. Spengler. You wanted to kill me. Now's your chance. I don't have all day."

Her impertinence in the face of danger aroused him. He was not sure how to play Joselyn; she was unlike any other woman he had ever encountered:

"What do I want with you? I think since you boarded my ship uninvited, it is the other way around."

A half smile: he did have a point: "You know why, Mr. Spengler."

"And let us please get things straight. I did not attempt to have you murdered. It was Peter Braun at the behest of Patrick Devlin."

"Devlin?" That name again.

He could see she was startled:

"Yes. Michael's father. A disgusting character. An obsessed Irish Republican fanatic, who wants revenge for the death of his son. But, you see, there is a lot more."

"Yes." For Joselyn, the mist was suddenly clearing.

"Walcott and the Devlins were financed by powerful Irish-Americans based in Boston and New York – the Donoghue family – wealthy and politically active. They were desperate to support their homeland against the evil British colonialists. And collaborate with Germany during the war. You must know this."

Joselyn sighed: "I thought you loaned Giles the money for Needle's Eye. I thought this was what it was all about. The trap with Braun, the fake lawyer."

"Oh, I did, back in 1933, when Rosa was studying at Dublin University. A trifling amount. They were in a romantic relationship, as you well know, and Giles was broke."

"Ok."

"The Donoghues are quite different; we are talking about a fortune. Not only funds collected at St. Patrick's Day Parades and other political rallies. But organised crime. The Donoghues control most of New York State and Massachusetts. It's called racketeering by the American press: gambling, drugs, liquor, prostitution. Oh, and extortion, I nearly forgot that."

"I see." Now it all made sense.

"They paid for half of the Vengeance Weapons Spengler GmBh manufactured to attack the UK during the war. You thwarted it. It's your blood Devlin and Donoghue want. Braun was really just the messenger who delivered. Or failed to, as it happened."

"I thought it was you."

"Me? No."

"Why should I believe you, Mr. Spengler?"

The old man looked tired. He went on to say he had nothing to lose, because he was suffering from degenerative spine disease:

"My doctors in Austria tell me the condition will finish me off if I don't do it first. I am in pain all the time – apart from occasional anaesthetic relief." And there was a hint of a smile. He was thinking of 'Paradise.'

But he was a businessman first and foremost, with the sole aim of growing his company while he could. And that meant expanding it into new fields: medicine: diagnostics and pharmaceuticals. There was a huge opportunity. He wanted Rosa to succeed him, but she seemed to have lost interest in running the business.

Spengler said he believed passionately that by 1980 Germany would be an industrial powerhouse in Europe and Spengler GmBh could be at the forefront of it. Because they were there at the beginning. He confessed he had no morals or scruples and was not ashamed to admit it. Business was business; take it or leave it. The fittest survive. Whatever the cost.

Spengler's revelation was a goldmine of information. His philosophy not too dissimilar to American business practice. She could not wait to tell Brim and the others, assuming she left the State Room alive.

"If you want answers, Joselyn Walcott ..."

"Just Joselyn, please. And yes, of course I do." She was playing for her life now.

The steely black eyes regarded her; he had disclosed much already:

"Peter Braun, my ex-business partner, has most of the answers to your questions. He has a valuable source inside the

American Embassy in London. His name is Samuel Donoghue, and he is part of the Boston and New York syndicate I told you about. A dangerous and duplicitous man, because of who he is. He will have diplomatic immunity and will go free. And there is nothing British Intelligence can do about it."

Joselyn thought about what Freddie had told her that day in the garden at the Landaus. What Brim had explained about Blue Raincoat and what was his name? - Rowlands. But she was confused by it all. Finally, she said:

"The Swiss police know Villa Languard in Pontresina is owned by a Dr. Schwartz. The name is a cover. It is surely owned by you ..."

"If it was ..."

The sound of machine gun fire shocked them both. A rapid cascade of bullets ripped into the side of the ship. Several rounds smashed through the portholes with an ear-shattering report. Joselyn dived to the floor and rolled for cover, as she had been trained, quickly assessing the situation: risk versus opportunity.

She leapt over to the table but could not see the Colt. The State Room was full of smoke. Somewhere on board a klaxon sounded – ship's alarm – she looked around; Spengler had vanished.

She dashed over to the door and opened it. At once, she made her way to the bridge; Edvard was at the wheel, Anders in the radio room, cursing that the Morse key had been deliberately broken.

Edvard said: "Look out of the port side door, a Schnellboot."

"A what?"

Edvard repeated: "A Schnellboot. I have stopped the engine. The alarm is sounding, but I told you, we have already launched a lifeboat and most of the crew abandoned ship in it."

"Yeah. A Schnellboot, huh?"

Joselyn looked outside from the bridge wing and almost alongside was the Schnellboot – a sleek grey shark - keeping pace beside Solveig.

On the Schnellboot, she could see Alistair was standing on the flying bridge above the wheelhouse, frantically waving his arms to get their attention. Beside him Manfred shouting words she was unable to hear.

Jensen fired a series of distress flares from a Very pistol. They tore into the sky one after the other, exploding into red. They reached their maximum altitude and floated gracefully down to the sea on little parachutes. Normally, particularly at night, they would have looked like festive fireworks.

But who were they signalling? Joselyn wondered.

At the bow of the boat, a man was reloading. She dashed back inside the bridge to be confronted by the dark face of Emran, clutching his machine gun. He pushed her violently out of the way, went out on to the port bridge wing and opened fire on the Schnellboot. He sprayed it with bullets randomly like a man possessed. The noise was deafening.

As soon as Emran started firing, the Schnellboot took off, full throttle.

Edvard turned to Joselyn with an expression of apology.

Scramble

Seefliegehorst Weddewarden airfield, Germany.

CHARLIE MORRIS HAD JUST lit a cigarette when he heard the ground radio crackle into life and a voice: “Contact.”

Charlie smiled at Freddie: “D’you want to go up and investigate, Group Captain?”

“Absolutely.”

“In that case: Scramble.” Swift and Freddie made their way as fast as possible to the Mossie.

In less than ten minutes the Mossie was airborne; Freddie pulled back the stick and felt exhilarated. Payback for the blessed Tiger Moth in the Fens, convalescence at the Royal Victoria Hospital, his prosthetic limb from Siebenthal in Basle. Payback for everything. Now was the moment.

And he desperately wanted his wings back.

“Nine hundred feet, Swift,” he yelled into the mouthpiece. “She doesn’t like it, does she? She wants speed.”

"Just keep her steady, sir. I don't have to tell you that."

The two Merlin engines sounded thunderous. Freddie held the stick, eyed the instruments: air speed indicator, artificial horizon, altimeter, compass. The Deutsche Bucht glistened; they were flying directly into sunlight. Any fighter pilots's worst enemy. At least there were no ME109s buzzing around his backside like irritating wasps. The Mossie flew past the Friesian islands to their port side. Then, in the distance two images: what looked like a large pleasure cruiser, grey, low in the water and a larger vessel, smoke billowing from the mid-ship accommodation.

"That must be Solveig ... but what the hell's the other boat?"

Freddie's headphones crackled with static: "Unless I'm going completely bananas, it looks like a Kriegsmarine Schnellboot! Hell! The Navy's arch enemy a few years back!"

"Jesus, really?"

They could see a tall man on the port bridge wing of Solveig firing on the smaller boat.

"I reckon that's your brother and Manfred, Freddie. It has to be. Who else would be chasing after Solveig?"

"Right, let's go around again."

Freddie took the Mossie into a steep starboard climb and powered into the hazy sunlight.

On the flying bridge of the Schnellboot, Manfred clipped the telescopic sights onto his rifle and focused on the portside bridge wing of Solveig. Not easy. Even for a marksman. The swell of the sea caused a rise and fall of both vessels. He steadied the barrel as much as he could. He aimed at the outline of Emran, his body exposed only from the chest up, firing his machine gun. Emran was wildly spraying bullets from left to right towards the Schnellboot, but it was surely out of range.

For Manfred this was not a clear shot. He squeezed the trigger and immediately reloaded - stock, action, bullet ... a matter of seconds.

Through the sights again, a few seconds later, he could see Emran now had his arm around Joselyn's neck in a stranglehold, her body in front of him acting as a shield. She was struggling frantically.

Jansen had his binoculars at his eyes again: "You hit him in the right shoulder. A remarkable shot and he's dropped the gun. Thank God. I presume that's Joselyn."

"Yes. And Emran."

Manfred re-loaded his rifle; held it with his left hand and flexed the fingers of his right, like a concert pianist about to perform a solo: "That's better."

"I need to get around to the stern of Solveig as close to the lifelines as possible. It looks like she has slowed to a virtual halt. And then move up towards the lifeboat lifelines."

Jansen issued the order and the Schnellboot immediately swung around to port to come up on her stern. Without another word, as they approached the hanging lifelines, Alistair dived off the boat and powered through the cold sea, front crawl. It was freezing, harsher than training in the loch at Sgian Dubh. Worse than anything he had ever experienced.

He opened his eyes, looked up. The salty water stung his optic senses. He scrunched his eyes shut and reopened them to try and clear his blurred vision. It was painful. He was desperate to get out of the water and in seconds saw the first lifeline hanging down into the sea. These lines were attached to a steel cable between two davits hanging over the ship's side. The lines had a figure-of-eight knot every yard or so for hands and feet. He swam and made a desperate grab for the first one ...

... It was cold and slimy, impossible to get a proper hold of. He sank and then, using every ounce of strength he had left, thrust himself up, partially out of the water. The lifeline was there now within his grasp. He immediately grabbed it with one hand, then the other. A herculean effort. He was gasping for breath and finally, hand over hand, found a foothold and hauled himself upwards. His body was shaking with exhaustion. With a last knot to go, he stopped and collected himself. And, finally, with the rise and swell of the sea, caught a roll which hurled him on to the deck. It was empty.

Alistair glanced over his shoulder and signalled to the flying bridge of the Schnellboot. Manfred, Jansen and Rosa stood there, immobile, dumbstruck at what they had witnessed. The superhuman effort of a man determined not to fail. Alistair had once again been pushed to the brink of his ability to survive and succeed. All the training in Scotland had paid off: the blood, the sweat, the salty tears.

A few deep breaths and, gradually, carefully, he made his way between the superstructure and number four hatch to the starboard side and climbed the stairways up towards the starboard bridge wing. The shooting had stopped. He hugged the side of the ship, inch by inch, quickly glanced inside the wheelhouse. The Captain stood at the wheel; another tall man was beside him. The Solveig was floating, almost motionless, no engine noise. Just rolling gently in the long, low swell.

Quickly looking through the wheelhouse again, from his side to the other Alistair could see Emran out on the port bridge wing, his back turned, still holding Joselyn in a stranglehold. At his feet was the submachine gun, where he had dropped it, a small puddle of blood beside it. Manfred's shot had been absolutely spectacular. But what was going on now? Was he trying to protect himself using Joselyn as a shield? The Captain briefly turned, saw Alistair and although shocked, said nothing. Alistair was about to move when the bridge door flew open. And there was Spengler, clutching something behind his back. The look on his face demonic.

In that second, Manfred fired another shot – deliberately wide – to distract Emran. It worked. He was caught off guard and Joselyn, still struggling, turned sharply, fell out of his grasp. She saw Alistair, her eyes wide with surprise and relief. He gestured with his chin toward Emran's gun. She made a wild grab for it, but Emran pushed her away.

Spengler held out the grenade, grasping it firmly as if it were a trophy. His black eyes shone; he was in control once again. But evidently in considerable physical pain.

The roar of the two Merlin engines was sudden, dramatic and unexpected. The Mossie cannot have been more than two hundred feet above them. Spengler, who was momentarily distracted, gave Alistair his chance. He rushed into the wheelhouse, grabbed Spengler's wrist and wrenched it sharply anticlockwise. The grenade fell to the deck and rolled across the bridge like a cricket ball heading for the boundary. It clunked to a rest, out of sight to all of them except Spengler ...

*

Nine hundred feet above the Deutsche Bucht, the Mossie was now in a descending flight path, having completed the sweeping 360-degree turn. Freddie was in his element and although still troubled by hazy sunlight, was busy listening to the VHF radio, awaiting the call from his friends below, on the pre-arranged frequency of 156 Mhz. Behind him, Swift sat in the navigator seat anxiously awaiting instructions.

Ten miles ahead, the Schnellboot was still idling just astern of

Solveig.

*

Aboard Solveig, after Alistair had disarmed Spengler, he ran to the portside bridge wing

door shouting: "abandon ship" to Langerhans and Anders, "starboard side." Spengler stood and watched him, rooted to the deck in shock at seeing the Mossie, powerless to do anything. Outside, Emran painfully clutched his shoulder, knowing now his plans to cause havoc and bloodshed in the Middle East were over.

Alistair grabbed hold of Joselyn's arm and they charged across the deck to ship's side. He turned to her and yelled:

"Hug yourself, Joss, like this," he crossed his arms, flat against his chest, palms facing inwards and smiled at her frightened face.

"We're goanna jump?" she said warily, still recovering from the clutches of Emran. "I'm scared of heights. Didn't I tell you?"

"No."

"Oh hell!"

Alastair yelled: "On three, two, one, NOW!"

They jumped simultaneously, feet first and dropped sixty feet into the freezing sea and sank below the frothing surface.

The tall Palestinian crossed the deck, holding his shoulder, hoping they would die on impact. He turned around, looked into the wheelhouse, and saw Spengler, der Jagdhund. He had picked up the grenade and held it in his hand, his finger crooked around the safety-pin ring. His face was wild with defeat and humiliation. How could it have come to this?

Spengler stared death in the face, just as he had done in the Great War. He flexed his thumb. Now he was ready to die ... what the hell.

On the flying deck of the Schnellboot, Manfred still held binoculars to his eyes, scanning port to starboard, astern of Solveig.

"There!" Rosa screamed beside him, "Port side. Joselyn and Alistair have jumped overboard. My God! Can they possibly survive from that height?" The anxiety in her voice was palpable.

Jansen called down to the wheelhouse and in a matter of seconds they were alongside Solveig. Joselyn and Alistair were treading water, visibly shaken, freezing cold. On the edge of death. Two S-Boot crewmen threw them lifebuoys and they were hauled onboard, Joselyn first and then Alistair, chivalrous as always.

"You must have an affection for the North Sea, Alistair. Second time today," said Rosa, handing them both thick blankets and a towel. "That was really something. Are you alright, Joselyn?"

She nodded, shaking with cold, but the famous blue eyes sparkled; no smile. Alistair knew she would be alright, she just needed time to recover. But she was particularly silent, even for her. Delayed shock, Alistair thought, and started to deliver instructions:

"Jansen, get on the VHF radio, search around 156 Mhz. Call sign..."

He paused, caught his breath, looking at Joselyn with concern. Her face and her eyes spoke to him in a way he would never forget ... you saved my life ... But more, you risked your own. Her eyes were fixed on him.

Alistair swallowed and for a split-second thought he had never felt more in love in his life than at that moment. Joselyn had jumped unquestioningly, trusted him implicitly about their chances of surviving. And they had.

Neither of them would ever forget a jump that might have killed them both.

Jansen broke the spell: "Alistair, you wanted me to radio someone?"

"Yes, yes. Sorry. The call sign is GOLF – Tango – Charlie – Romeo – Whisky. Freddie will be listening, up there somewhere."

He panted the words out, simultaneously drying his face and hands. He noticed they were shaking and hid them in the towel. Joselyn noticed and gave him a wonderful look of care and intimate understanding. It was as if she had read his mind. He shivered: Oh yes, she knew.

"Ja, will do," said the old sea dog. "Message?"

"Crimson Wing – clear."

"That's all?" Jansen questioned.

"Yes ... but please swing the S- Boot around to starboard of Solveig. Pick up two crew – the captain and his crewman. If they haven't already frozen to death."

Rosa looked down at her feet. She knew her father was still on board and so was Emran but said nothing. She was powerless.

Jansen went below to the wheelhouse, picked up the radio mike and made the call as requested. The S-Boot jumped into life to recover the crewmen.

Rosa took Joselyn's arm: "I should have come with you earlier, I'm sorry. I should have known it might be dangerous. Emran and ..."

Joselyn interrupted her: "I did what I did because I'm stubborn. Ask my father, Grizzly."

"Or me," said Alistair with his winning smile.

Joselyn ignored his comment: "Did I seriously just jump off the side of that ship?"

"You did," said Rosa, wondering why Joss had interrupted her so rudely. Maybe it was nerves, she thought, and wondered what her father had said to her on the boat: what lies had he told her to mislead her?

Alistair passed Joselyn one of Jansen's flasks: "Have a drop of this, it will calm you down, Joss."

"What is it?"

"Coffee, with a Commodore's nip," Alistair said with a grin.

*

The Mossie was descending fast. Freddie had received the message and prepared to attack the now motionless Solveig.

"Bombs fused, bomb doors down." Freddie said, a tremor of nerves in his voice. He looked through the bomb-release sight. Low cross winds caused the airframe to vibrate slightly, but she was steady.

"Alright, I have clear visual ... wait for it ... left, left, steady, I'm holding her, finger on the button ... right, three, two one ... bombs gone!"

Eleven seconds later, a massive explosion below as two 500lb bombs hit Solveig.

"Direct hit!" Swift yelled.

A split second later, a second massive explosion suddenly ripped through Solveig's wheelhouse. A huge surge of fire blew all the windows out in a blinding flash.

"What the hell was that?" Freddie yelled and rapidly took the Mossie out of descent and pulled away to starboard again.

"It's certainly not a gas main," Swift replied, binoculars at his eyes. "The Schnellboot is heading back east again – away from Solveig – God! She is moving fast. She must be making at least forty knots."

Freddie: "Let's go around and take another look."

"You've still got the rockets."

Swift was referring to the 8 high-explosive rockets mounted under the wings, specifically made for anti-shipping, with armour-piercing heads, which can punch clean through a ship's hull.

"I know," said Freddie, his thumb hovering over the button, "but I don't think we'll need them. That was almost incendiary down there, like a grenade exploding."

He took the Mossie into another 360-degree turn; the plane was agile, fast, and responsive to the lightest touch of the stick. In minutes she was eight miles astern of the smoking vessel, descending from two hundred miles per hour to one hundred and fifty ...

"Dead ahead," Freddie yelled.

"Alright."

The Mossie vibrated in protest, almost on stall, a hundred feet above the sea. Freddie held her true: concentration fixed, watching the target, then instruments: air speed indicator, horizon, altimeter, compass. All good. He swallowed. The Solveig was an absolute fireball.

"Pulling out," said Freddie. "Job done."

Freddie pulled back the stick and the Mossie powered back up into the sky like a rocket. Was it the explosion below, or the wooden airframe struggling with the massive acceleration. Freddie felt the old buzz of exhilaration. He sighed. Felt the adrenalin. They had done it. But what was the second explosion? Freddie wondered. Surely not the missiles, they had been deactivated for the journey.

"We've just prevented a major war in the Middle East, Swift. Good job!"

"Joint effort, sir."

The VHF radio suddenly hissed static: "Crimson Wing, come in please,"

"GOLF – Tango-Charlie-Romeo-Whisky, receiving."

"Northolt Tower. Return to London. Repeat – return to London."

"Wilco," said Freddie. He was surprised by what was clearly a direct order from Squadron Leader Squires, and consequently Brim. But he said nothing. Had Alistair contacted London?

Swift, now communicating on the intercom, produced a chart and said he would plot a course back to London which would be quite different from their journey out. Freddie held the stick and once again checked his instruments: altitude fifteen thousand feet; airspeed two hundred and twenty miles per hour. The sun had dropped, and visibility was clear. After ten minutes or so Freddie broke the silence. He thought Swift might have been asleep:

"What about Charlie?"

"I suppose he'll be getting the train back," he said, unconcerned. Freddie would later learn that had been the intention all along.

When they touched down at RAF Northolt both Squires and

Brim were there to meet them. Squires looked relieved; Brim concerned. Something was up.

*

Simultaneously on the Schnellboot a similar conversation had quietly taken place between Alistair and Joselyn. She had asked him about Freddie and the Mossie.

'Oh, back to London,' he had said casually. 'Squires insisted I send him a Morse signal as soon as it was mission complete. Which I did. Freddie and Swift will be at Northolt by now. Don't worry, Joss. All will be alright.'

But Joselyn harboured a number of concerns. Not just the question of trusting Rosa. She still wasn't entirely sure about her. Spengler and Emran were dead. But Spengler had confided a lot before the sudden gunfire on Solveig: it was Peter Braun who had planned and organised her attempted murder in Pontresina. Not Spengler. But was that true? Then there was the Irish connection. Not only Patrick Devlin, but Samuel Donoghue, the man being held at the American Embassy. Suddenly it was a much bigger picture. Now she wanted to speak to her father. Yes, Grizzly would have all the answers. He always did. And she had his private line at Macdonald House, Grosvenor Square. But it would be a phone call not a visit. And Joselyn had her reasons. Because she always did.

Headline

Hotel Landaus, Mitte-Nord, Germany.

ALISTAIR, JOSELYN AND Manfred were sitting once again in the rear garden of the Landaus. A fresh pot of coffee and cups stood on a tray on the familiar wrought-iron table. It was civilised, as ever.

Except that there were now only three of them.

A copy of 'Die Welt' newspaper lay on the table, half folded. It had been read by all of them.

ERICH SPENGLER COMMITS SUICIDE AT SEA.

The owner of Spengler GmBh killed himself when a grenade exploded on board his ship, the SS Solveig, according to statements made by the only two surviving crew members. Captain Edvard Langerhans and his Second Officer Anders were shocked when Spengler entered the wheelhouse clutching an old grenade and told them to abandon ship. There was no explanation as to why. The Quartermaster Martin Zimmer had launched one of the ship's lifeboats earlier after the crew had heard gunfire from a pirate boat and believed they were under attack. Spengler's daughter Rosa, a senior executive in the company, was said to be too distressed to make a comment.

Alastair said: "You've obviously all read this article?"

But it was only Manfred who replied in his deadpan way: "Yes. But it is what they omitted that was the most important. The real story."

"Selective?" suggested Alistair.

Manfred raised his bushy eyebrows: "Selective, yes. And fortunate that the editor and Helmut Siebenthal are such good friends."

Joselyn laughed quietly to herself; Alistair was right about Nexus.

Envelope

Hotel Landaus, Mitte-Nord, Germany.

ON THE LAST NIGHT OF THEIR STAY, Alistair and Joselyn were in their room at the Landaus, dressing for dinner. Joselyn had not been herself since the Schnellboot journey back to Cuxhaven six days earlier. Alistair knew she was in an odd mood. Maybe not odd, but certainly preoccupied with something:

"I've been thinking about London, Alistair."

"Oh?"

"I don't want to go back there. Not yet." She was brushing her hair, looking into a long mirror, and seeing him in reflection.

He was surprised: "I thought you wanted to see your father. To ask him about this Donoghue character and the question of diplomatic immunity. Brim and your father are meeting in a couple of days with Freddie. Your father will want to know everything."

She turned to face him: "I know. Of course, I do. But I might just telephone him when he returns from Paris. I – I think he might be seeing someone over there. You know, a lady friend. I just hate the thought of that. I cannot imagine the idea of even seeing him with another woman. And as for public displays of affection ..."

He walked over to her: "I understand. Whatever you want, Joss."

"I don't know what I want at the moment, that's the problem. I am out of sorts, as my Uncle Mark would say. He'd understand."

Alistair took her arm and looked her in the eye: "I understand, Joss."

"Sure?"

"You know I do. But just don't forget we have to see Brim for a debrief after all this. And Freddie, of course. He is back at that bloody Baker Street safehouse. Brim wants him close."

Joselyn gave him a half-smile and remained quiet for a long time. He knew not to intrude into her private world when she was in this mood.

"Let's go down to the bar and meet Manfred. I fancy a drink. In fact, I feel as if I need a few drinks," she said testily.

Alistair: "You want to go back to St. Moritz, don't you? To see Peter Braun in prison?"

She nodded and those famous blue eyes glistened once again. Alistair agreed, but on one condition: "We meet Brim and Freddie first, ok?"

"Yeah. But not London. Somewhere else, please."

"Why not St. Moritz? Kill two birds ... I'll contact Leo

Hoffmann." He touched her cheek, the way he did, and she smiled. He realised the prospect of Joselyn confronting her father was extremely delicate at the moment, particularly with the lady friend issue. What was it she had just said? And she had made her feelings quite clear.

She appeared to mull the idea over: "Good idea, yes. Brim would approve of Badrutt's. He can see what he's been paying for."

"I'll call London tomorrow," Alistair said to show that they had an agreed plan of action.

Joselyn turned and hurried to the bedroom door. That was what she had wanted all along and he had not seen it. He followed her, realising she had twisted him round her little finger.

And the very thought of it amused him.

The prospect of a few aperitifs in the hotel bar with Manfred and her suddenly seemed appealing to both of them, all the same. It was their last night at the Landaus, after all.

But when they arrived at reception Rosa was standing there clutching an official-looking envelope. It bore the name and address of a law firm. As they got closer, they could see she appeared to have been crying.

"From my father's lawyer in Berlin," she said, poking the envelope in their direction and sniffing. "It seems he's left a large amount of cash to a certain Fräulein Stefanie ... I am unable to understand his logic." It seemed a very precise thing for her to say.

"Who is Fräulein Stefanie?" Joselyn asked, taking hold of the proffered envelope, noticing the name and address.

"I understand from Werner, father's lawyer, that she owns Die Paradise Klinik," she sniffed again, her voice shaky, the words broken, "in Königsee, Austria."

"And what is Die Paradise Klinik exactly?" Alistair asked innocently. "A hospital? Some sort of recuperation clinic?"

"Don't be ridiculous. It's a euphemism for whore house. My father thought I didn't know what he got up to when he was on business in Austria. Scandalous!"

"Oh?"

Manfred came bounding down the spiral staircase, dressed like something out of an Italian opera. His bushy black hair had been cut and elegantly styled:

"I am ready for a gin and tonic like the ones we had at Skindles, Alistair ... What? Did I miss something?"

Rosa plucked the envelope out of Joselyn's hand and said: "Nothing, Manfred. But you can certainly buy me a gin and tonic. The bigger, the better. I'm in shock."

*

Later, in their bedroom Alistair could hear Joselyn in the en-suite bathroom. She was brushing her teeth and gargling a fresh mint mouthwash provided by the Landaus. Soon she would appear in her towelling bathrobe, her hair wrapped up in a towel like a turban, the way she did every night. It was her bedtime routine.

He noticed a piece of paper among her things, and her distinct handwriting:

Werner Kauffmann
Advokaturbüro und Notariat
Friedrichstrasse, Berlin.

"Didn't Herr Seiler teach you not to pry into other people's personal belongings, Mr. Valentine?" Her voice smouldered ...

She looked eminently desirable leaning against the bathroom door, one leg crossed over the other. She was still holding the tooth glass as if she had been interrupted, mid-swill. He ignored her question and walked over to her.

He narrowed his eyes and suggested: "Erich Spengler's lawyer in Berlin, perhaps?"

"Uh-huh." Something in her eyes spoke to him again.

He took her hand: "I love you, Joselyn."

The front of her bathrobe fell open; she was naked underneath: "Yeah? Prove it."

Embassy

Macdonald House, Grosvenor Square, London. England.

THE TRUSTY OLD Humber was ticking over outside Brim's office building in St. James's. Captain Clitheroe, Brim's driver, got out when he caught sight of him struggling with his umbrella. Beside him was Freddie Valentine who had walked from the Baker Street safe house.

Brim was wearing his pre-war tan-coloured mackintosh, which had certainly seen better days and Freddie wore an oilskin he had borrowed from one of Hugh Dalton's team. The rain was cascading down in this part of London, a summer storm, flashes of lightning, rumbling thunder. An angry grey clouds hung over St. James's Park. Mothers with their prams struggled against the wind; ubiquitous city gentleman, bowler hatted, brollies unfurled attempted to flag down the occasional passing taxi.

"Good afternoon, Professor. And Group Captain Valentine."

"Oh, hello, Captain Clitheroe. Sorry to drag you out on such a filthy afternoon. We're only going to Grosvenor Square, but this downpour isn't going to ease."

"Never a chore, sir." Clitheroe held the rear door open and they were soon turning into Berkeley Square up towards Davis Street, a stone's throw from Claridges. Wet raincoats and sheltering newspaper vendors greeted them at the next junction. Brim glimpsed one of the Evening Standard's newsstands through the steamed-up window of the Humber:

> *Wimbledon Women's Tennis: In an all-American match Pauline Betz beats Louise Brough – 6-2, 6-4. Her only Wimbledon Crown.*

"Do you follow the tennis, Clitheroe?"

"No, sir. Be glad when the football season kicks off, to be honest. Me and the Missus are keen Chelsea supporters. But we don't mind watching a bit of cricket on a Sunday afternoon at the Oval - 'cept Sheila dozes off. So do I if I've downed a few pints lunchtime at the Nag's 'Ead. I can't understand them rules, can you? ... Here we are ... Grosvenor Square." The car pulled up in a puddle, splashing rainwater over the damp pavement.

"Would you mind waiting?" said Brim, fiddling with his umbrella, as he climbed out of the car. "Don't worry. I can manage ... We shan't be a jiffy, shall we, Freddie?"

Freddie slid along the rear seat after him. Clitheroe had heard Brim's expression jiffy before. It could describe a timespan of anything from ten minutes to two hours, depending on whom he was visiting. An Agatha Christie novel was always to hand, together with a flask of tea, care of Sheila Clitheroe.

*

Charles Foster was at his most urbane on this dreary day. He was attired in what looked like a new handmade Savile Row suit, customary pressed white shirt, his Stamford tie, tied with a Windsor knot, Brim observed without comment. Foster had caught the sun; with his weather-beaten features and coiffured silver-grey hair, he looked a picture of health and energy. The tall New Englander had greeted them in the lobby of Macdonald House. An American secretary had relieved them of their soaking mackintoshes and dripping umbrellas on to a busy hat stand.

They shook hands and took the elevator up to the sixth floor. Once in the office, Brim was offered his favourite leather armchair. Freddie admired the impressive – if rainy – view of the Square below.

"Charles, you're looking very well. What's the secret?"

Foster had a look in his eye which Brim recognised. It was either the good fortune of an unexpected inheritance or romance. He suspected the latter, since, he assumed, Foster was already wealthy.

"A glimmer of light in my lacklustre world of diplomacy and politics, Brim. Let's just say France suits me better than London.

And probably Boston too."

"France?" Brim took out his battered silver cigarette case and lit a Senior Service. Freddie sat on a button leather chesterfield.

"Yes. Firstly, a little tête-à-tête at our Embassy in Paris and then, Ile de Ré, four days' sailing with a companion, off St. Martin. Do you know it?"

"Only from the air during the war, but we certainly weren't sailing," Brim responded a little more brusquely than he intended.

"I can imagine, Brim." Foster was anxious to share the reason for his joie de vivre but could see now was not the time to share such secrets.

"You wanted to see me, Charles?" Brim asked formally. "You've got two for the price of one because Freddie here only arrived back in London yesterday. We'll explain the details later."

Foster made himself comfortable behind his busy desk and shot his cuffs, immediately business-like:

"Samuel Donoghue – Blue Raincoat – has left the Embassy, as he is entitled to do under current legislation. Yesterday afternoon."

Brim was riled: "In spite of my written protestation and lengthy meeting with the Home Office. Diplomatic bloody immunity. It's scandalous."

"I know and it was damn selfish of Clive Rowlands to throw himself under a taxi," Foster said without humour. He meant it.

Brim pursed his lips and puffed out his cheeks. He was livid:

"Would it have made any difference if he hadn't?"

Foster shook his head with a sigh: "I guess we'll never know, will we? But what is interesting, Donoghue did not fly back to the US direct from London, as he was obliged to do under rules from Washington D.C. Protocol."

"Oh?"

Foster consulted some papers and a few photographs. "He walked from here to Euston Station and then Kings Cross. I had two of my people follow him. Army, but plainclothes."

"But they lost him?"

"Yes."

"He knew he was being followed."

"Yes. But it's a fair hop from Grosvenor Square to Euston Road."

"Agreed. But easier to lose two followers at major railway stations than Great Portland Street or Tottenham Court Road. Both are straight, more or less. No hiding place. The stations provide Main Line and Underground as a means of escape. And temporary concealment. Donoghue knew what he was doing; that's obvious."

Foster pushed the papers away angrily. He was now only too aware he had been deceived by Donoghue. The man had high security clearance and access to sensitive material, some of which he had passed through Rowlands to Erich Spengler. A first-grade traitor.

"We let you down."

Brim ignored the admission: "I presume he was carrying his passport, ID?"

"I would assume so."

"Then he'd be at liberty to travel to anywhere in Europe."

"From King's Cross?"

Freddie said: "You know, Charles, if I were him, I know exactly what I'd do."

Foster's blue-grey eyes regarded Freddie respectfully: "What?"

"Perfectly simple really. I would lose my pursuers at Kings Cross – among a throng of travellers - and hop into a taxi down to Victoria. Catch the boat train to Calais. Or wherever I wanted."

"I see," said Foster.

"Did Donoghue have any luggage?"

"I'm not sure."

Freddie mused: "Hm, although does it matter? He could easily have left his cases in a storage locker somewhere earlier on. Did he stop off anywhere after he left here?"

Foster picked up the telephone: "I'm going to get one of the ... oh, Suzanne, ask Captain Kosinski to come up here will you ... yeah, right away. It's urgent."

After what seemed like only a few minutes, there was a knock on the door and a tall man with a military-style crew cut entered. He wore Army uniform, his cap under his arm and saluted:

"Kosinski, sir."

"These gentlemen wish to ask you a few questions about the

man you tailed yesterday."

Kosinski looked down at his boots, embarrassed and Freddie felt for him. A young American in London, unfamiliar with the territory.

"At ease, Captain," said Foster and the man relaxed an inch, still uncomfortable, not knowing who the Ambassador's visitors were. Or why they were there.

Freddie said: "Mayfair up to Euston is a maze of streets; easy to get lost and even easier to lose someone you're following. But maybe you can help us with two things; did Donoghue carry any luggage?"

The young soldier was direct: "No sir, not to begin with."

"So, he stopped off somewhere en-route to the station?"

"Sir, yes, he did, twice." He looked at Foster as if to seek permission to go further.

"Go ahead, Captain Kosinski, tell them all you know."

The young soldier unbuttoned his front tunic pocket, took out a piece of notepaper and started to read, a little self-consciously:

"Sir. The first stop was a shop called – 'John Bell and Croydon' on Wigmore Street."

"And what do they sell?" asked Foster.

But it was Brim who answered: "A famous old company. Medical supplies, Chemists. They used to supply many of the doctors on Harley Street. Probably still do."

Kosinski, still at ease, was staring directly ahead: "Sir. Yes, sir. Medical supplies."

"You said there were two stop-offs, Captain?" Freddie asked.

Kosinski consulted his note: "A private address on New Cavendish Street. Donoghue was in there ten minutes and came out ..."

"With another parcel?" Brim asked, taking out his silver cigarette case once again.

"Sir. Yes, sir. Correct," Kosinski said.

"What size?" Brim pressed.

"Like a shopping bag, with a handle. You know, grocery-bag style."

Brim lit a Senior Service: "And then he went up to Euston and Kings Cross Stations?"

The young soldier nodded.

"Good work, Captain," said Freddie. "The question is, where did he go after that? You couldn't have followed him forever."

"No, sir."

"Is that all?" asked Foster.

"I have no further questions. Thank you, Captain," Freddie said, and Brim shook his head, exhaling smoke.

"Dismissed, Captain Kosinski."

Brim: "Don't count on Donoghue making mistakes, Charles. The man is thorough. It took a lot of risk doing what he did; he must have had a damn good reason not to go straight back to America."

"But what?"

Foster's secretary entered the office after a soft tap and served them iced tea. It was peach- flavoured and a first for Brim. He sipped some with apprehension, not convinced about the addition of ice since the Skindles gin-and-tonic evening.

"Delicious," said Freddie.

"I want to hear about my daughter, Brim. I sense I am not top of her mailing list since my trip over to France." A trace of sadness briefly crossed his handsome features.

"Oh?" Brim said simply, immediately comprehending the reason for that sadness.

"But first tell me about the Crimson Wing operation."

Brim and Freddie detailed all the events that occurred in Northern Germany, culminating in the Mosquito flight back to RAF Northolt. Foster knew Freddie's history:

"It must have been great to fly again, Freddie. Especially an air to sea confrontation?" Foster was clearly impressed.

"There are no superlatives to describe the efficacy of my team, Charles," Brim said, answering for him. "As we have just explained Joselyn was crucial to the operation, everyone played their part. The Nexus input was invaluable, even influencing the German Press post- event. Helmut Siebenthal knows the editor of Die Welt. And the reporting of Spengler's death was economical, to say the least."

"Your network is impressive, Brim," said Foster.

"My network has to be impressive, Charles."

"Precisely. Now, you said on the phone Joselyn and Alistair

have gone to St. Moritz? Direct from Bremerhaven? They are not coming to the UK?"

"No," said Freddie. "I spoke to Alistair this morning. This arrangement seemed more logical. He was keen for you to be kept up to speed with what had happened in Germany."

"I see." Charles Foster could not hide his disappointment.

Brim placed his unfinished drink on the desk and rose to leave. "Our driver, Captain Clitheroe, will be getting concerned. I told him we'd only be a jiffy."

"Of course. I wanted you both to know the exact position with Donoghue. And it made sense for you to speak to Captain Kosinski."

Freddie grinned: "He's certainly given us plenty to think about."

Brim seemed to stall their leaving and glanced at Freddie, then Foster:

"Do you feel inclined to tell us about your new sailing companion, Charles? I am sure we have time for that."

Foster raised his eyebrows and his walnut face creased into a smile: "She's a French anaesthetist I met at an Embassy pow-wow a few months ago ...

Her name is Dr. Michelle Labrut. She is forty, married to her job at a hospital in Paris and loves nothing more than sailing. Oh, and her parents have a summer house at St. Martin. That is the story, in a nutshell."

Brim glanced at the 10x8" photograph of Foster's late wife

Maria. And noticed once again the uncanny resemblance to Joselyn. She had probably inherited her mother's Mediterranean temperament too, he thought to himself.

"Do you suppose your new companion is the reason why you have been temporarily demoted on your daughter's mailing list, Charles?"

"You're on the money there, Brim."

Freddie and Brim took the elevator back to the entrance lobby where Suzanne greeted them with their belongings:

"You won't be needing these, Professor Brimblecombe. Look out at Grosvenor Square: sun, glorious California sun. Just like home!" Suzanne smiled deliciously.

*

Once back at the office, Brim and Freddie drafted a telegram to Alistair and Joselyn at Badrutt's in St. Moritz. The content summarised their meeting with Charles Foster; particularly the information Kosinski had relayed to them about Samuel Donoghue's disappearance. Not that it would do much good; the trail had gone cold at Kings Cross. Miss Trueblood would alert her contact with the Police and they would inform Passport Control at the airports just in case.

Kreisspital

Kreisspital Oberengadin, Via Nova, Samedan, Switzerland.

DR. P. J. O'BRIEN was sitting in his new office at the Kreisspital Oberengadin, a hospital outside the town of Samedan. The elevated position of the traditional-style building gave him astounding views of that part of the Maloja region: mountains, lakes, lush green meadows, and the picturesque railway line he had so recently travelled on from Chur.

He wore a collar and tie under his white lab-style coat: 'Cavendish Clinic, London' embroidered on its pocket. A stethoscope hung around his neck. O'Brien was of average height, with auburn hair cut short and straight, almost military. He had energetic eyes and an academic manner.

His office was adjacent to the new experimental Cardiac Clinic, inspired by the pioneering work of Dr. Werner Forssmann, the renowned German surgeon and inventor of the cardiac catheter. O'Brien had made it known he was a great advocate of new technology and keen to be involved with the sort of international clinical trials that would put Samedan on the map.

His paperwork was, of course, impeccable. Dr. O'Brien's credentials described him as having trained at Yale-New Haven Hospital in Connecticut, a brief spell in Boston and then a post at St. Bartholomew's, London, where he qualified as a Consultant. His most recent medical appointment at the Cavendish Clinic near Harley Street had given him a glowing written reference. A certain Dr. Meyer had described how they were desperately sorry to see him go but wished him good luck for the future. His letter was full of praise.

Dr. O'Brien had also made it known he was keen to work in Switzerland, having become engaged to a physician from Berne. But there was one other clinical asset which had clinched it for hospital management in Samedan. O'Brien had worked – very briefly - he admitted, for André-Frédéric Cournand, a famous physician at New York Presbyterian Columbia.

The Senior Administrator at Spital Oberengadin, Anna Taussing, had no hesitation in appointing Dr. O'Brien to work at their new clinic, given his experience.

At the end of their 'welcome interview' Dr. O'Brien said he had a special 'if embarrassing' favour to ask her. He was charming and persuasive, with his slight Irish- American accent and polite manner. Anna felt she could detect a slight ecclesiastical propriety in his words; she was a devout Catholic.

“A family friend is in Police custody in Pontresina and I have been asked to go and see him. His family have a history of congenital heart disease ...” He paused for effect ...

“... I feel it is my moral obligation to help them if I can.”

“I see. My Goodness. What has this person done to be in Police custody?” There was a trace of concern in her voice.

“Oh, I have no idea,” Dr. O’Brien replied softly, compellingly. He looked at her. “If there is a problem ...” his words trailed off, “... Whatever happens, I don’t want him to die in prison. His mother would never forgive me.”

A self-deprecating sigh: you must understand, was the impression conveyed.

“No, of course not,” Anna said, unscrewing the top of her fountain pen. “What’s the patient’s name?”

“Peter Braun,” he said calmly. His eyes met hers and he knew he had an ally.

Journey

Zürich SBB via Chur to St. Moritz, Switzerland.

"ALL I AM SAYING, Alistair, is that one way or another, Rosa Spengler has seen off all her adversaries." Joselyn's tone was adamant. They were on the same SBB train they had journeyed on back in December 1945: from Zürich via Chur to St. Moritz. The stop at Chur was the connection.

"Not all," Alistair countered. He enjoyed challenging her even when he knew she was most probably right.

She raised her eyebrows, looking out of the First-Class carriage window, as she had done before: "You think about it. Spengler, Gertrud, Schaffer, ... oh and Harald Wolf, of course, we can't forget him. Even though I was responsible. He was no friend of hers, was he?"

"Emran?" Alistair suggested.

Joselyn turned away from the window and looked at him: "I wasn't even considering that bloody warmonger. He was accidental."

"Accidental? How do you mean?"

"Sure, yeah. Collateral fall out. Not planned." She paused, biting her bottom lip. "Not forgetting the solicitor guy in – where was it – Weybridge?"

"Clive Rowlands."

"Yeah, how many is that?"

"Try not to worry about it, Joss. It really doesn't matter. It's part of what we do. We have a job to do. Leo Hoffmann has arranged for us to see Peter Braun. Hopefully today. That's our mission."

"I know and I can't wait to see his face. The last time I had my knee in it."

Badrutt's

Badrutt's Palace Hotel, St. Moritz, Switzerland.

LEO HOFFMANN hadn't changed at all, except this time there was no fur greatcoat and chunky leather gloves. The temperature outside the hotel on Via Serlas was upward of twenty-five degrees. But still the dome-shaped head, and customary cigar, courtesy of his protégé investigator Heinz Johner.

He greeted them both like old friends in the opulent wood-panelled reception of the hotel, a handshake for Alistair and a light kiss on both cheeks for Joselyn.

"No Freddie?" asked Hoffmann with a trace of disappointment.

"On his way," Alistair said.

Joselyn linked her arm through Hoffmann's, and they strolled across the marble-tiled floor under high white archways into the palatially appointed lounge. It was busy with visitors of all ages and nationalities. Affluence was all around: well-dressed men and chic-looking ladies; Parisian haute couture. There was a background murmur of French, Italian, German and a smattering of English.

A green-liveried waiter approached them and quietly escorted them to a table by the window. It overlooked the lake, with a panoramic view of the mountains beyond. They were bathed in soft late afternoon sunlight. Joselyn took in the peaks of Piz Bernina, and Piz Roseg across to Monte Sissone.

"Joss, the waiter is offering you a seat," Alistair said, breaking her reverie.

She turned from the window, her lips parted: "Mi dispiace, signor, la vista è bellissima."

The young man was smiled: "Si."

They were served traditional tea and cakes; no milk with the Lapsang Souchong, the smoky Chinese tea normally served with lemon. Joselyn discreetly said she could not bear the taste of it. The waiter politely persuaded her it might be a good idea to have a glass of chilled Bollinger instead and dashed to the bar with the order. It all happened in an instant:

"Sorry to be a pest," she said, as the young man, presented her drink on a silver platter.

"You can see Herr Braun tomorrow morning at nine," said Hoffmann, sipping his tea.

He watched Joselyn sip champagne. He had forgotten just how beautiful she was and today was no exception: sky-blue eyes; her skin, kissed by the sun had freckled slightly. She wore a ruffled silk blouse and a figure-hugging pencil skirt that looked perfect in such fashionable surroundings.

"I thought you said we'd be able to see him today?" Alistair asked with undisguised irritation. "When we spoke on the phone."

"I'm sorry but that won't be possible, Alistair." Hoffmann said, replacing the tiny cup on to its saucer.

"Why not? Where is he?"

Hoffmann steepled his hands: "He's being examined by a Doctor."

"Doctor? What Doctor? Why?"

"We had a request from the senior administrator at Kreisspital Oberengadin in Samedan. The doctor is apparently a heart specialist."

"What's his name?" Alistair's face furrowed into immediate concern, his mind calculating possibilities. And inconsistencies.

Hoffmann consulted a piece of paper: "Dr. O'Brien. Just moved here from London. St. Bartholomew's Hospital."

"Where is Braun now?"

"He was transferred from Kantonpolizei here in St. Moritz to Sennhof, the prison in Chur Old Town. We didn't have room to ..."

Alistair shot out of his chair: "We need to go there now, Leo."

"But why?" Hoffmann also stood, catching the panic.

"I'll tell you on the way. Come on. Joss, quick. Come."

Hoffmann: "Right."

Before he could utter another word, Alistair was half-way

down the elegant hallway, almost running, heading for reception. Joselyn and Hoffmann followed in his wake.

Sennhof

Sennhof Prison, Chur, Switzerland.

THEY WERE TOO LATE, of course. Blue Raincoat had already disposed of his target with brutal, surgical precision and fled the scene.

Sennhof prison in the old walled town of Chur was in chaos. Hoffmann's deputy, Heinz Johner, met them outside the room where Braun had been killed:

"Apparently Dr. O'Brien arrived here just after four pm, by appointment, to see his patient, Peter Braun. He was escorted to this interview room, where Braun awaited him. There was a question of patient-doctor privacy for physical examination and the prison guard waited just here outside. They were left alone for a matter of minutes. I'll show you."

Johner showed Hoffmann, Alistair and Joselyn into the interview room; Braun's body was there together with the instruments of his murder.

"Thank you, Heinz," said Hoffmann.

"Sir. This evidence was found just as you see it: a pharmacy bottle marked 'Chloroform,' that pad, a hypodermic needle and syringe; that glass phial marked 'Insulin' made by a well-known British pharmaceutical company."

"Insulin?" Alistair asked.

"Yes. According to the guard, Dr. O'Brien banged on the door and said he needed to get urgent help from the hospital. Braun had suffered a heart attack. There was confusion and O'Brien darted outside to a car and vanished. That is all I know, sir".

"Timings?" asked Hoffmann.

"More than an hour, sir. I tried your office. Monika said you were out."

"I was," said Hoffmann, "with Alastair and Joselyn here. Having tea."

"You weren't to know," Alistair said, reading the implication. "More than an hour or less. This was the perfect murder. And the perfect place. Because it's secure."

"And private," Joselyn said, looking at the surroundings.

"I bet Braun couldn't believe it," Alistair continued. "He must have thought Donoghue had come to help him escape ..." He paused ...

"... The chloroform-soaked pad would have quickly disabled him; 100mls of insulin to finish him off. Clever and quick. I take it you checked his pulse when you found him?"

Heinz Johner: "First thing I did Herr Valentine. Neck and radial. My colleague double- checked. He wasn't breathing, quite clearly he was ..."

There was a knock on the door; another officer said: "There's a lady to see you, Detective Hoffmann. Anna Taussing from Kreisspital Oberengadin. Matron in charge."

"Show her in, Klaus."

A lady entered the room: tall, meek and mousy. She let out a cry of shock when she saw the crime scene. She nodded at Hoffmann, introduced herself and asked if she could have a look at the body. It was immediately evident she was competent and experienced. After checking Braun's pulses, she lifted his head and sat him back in the chair with the help of Heinz Johner.

Braun's skin was grey, eyes closed. There was dried, sticky saliva around his blackened lips. She listened to his chest with a stethoscope as a formality and finally turned.

"I cannot tell you how long he has been dead, for certain. Maybe an hour? A physician will pronounce accurately ..." Taussing paused and regarded the others, before continuing, her voice hesitant ...

"I am, of course, extremely sorry about this. Dr. O'Brien's references were impeccable. America, England ..." She spoke delicate, precise German.

"He wasn't a doctor, Frau Taussing," said Alistair. "Far from it. He was a conman. An Irish-American criminal called Samuel Donoghue. Any documents you may have received and read were fake. That is to say they belonged to the genuine Dr. O'Brien who practiced at a hospital in London."

Taussing's head fell forward with a heavy sigh of disbelief: "This is quite unbelievable; he was so convincing. I was sure he was a real doctor. I have interviewed so many ... his CV was impressive. That was precisely the reason why we wanted him to work here; his research and clinical experience."

"That is the nature of the clever confidence trick. As you say, convincing."

Joselyn wandered over to Anna: "If it's any consolation, Frau Taussing, he conned my father and he is the American Ambassador in London. Not a man to be easily fooled and neither were his staff."

Anna looked shocked to suddenly hear American-accented English. It was as if she was suddenly aware of Joselyn's presence in the room.

"Oh," was all she said to her, overwhelmed by the magnitude of such a swindle.

She addressed Hoffmann: "There will be a Police enquiry, I assume?"

"Yes, there is no question. This is a murder, Frau Taussing."

Again, her head fell forward; a stupid question, but she was clearly shocked. Alistair waited a few moments before asking the obvious.

"Do you have any sort of identity photograph of Dr. O'Brien? Something we can use to show potential witnesses?" He chose his words guardedly; he did not want her to appear foolish in front of Hoffmann and the others.

She shook her head: “No. He only arrived at Samedan yesterday. There just hasn’t been time yet.”

Alistair: “Exactly what he was counting on. A swift execution; in and out.”

Hoffmann agreed with this summation as Alistair continued:

“There’s no point in alerting railway staff or creating roadblocks. Nobody knows what he looks like. The railway is busy with tourists; we’ve just come from Chur and it was packed. He won’t even be noticed.”

Hoffmann seized control: “Right, let’s get Braun’s body to the mortuary. Are you able to officially pronounce death, Frau Taussing?”

She shook her head again: “No this must be done by a doctor. I will telephone the hospital to arrange. The deceased must not be moved or touched again until that happens.”

“Herr Valentine, do you have any further business here?” Hoffmann asked formally for the benefit of all concerned.

“No. A wasted journey,” Alistair replied solemnly. “We should have realised Braun was an obvious target.”

“Thank you, Detective Hoffmann,” Joselyn said in English.

A trace of something crossed Frau Taussing’s pale features and it was obviously annoyance. She was clearly irritated she had been deceived so easily by a man like O’Brien and it had led to the death of a patient. Even though that patient was a prisoner and not her responsibility, she felt humiliated.

Joselyn picked up on her expression, but Taussing turned and left the room without another word.

Blue Raincoat

Heston Aerodrome, Middlesex, England.

CHARLES FOSTER, BRIM, FREDDIE and Captain Clitheroe flew from Heston Aerodrome to Zürich on a privately chartered Beech Model 18, an ex-US military aircraft. The charter had been organised by Foster and the American Embassy. The extravagance was justified: he was desperate to see Joselyn after he had learned of all she had been through in Northern Germany. He had another agenda; he was keen to tell her about Dr. Michelle Labrut and the development of their relationship. Joselyn had to be 'on side' if they were going to continue seeing one another.

At the last moment Brim had asked Captain Clitheroe, his driver, to accompany them. A wise afterthought. Senior Intelligence Staff were advised to engage protection when travelling abroad on HM Government business. Brim was in no doubt about his decision. Clitheroe was capable, loyal, and armed.

Brim urgently needed a debrief with Freddie and Alistair. The PM required answers to some tricky questions regarding events in Northern Germany, the loan of the Mosquito from RAF Northolt and the situation with the traitor at the American Embassy. Joselyn was a crucial part of the team and would also need to respond. Manfred had provided Brim with a detailed statement of his participation before leaving for Baden.

Equally, Freddie wanted to see Alistair. He had not seen him since he had flown the Mossie from Seefliegehorst Weddewarden to attack SS Solveig.

*

The train rattled up from Zürich to Chur Bahnhof, as it had done earlier for Alistair and Joselyn. They also waited the scheduled ten minutes for the narrow-gauge connection to St. Moritz.

A split second later and Charles Foster would have missed him: a man of average height, with auburn hair cut short and straight, almost military.

"Christ! There's Donoghue, over there. Other platform!"

Foster, Freddie and Clitheroe were out of that carriage in an instant.

"Don't let him get away," Foster barked.

*

On the other platform, Donoghue could not believe what he was seeing. Foster, the American Ambassador from London, a soldier in British Army uniform waving a gun and another man with a limp crossing the narrow-gauge railway track towards him. What the hell could he do?

"Don't let him get away," someone shouted. He knew that voice only too well. There was a whistle, somebody fired a shot. He could see two Graubünden Police running towards him. An older man looked out of the carriage window. He had seen that face before. Where? A middle-aged woman was two feet away from him. He grabbed her roughly around the neck and dragged her towards him. She screamed in German, then Italian. Panic. Terror: "No! Please don't kill me! No!"

"Let her go, Samuel," Foster shouted; American- English, forceful, direct, commanding, "or I swear you will not leave this station alive."

The two Police unholstered their weapons, stern-faced, walked towards Donoghue fearlessly. One of them shouted in German: "Let the woman go" - then repeated it in English. Donoghue felt his grip relax. Trapped.

The English soldier was a few paces away, gun drawn, pointing at them both, the woman was panting with fright. And screamed.

"It's over, Donoghue," said Foster, a little less aggressively. "Let her go. Just let her free."

Donoghue pushed her away with such force that she fell to the ground. A split second and he ran. Clitheroe raised his weapon: "Stop or I shoot."

No response. Donoghue was getting away.

Clitheroe carefully took aim, squeezed the trigger. The single round caught Donoghue in the back of the thigh. The sound was thunderous, unexpected to the cowering passengers on the platform and in the station ...

Donoghue was thrown flat on his face with the impact of the bullet. Clitheroe walked towards the felled figure, adrenalin pumping, hands shaking, pointing the weapon. His eyes darted left and right, looking for support.

"Hold your fire, soldier," Freddie called, walking towards him. What happened next was unclear when Hoffmann questioned them all later. The Graubünden Policeman bent over to cuff Donoghue, and, as he did so, Donoghue somehow turned to try and grab the officer's gun. But Foster was there and kicked Donoghue square in the jaw, shattering bone with a chilling crack. Donoghue spat blood and teeth as Foster bent down and whispered,

"Fucking traitor."

Within seconds Brim was there and the Police had called for backup. Donoghue was cuffed to a post and Clitheroe sat quietly on a bench, his face creased with disbelief. Brim leant over Donoghue and puffed out his cheeks:

"I don't think you'll get diplomatic immunity here, old sport."

Freddie laughed. Foster said nothing, inert with sheer anger.

A black Mercedes-Benz type 170 pulled up outside Chur Bahnhof and a senior officer got out and said in German:

"Dr. O'Brien – or whatever your name is – I am arresting you for the murder of Peter Braun at Sennhof Prison, Chur today. You have ..."

Dr. O'Brien?

Brim took Foster and Freddie to one side: "You remember Captain Kosinski told us Donoghue made two stops on his way from the Embassy to Kings Cross? One was to John Bell and Croydon on Wigmore Street, medical suppliers; the other ..."

"What turned out to be a private hospital on New Cavendish Street. Yes, I checked," said Charles Foster. Now it was clear. Donoghue had an inside contact where he could source the drugs and medical devices he must have needed".

"That's why Donoghue was so desperate to escape." Brim pursed his lips the way he did and smiled; problem solved.

"To collect a doctor's paraphernalia. White coat and stethoscope?" Freddie suggested. "Is that what you mean?"

"Yes, exactly. But more importantly, to steal a real doctor's identity, from a credible hospital," Brim said. "You see if I'm not right. Come on, let's get up to St. Moritz and meet Alistair and Joselyn ..." Brim's mood melted into one of good humour and bonhomie now he had fathomed the mystery. He paused a moment ...

"Do you know, I rather fancy a Skindles-style gin and tonic, with ice. To celebrate our success."

"Good idea," Foster agreed.

"Do you think Badrutt's would serve such an American-style cocktail, Freddie?" Brim asked with mock incredulity.

"Only one way to find out, Brim," he said, looking at Foster.

Foster smiled; he was going to see Joselyn, always his little girl, no matter what. And all he ever wanted in the world was her love.

Letter

Nordenham, Germany.

ROSA SPENGLER KNEW once again that something was wrong outside as she sat in her little kitchen sipping whisky. The gramophone played; her book still lay unread. And for good reason.

It was Fritz's bark and then the ensuing silence which alerted her. She looked out of her kitchen window; her trusty dog was devouring a large piece of bloody meat. Again, someone was sitting on one of her sun loungers. She could not see who it was. She opened the screen and kitchen door, stepped out into her neat garden, and squinted her eyes.

"Hello, Rosa," Patrick Devlin said in his thick Dublin accent. "I thought we might have a little chat."

His owl-like eyes regarded her with a combination of lust and venom.

"Oh."

The tough old man stood, spat the remains of a roll-up

cigarette on to her lawn and walked towards her. The blade glinted.

"What do you want?" she asked, stepping back, apparently wary.

"You and Braun were supposed to kill the Walcott bitch. You didn't."

"We have already been through this, Devlin. It's history."

He cleared his throat: "Braun's dead; Donoghue charged by Swiss Police for his murder. No extradition, no immunity. He'll stay there."

Rosa concealed her surprise: "What do you want?" she asked again.

"Money. You're loaded, now."

"Are you threatening me, Devlin?"

He licked his lips salaciously: "You have no choice."

"Oh, I think she does." Edvard Langerhans emerged from Rosa's kitchen; a towel wrapped around his waist. His tall frame dripped water from the shower; Devin could not hide his shock.

"Well, Mr. Devlin?" Rosa asked, "Cat got your tongue?"

"I'll be back, Rosa Spengler. You can be sure of that."

*

Rosa and Edvard walked back into the kitchen as Devlin left the garden. Even though it was August, there was a sudden chill in the air, from the sea. She sipped her whisky and poured one for him. Propped up against her Adler was a cream-coloured envelope, embossed on one side: Spengler Corporation. In typed letters it was addressed to:

Werner Kauffmann
Advokaturbüro und Notariat
Friedrichstrasse
Berlin.

"Joselyn held a similar envelope in her hand for less than two minutes. It had that address on it, my father's lawyer in Berlin."

"And?" Edvard sipped whisky with pleasure.

"My guess is she memorised the address. She will go there, with Alistair, to see Werner in an attempt to find out if what I told her was true."

"Was it?"

"No. My father bequeathed me the entire Spengler empire. There was no provision for Fräulein Stefanie at the Die Paradise Klinik in Königsee. I lied. But what Joselyn will discover when she goes to Berlin – which she will – is that letter from me." Rosa treated herself to a rare smile of satisfaction.

"What's in it, may I ask, Rosa?"

"An idea. Joselyn is brave, resourceful, inventive and, I am sure, trustworthy. Independent but respectful. By the late Seventies, we will be one of the biggest companies in the world.

Europe will be run by Germany. My father always said that. Believed it without question."

"Really? Will the world forgive Germany? Will Europe?"

Rosa: "Yes. And do you know the irony?"

Edvard shook his head, out of his depth; he was a sailor, not a businessman. Rosa was complex; he had seen a new side to her.

"My father would approve of my idea, because secretly, like me, he admired her ..." Rosa topped up their glasses ..." Joselyn boarded Solveig, not knowing what danger she would face. Even her death, but she went undeterred. But I bet she encountered my father and they actually got on."

"But they were sworn enemies. Joselyn was there to prevent the voyage, which she did. The ship was destroyed and he and Emran's plans sunk."

"I know, but only two lives were lost." She did not acknowledge that one of them was her father, who had, effectively, committed suicide.

"True."

"And I would love to know what they spoke about in those final moments, although I can guess."

"Maybe one day, you'll be able to ask her," said Langerhans.

Rosa smiled again, finished her drink: "Oh yes, I will. But I'd just like to see her face when she reads this letter."

Langerhans smiled, but he could not really comprehend what Rosa was talking about.

"By the way, Edvard. That man you and my father knew in

Malmo ...”

“What about him? I stay away from people like that, Rosa.”

“Do you think he’d like a trip to Dublin? I’d pay well for his services. My father used to call it a loose end. And Erich Spengler didn’t like them.”

Dotted Line

Friedrichstrasse, Berlin, Germany.

ALISTAIR, FREDDIE AND JOSELYN are walking by Weidendammer bridge; the River Spree runs fast with debris: broken branches of trees, discarded boxes. The streets are a wasteland of rubbish and fallen masonry after aerial bombardment by the British, Americans and Russians.

The three of them are nearing their destination. Extensive reconstruction and rebuilding of Friedrichstrasse Station has begun over a year ago, in the summer of 1945. All around them are shattered landmarks, sad relics of a once-elegant city. The streets are war torn; people everywhere; the sound of a half dozen different tongues. Malnourished children push carts and prams bulging with their meagre possessions.

Alistair remembers Unter den Linden and his encounter with Admiral Canaris three years ago. What would it look like now, he wonders? The same as the Reichstag probably. They walk wordlessly and eventually find the correct address, climb the stone steps of a building that has only just avoided destruction. Once inside, a secretary greets them and, without further ado, passes Joselyn a cream-coloured envelope. It bears the name: Spengler Corporation. And a trademark image unfamiliar to them.

"This is for you," she says in English, "from Dr. Spengler." She beckons them to sit in a waiting area; it is candlelit and smells musty. There is a feeling of impermanence, that the building may collapse at any moment.

"Is Herr Werner Kauffmann not here? I understood he was expecting me. I sent a telegram."

"No. He sends his apologies." The lady turns and walks to her down-at-heel office. Something is in the air and Joselyn cannot work out what. She has made an appointment and it has been accepted.

Joselyn carefully cuts the seal of the envelope with her Swiss Army knife and quickly reads the contents. It has been typed on a pre-war Adler typewriter and is elegantly presented. Alistair and Freddie watch her as she reads and re-reads the contents. A frown brushes the contours of her face. And then a delicious smile.

"It's from Rosa. She has applied for planning permission to build a hotel in Boston: Copley Square, to be precise. 100 bedrooms, marbled-tiled reception area, two restaurants and an indoor swimming pool ..." Joselyn pauses, as if reading on ...

"Spengler Corporation have applied for permission to trade in the state of Massachusetts."

"And?" Freddie asks, fascinated. A trace of concern crosses Alistair's face.

"She wants me to be President of her American operations ... it was her father's wish to expand the business into the US after the war: hotels and restaurants ... I can't believe it. Why would she choose me?"

Joselyn looks up from the page at Alistair and Freddie, glancing from one to the other with a what-shall-I-do expression.

"You must accept," Alistair says. "It's the opportunity of a lifetime. And so completely out of the blue. And she chose you because you are you."

"I don't know ... Rosa writes that the Spengler Corporation will have some kind of partnership with an American bank to ensure ..."

The door of the lawyer's office opens gently, cautiously. Joselyn does not hear it at first and neither do the others. But suddenly her uncle Mark is there, as large as life. Like her father, he has a lumberjack build and a big grin. His presence suddenly fills the room, and the secretary looks up, but she is not surprised. Another man, presumably Werner Kauffmann, follows him in, a little sheepishly, with file of documents.

"Hello, pussy cat." Mark beams at her, relishing her surprise. His dialect is carved out of Boston, a deep mellifluous timbre that resonates.

"Uncle Mark?" For once, Joselyn is dumbfounded. Alistair

and Freddie watch her with amusement.

Mark introduces himself to Alistair and Freddie and perches on the corner of the table. He wears beige slacks and a club blazer – another elegant New Englander. In a way he is a carbon copy of his brother.

"Yes. Mark Foster Associates and the Bank of America Boston are putting a package together to finance the deal with the Spengler Corporation. And I have suggested something I am sure you will approve of, Joss,"

Foster pictured a certain 10x8" photograph which sat on his brother Charles's desk in London. He cannot conceal the smile which crosses his handsome features.

"What suggestion?" Joselyn rises and walks over towards him.

"That we call it the Hotel Maria, Copley Square, Boston. The first in a chain across the north-east of America. New York could be next; who knows?"

Those famous blue eyes shine with tears, but not with sadness. With pride. If only Grizzly were here to share this moment. Alistair and Freddie join her, themselves overcome with the power of the moment. They know what the memory of her mother means to her.

She looks at Alistair, her voice a whisper: "Will you come with me?"

"Yes, if that's what you want, of course I will." He glances at Freddie who nods in approval.

"Alright," she says, wiping her eyes. "Where do I sign?"

"Just here," says Kauffmann, holding a contract, "dotted line."

THE END

Bibliography

'Inside the Third Reich.'

Memoirs by Albert Speer. Published by The Macmillan Company 1970

'Battle of Wits – the complete story of codebreaking in World War Two.'

Stephen Budiansky. Penguin Group 2000.

ISBN 0-670-88492-8

'Enigma – the battle for the code.'

Hugh Sebag-Montefiore. Weidenfeld & Nicholson 2000.

ISBN 0 297 84251 X

'Ian Fleming and SOE's Operation Postmaster.'

Brian Lett. Pen & Sword Military 2012.

ISBN 978 178159 000 3

'The Nazis – the rise and fall of history's most evil empire.'

Paul Roland. Arcturus 2019

ISBN 978-1-78828-483-7

'Valkyrie – the plot to kill Hitler.'

Philipp Von Boeselager. Weidenfeld & Nicolson 2009.

ISBN 978-0-297-85546-7

'Hitler's spy chief – The Wilhelm Canaris Mystery.'

Richard Bassett. Cassell Military Paperbacks. 2005.

ISBN 978-0-3043-6718-4

'Hitler's last days – an eyewitness account.'

Gerhard Boldt. Rowohlt Verlag GmBh 1947

ISBN 0 7221 1735 3

'The secret war of Charles Fraser-Smith – the real Q of WW2.'

Charles Fraser Smith. Michael Joseph Ltd. 1981.

ISBN 978 0 9528408 0 0

'The Debs of Bletchley Park.'

Michael Smith. Aurum Press Ltd. 2015

ISBN 978 1 78131 388 6

'What if? Military historians imagine what might have been.'

Edited by Robert Cowley. Pan Books. 2001.

ISBN 0 330 48724 8

'The heroines of SOE – Britain's secret women in France

F Section.'

Squadron Leader Beryl E. Escott. The History Press 2010.

ISBN 978 0 7524 8729 8

'The Secret life of Bletchley Park – the men and women who worked there.'

Sinclair McKay. Aurum Press Ltd. 2010.

ISBN 978 84513 633 8

'Between Silk and Cyanide – a codemaker's war 1941-1945.'

Leo Marks. Harper Collins 2000.

ISBN 0 00 710039 6

'Inside Hitler's Bunker – the last days of the Third Reich.'

Joachim Fest. Pan Books 2005.

ISBN 978-1-4472-1860-9

'Secret Weapons – Death Rays, Doodlebugs and Churchill's Golden Goose.'

Brian J. Ford. Osprey Publishing. 2011.

ISBN 978 1 78096 721 9

'McIndoe's Army – the story of the Guinea Pig Club and its indomitable members.'

Edward Bishop. Grub Street London 2001.

ISBN 1 902304 93 4

'He was my chief – the memoirs of Adolf Hitler's secretary.'

Christa Schroeder (Introduction by Roger Moorhouse.) Langden Müller 1985.

ISBN 978 1 84832 631 6

'I was Hitler's chauffeur – the memoirs of Erich Kempka.'

Erich Kempka (Introduction by Roger Moorhouse.) Kyrburg, Munich. 1951.

ISBN 978 84832 630 9

'The wisdom of Winston Churchill – words of war and peace.'

Edited by Sean Lamb. Arcturus Publishing Ltd. 2019.

ISBN 978-1-78888-785-4

'The last enemy.'

Richard Hillary. Macmillan and co. 1942.

ISBN 0-7126-7344-X

V

LIST OF CHARACTERS:

Joselyn Foster	British Intelligence Field agent
Mark Foster	Joselyn's Uncle in Edgartown, USA,
Charles Foster	Deputy Chief of Mission, US Embassy, London, Joselyn's father
Nicholas Brimblecombe	Head of British Intelligence
Alistair Valentine	British Intelligence Field agent
Freddie Valentine	RAF 'Ace' and B. I. Field agent
Peter Braun	'Lawyer' in St. Moritz
Wolfgang Koch	Carriage driver in Pontresina
Leo Hoffmann	Detective, Graubünden Police
Dr. Rosa Spengler	Erich Spengler's daughter
Patrick Devlin	Irish Republican fanatic
Dieter Schmidt	Hired killer from Berlin
Werner Kocher	Hired killer from Berlin
Heinz Johner	Leo Hoffman's protégé
Manfred and Ingrid Lochar	Nexus spies from Baden
Clive Rowlands	Spengler's contact in England
Gertrud Wolf	Half of London sleeper cell
Captain David Fox	Army Signals, Beaufort Lodge
Lt. Col. Andrew Kirkpatrick	Assistant Commandant (Intel.)
Ali Emran	Palestinian terrorist
Erich Spengler	Owner of Spengler GmbH
Gisela	Rosa's secretary
Captain Clitheroe	Brim's driver and factotum
Squadron Leader David Squires	RAF Northolt, London
Peter Schaffer	Former SS killer / bodyguard
Harald Wolf	The other half of sleeper cell
Captain Edvard Langerhans	Skipper of SS Solveig
Charlie Morris	Pilot of Mosquito FB V1
David Swift	Navigator

Commodore Folker Jansen	Harbourmaster, Cuxhaven
Martin Zimmer	Quartermaster SS Solveig
Captain Kosinski	Soldier based at US Embassy
Anna Taussing	Kreisspital Oberengadin,, Samedan
Samuel Donoghue	Blue Raincoat

Thank You

Especially to my wife Pam for her love and patience; and to Marianne, always my first and trusted reader.

To J.P. for such a great edit and providing so many suggestions.

Len Greenwood for the original artwork, layout and continued enthusiasm for the Valentine Series.

Stuart Amesbury for his meticulous research and feedback.

As all historians know, there was a secret meeting 20th February 1933, where 24 German industrialists assembled secretly to hear AH speak. They represented household companies which exist today. The meeting is described in 'The Order of the Day' by Éric Vuillard, published by Picador.

The Hotel Monte Rosa in Zermatt is a fabulous retreat at the foot of the Matterhorn. It was where Edward Whymper stayed during his pioneering ascent of the mountain. I have named Herr Seiler's chalet after this hotel and thank Simone Seiler for permitting me to borrow both names.

I would also like to thank Sally Brimblecombe for not only being a constructive reader, but also allowing me to use her late husband's name. Nick was a great friend too, but he was never known as 'Brim'. That was purely invented for the Valentine Trilogy.

I would like to thank Robert Glasby, the curator of the de Havilland Museum. He helped me with everything to do with the DH 98 Mosquito FB MK V1.

Similar thanks to Dora Filli at the Library in St. Moritz. She carried out much of the research to do with the Graubünden Police and historic geographical locations and buildings.

Kristin Linger, PR manager, Badrutt's Palace Hotel, St. Moritz; for furnishing me with information about how the hotel looked in 1946.

Jin Chei, archivist at SBB Historic Archive, Zürich; thorough research, thank you.

My friend Tony Prosser in Bristol devised the layout of the (mythical) SS Solveig. This was for the action scenes on the bridge and wheelhouse. Tony spent many years as a Merchant Seaman and was able to provide nautical and technical input.

Robert Wallace.
10th May 2022

X

Printed in Great Britain
by Amazon

80485665R00234